FOUR
YOU SAY WHICH WAY
ADVENTURES

❖ PIRATE ISLAND

❖ IN THE MAGICIAN'S HOUSE

❖ LOST IN LION COUNTRY

❖ ONCE UPON AN ISLAND

BY
BLAIR POLLY & DM POTTER

FOUR YOU SAY WHICH WAY ADVENTURES

ISBN-10 : 1512256145
ISBN-13 : 978-1512256147

How This Book Works

- These stories depend on YOU.

- YOU say which way the story goes.

- What will YOU do?

At the end of each chapter, you get to make a decision. Turn to the page that matches your choice. **P233** means turn to page 233.

There are many paths to try.

Your first decision is to pick which story to read. Things get trickier after that.

Oh ... and watch out for giant squid, pirates, lions and that pesky magician!

List of Books

Pirate Island – Go exploring for treasure on a Caribbean island where you meet the locals, dive with sharks and come across lots of interesting creatures. Will you choose to investigate an old Spanish fortress, or will you head off into the jungle? Will you find pirate treasure? Or will your decisions land you in trouble? **Turn to page 7.**

In the Magician's House – The magician's house is steeped in magic. There are many rooms inside, but you have to find them first. Things change. Dreams swirl around in the magician's house just like dust in the corners of other houses. Little stories get stuck in the crannies. **Turn to page 97.**

Lost in Lion Country – You are on safari in Africa, but when you step out of the truck to take photos of a giraffe, the vehicle accidentally takes off without you. Now you are on your own. There are hyenas, cheetah and lions out here ... lots of lions. You wanted to see animals up close and now you're getting your wish as you try and find your way back to civilization. **Turn to page 163.**

Once Upon an Island – You have been invited to New Zealand to stay on a beautiful island. Right from the start you get to pick what happens. Watch out. Not every path is safe. You could be dragged to the bottom of the sea by a giant squid, go back in time, get kidnapped by poachers and a whole lot more. If you survive there are rich rewards. Good luck. You'll need it! **Turn to page 247.**

Pirate Island

At the Resort.

Your family is on holiday at a lush tropical island resort in the Caribbean. But you're not in the mood to sit around the pool with the others, you want to go exploring. You have heard that pirate treasure has been found in these parts and you are keen to find some too. You put a few supplies into your daypack, fill your drinking bottle with water, grab your mask and snorkel, and head towards the beach.

You like swimming, but you've been planning this treasure hunt for months and now is as good a time as any to start. The beach outside the resort stretches off in both directions.

To your right it runs past the local village, where children laugh as they splash and play in the water. Palm trees line the shore and brightly colored fishing boats rest on the sand above the high tide mark. Past the village, way off in the distance, is a lighthouse.

To your left, the sandy beach narrows quickly and soon becomes a series of rocky outcrops jutting into the sea. Steep cliffs rise up from the rocky shore to meet the stone walls of an old and crumbling fortress.

You have four hours before your family expects you back.

It is time to make your first decision. Do you:

Go right and head towards the lighthouse? **P8**

Or

Go left and head towards the rocks and the old fortress? **P12**

You have chosen to go right and head towards the lighthouse.

After deciding to turn right and walk out to the lighthouse you make your way down to the hard, wet sand where the walking will be easier.

Off in the distance, past the local village, the palm trees gradually thin out and the lush vegetation gives way to low sand dunes, scrub, and hardy grasses. A narrow sand spit, with a lighthouse on its far end, juts out into the ocean. The spit curves around in a gentle arc, forming a protected bay sheltered from the full force of the ocean beyond. Seabirds dive into the bay's sparkling blue waters as they hunt for fish.

As you walk down the beach, you pass resort guests lying on beach towels, swimming in the ocean, and playing games in the sand. You're not interested in all that, you want to find treasure.

You're pretty sure there is unlikely to be any treasure so close to civilization, so you pick up the pace. You want to get as far away from the others as you can and check out the windswept sand spit where it's far more likely you'll find treasure. What clever pirate would bury his treasure so close to the village?

Coconut palms line the shoreline and you hear birds and other animals in the jungle beyond the trees. Out in the bay, small fish are leaping out of the water trying to escape bigger fish below. Hungry gulls dive bomb the little fish from above. Then even bigger fish are leaping from the water, and you wonder what is chasing them. You've never seen so many fish and birds in one place before.

After walking for about half an hour you reach the sand spit. The jungle further inland starts to thin out and you can see water through the trees on the other side of the peninsula. Gradually even the palm trees are left behind and the only plants you see are low scrub and tough grasses whose roots cling for dear life onto the sand.

An old weather-beaten sign explains that the sand spit is the nesting place for migratory birds. It asks you to watch where you walk so you don't disturb any nests by mistake.

Not wanting to frighten or harm the nesting birds, you are careful where you step, keeping to the water's edge and away from the dunes. Small grey birds with pale yellow plumage on their chests scurry around, screeching at you whenever you get too close. You admire these mother birds for their bravery in chasing off something so much larger than themselves.

The sand spit is littered with bleached shells that have been washed up over time. In the wet sand you can see bubbles. The bubbles and the old shells lying about make you think there must be quite a few shellfish hiding under the sand. You dig in your toes and sure enough a small scallop is uncovered. You pick up the shell and inspect it. It is a half circle with ridges in the shell radiating out like a child's drawing of the sun. The other side of the shell is the same and you notice a small hinge that holds the two side of the cream and pink shell together.

After looking at the shell for a few moments, you drop it back onto the wet sand and are amazed at how it manages to wriggle its way back under the sand and disappear. Then, with one last bubble, it's gone.

The sun is hot so you pull your floppy hat and sunglasses out of your daypack and put them on. You are pleased you brought water and take a long sip. The sunglasses make it much easier for you to look though the water to the seabed below. You decide to walk with your feet in the shallows to cool off a bit as you continue towards the lighthouse.

A flash of color glints from under the crystal clear water a little way off shore. You stop and stare, trying to see what has caused the sparkle. Little fish dart left and right.

Was it just the light catching the side of a silver fish, or could this be the treasure you are looking for?

You drop your gear and wade in to the water to get a better look at whatever is reflecting the light. By the time you are waist deep, you realize the water is far deeper than you first thought.

Back on the beach you take your snorkeling gear out of your bag and strip down to your bathing suit and then wade out into the bay. After rinsing out your mask, you fit it to your face, pop in the snorkel's mouthpiece and stick your head under the water to try to see what is glimmering.

Out in deeper water you see a twinkle of sunlight reflecting off something. The glimmer isn't moving so you figure it isn't a fish. You lie on your stomach and paddle out along the surface with your face in the water, breathing through your mouthpiece, until you are directly over what looks like a gold coin resting on the sandy bottom.

You can feel your heart beating in your chest. You can't believe your eyes. Could this be your first discovery?

After taking a deep breath you dive. Down and down you go. The water is so clear everything looks much closer than it actually is. As you dive you kick with all your strength, scooping water with your cupped hands. You are so deep the pressure is starting to hurt your ears.

Just as your hand reaches for the coin, a shadow races along the sandy bottom. The shadow is huge and moving quickly. You snatch the coin off the sand and flip onto your back, looking for whatever it is that is causing the shadow. You hope it isn't a shark.

It only takes a moment to find what you are looking for. Near the surface, a manta ray flies like a bird, its wings barely moving as it glides through the water. The ray's mouth is as wide as the front grill of a car and it wings stretch out and then curve up at their tips. Behind the ray swishes a snake-like tail.

You relax a little. You know that despite being big, manta rays aren't dangerous. You watch entranced as the manta ray passes, but then your lungs start to burn. You push off the bottom and head for the surface, desperate for air, clutching the coin in your hand.

After your head breaks the surface, you spit out your mouthpiece and gulp in air. After a few deep breaths you take off your mask and hook its strap over your wrist and start dog paddling back towards the beach, happy with your discovery.

Sitting in the sand at the edge of the water, you study the coin. It is quite rough and looks handmade, not perfectly round like modern coins. On one side there is a cross made from what look like two capital I's. You're pleased you did an online search for treasure before coming on holiday and remember that this type of cross is called a Crusader's Cross, which signified the union of the Catholic Church and the government of Spain back in the old days.

What's even more exciting is the picture of a Lion and a Castle on the back of the coin. This means you've found a gold Spanish doubloon! The doubloon was a common coin at the time of the Spanish conquistadors. The Spanish exchanged them for trade goods in the New World for nearly two hundred years.

Have you found part of a pirate's treasure? Or is it a coin washed up from some ancient shipwreck? The coin looks pretty knocked around.

You're keen to go and look for more coins, but just as you put on your snorkel again, you see a triangular grey fin cruising back and forth along the beach. It's hard to tell if the fin is a shark or a dolphin. You wait for a while to see if you can get a better look at what sort of fish the fin belongs to, but whatever it is swims off before you can identify it. You wait a few more minutes to see if it comes back, but it doesn't.

It's time to make a decision. Do you:

Go back into the water and look for more coins? **P15**

Or

Keep walking towards the lighthouse? **P17**

You have decided to go left and head towards the old fortress.

You head down to the firm sand where the walking is easier and start your journey towards the old fortress. It is an imposing looking place even if it is in ruins. Stone walls rise vertically out of the cliffs almost as if they grew there. Only the crude joints in the massive stones used to construct the fortress walls give any hint to them being manmade.

The tower at one end of the fortress is still standing, although its roof has long gone. Along one wall, three ancient cannon point out to sea. These cannon once protected the fort and the village from pirate raiders that used to sail these seas many years ago.

The waves are bigger down this end of the beach. You can see white water spraying high into the air when the waves crash onto the rocks ahead. Further inland, the rugged slopes that lead up the fortress are covered in dense jungle. A layer of mist hangs near the fortress as steam rises from the humid jungle below.

In the ocean, not far from the fortress, is a small island with lush vegetation growing on it. Much of the island's shoreline is steep and rocky, but you notice a small patch of sandy beach at the near end. You can't see any huts on the island, and it looks too small to have fresh water on it, so you doubt anyone lives there.

The sun shines in your eyes as you walk, so you pull a pair of sunglasses out of your daypack and put them on. This makes everything so much easier to see.

Before long, the sandy beach becomes rocky and you are hopping from rock to rock across the tidal pools. You are pleased you wore runners rather than sandals because the surface underfoot is sharp and slippery with spray.

As you work your way around one of the larger pools you look down into its clear water and see tiny fish, starfish, urchins and miniature crabs. The pool is like a little village. The small fish swim in schools around the pool, darting here and there in perfect unison.

You stop for a moment to watch the animals. One little hermit crab has found a discarded shell to use as a home. The shell is much larger than the little crab and he struggles to carry its weight. A fish comes to investigate and the crab disappears into the shell for protection until the fish leaves. You watch as a delicate starfish moves, one tentacle at a time, over the rocks, and see small limpet shells stuck firmly to the rocks, waiting for the tide to come in and refresh the pool. Seaweed necklaces drift on the pool's surface like strings of brown pearls.

After negotiating your way around the tide pools, you find a rocky shelf to walk on. This shelf runs along the bottom of the cliffs and is worn smooth from the action of the waves. In some places where the rock is softer, caves have been eroded into the hillside. You poke your head into one cave, but it only goes back a little way and is dark and damp.

As you near the old fortress, the cliffs get steeper and higher, and the waves breaking on the rocks further out to sea get bigger and wilder. You wonder how safe it is to walk here, and if there are rock falls from time to time. You see quite a few rocks along the shelf, but you're not sure if they've tumbled down from above, or been tossed up by the sea in a storm. The rocks don't have the remains of barnacles or other sea life on them so you suspect they've fallen from high above.

When a fist-sized rock smacks into the ledge twenty yards ahead, your suspicions are confirmed. The shelf is getting narrower and narrower with each step you take. With rocks coming down from above, you realize there is serious danger in going any further.

You are about to turn around when you notice an unusual looking cave. It is unlike all the other caves you've seen. This one has light shining into to it from above somehow. The other caves you've seen are just shallow holes that narrow quickly and go nowhere, but you can see well into this one. The cave interests you, but you are unsure of what to do. Do you investigate further?

As you think, you kick the ground just inside the mouth of the cave with your toe. When you see a glint of light at your feet, you bend down to see what your kicking has uncovered.

It is an old coin. On one side is a cross, on the other a castle and a lion. You've seen these before online and can't believe your luck. You've found a gold doubloon!

Did the pirates drop this coin when they went into the cave to stash their treasure? Was it tossed up by some big storm?

You have a decision to make. Do you:

Go inside the cave to investigate? **P45**

Or

Go back past the rock pools and try to find another way up to the fortress? **P47**

You have decided to go back into the water and look for more coins.

The fish fin hasn't returned for over ten minutes. You wade into the water and put on your face mask and snorkel. As you paddle back out to where you found the coin you scan left and right for sharks. You're scared, but you also want to find more coins.

Floating on the surface, you scan the sea floor below. You scan again for sharks before swimming further away from shore. A little further out you see that coral is growing on something sticking up from the bottom. It looks man-made. Could it be part of a sunken ship?

You kick your feet and head out towards the outcrop. The sandy bottom has given way to rocks and coral. Flower-like anemones sway in the current and tiny fish are everywhere.

There are fish with orange and white stripes, fish of bright blue and others of yellow and red. Schools of bright silver fish race past, zipping one way and then the other, moving together like a troupe of dancers. Some fish weave around the tentacles of the anemones for protection, others pick at the algae growing on the rock.

Occasionally there is a flash of silver as a larger fish swoops in for a meal. The smaller fish scatter quickly in all directions, but once the danger has passed they reform into schools again.

When you reach the outcrop that has caught your attention, you see an old anchor, encrusted with barnacles and other sea life, jammed between two large rocks.

You take a deep breath and dive down towards the anchor. As you swim down, you wonder if the anchor is from an old Spanish galleon or from a more modern vessel. As you reach the anchor, you grab on to its shaft to keep yourself from floating upward as you look around. With so many things growing on the surface of the anchor, you can't tell its age. You can't even tell if the shaft is made of wood or metal.

You've decided to have a quick look for coins before your air runs out, when you see a shadow moving across the seabed. This time you can tell it isn't another manta ray, but that of a large shark.

Your air is nearly gone. You have no option but to head for the surface, but before you head up, you grab a rock to use for protection should the shark attack. The rock can't be too big because you won't be able to reach the surface with too much weight, but too small a rock won't be of much use for fighting off a hungry shark.

You grab a medium sized rock and push off the bottom. As you kick up towards the surface you scan the surrounding water for signs of the shark.

But sharks are the ocean's most effective predator. You don't stand a chance. The shark hits you from behind and drags you out into deep water. You try to swing the rock, but everything goes black.

Sorry but this part of your story is over. You made a poor decision and went back into the water after seeing a fin that could have been a shark. Now you've become the shark's lunch.

It is time for you to make another decision. Do you:

Go back to the very beginning of the story? **P7**

Or

Go back to your previous decision and make the other choice? **P17**

You have decided to keep walking towards the lighthouse.

You are pleased that you've decided to keep walking rather than go back into the water. The fin has returned and is cruising just off the beach. You can see now that it was not a dolphin but a big and hungry looking shark. Smaller fish in the shark's path are jumping out of the water in their attempt to get away. This has brought the birds back.

You tuck the gold doubloon safely away in your pocket and start walking towards the lighthouse, eager to find more treasure.

As the spit curves around, you can see the resort and the local village far across the bay. The houses of the village are small compared to the multi-story buildings of the new resort. You can just make out the small fishing boats pulled up onto the sand. Wet fishing nets glisten in the sun as they dry, strung out on poles in the warmth of the sun.

You are so busy looking back at the village as you walk you almost step on a nest. It's only the desperate call of the mother bird that alerts you to it.

Then you hear a voice call out. "Hey watch it!"

When you turn towards the voice you see a boy about the same age as you carrying a net bag of shellfish. Around the boy's neck is a string of shells. His skin is burnt brown by the sun.

"Sorry," you tell the boy and walk around the nest. "I was busy looking at the village and not watching where I was going."

The boy shrugs. "These birds are endangered you know. Didn't you read the sign?"

You explain how you've come out here on the spit to look for pirate treasure, not to harm the birds. You ask the boy if he has ever found any gold coins out here on the sand spit when he's been digging for shellfish.

"No," the boy says shaking his head. 'But the village elders tell stories about pirates and treasure, stories that their parents told them.

I've heard them repeated all my life.'

"Could you tell me what you've heard?" you ask the boy.

"I could, but I've got to get these scallops back to the village. My mother will be annoyed if I'm late."

You nod your head and frown.

"But if you want to come by the village when you get back from your walk, I can tell you some stories. How does that sound?"

"That would be great," you tell the boy.

"My house is the one nearest the red and blue fishing boat. You shouldn't have any problem finding it."

You thank the boy and he heads off toward the village, turning once to give you a wave. You carry on toward the lighthouse.

As the sun rises higher in the sky, the heat of the day increases. You take the water bottle out of your pack and drink. The water is lukewarm but at least it's wet. As you drink, you watch a family of crabs scuttle sideways across the sand. Their eyes are black and stand out bead-like on stems. Their bodies are bright orange and shiny. When you approach for a closer look the crabs turn towards you and lift their pincers into the air for protection. You imagine the nip those big pincers could give you and stay well clear. One crab advances on you, and you laugh at his antics as he waves his arms around and snaps his claws.

You walk around the crabs and pick up the pace. Before long you reach the lighthouse.

The lighthouse sits on a base of large rocks concreted together to form a wide flat platform. The platform is taller than you, but a narrow set of steps lead up to the base of the building on one side. Rusted handrails allow you a handhold on the slippery algae covered steps.

The lighthouse tower is white with bright red stripes running around it. A structure made of glass windows with a peaked roof and a white balcony crown its top. There is a brass plaque mounted on the outside wall near a big steel door.

You climb up the steps to investigate further.

The brass plaque has gone a little green over time, but the engraved words are still quite clear. You step a little closer and read.

Beware of the sea. For under these calm waters lay many shattered dreams.

As you think about the words written on the plaque you walk over to the lighthouse's door. Its surface is bubbled with rust, but it hinges are big and strong and its paint is fresh and white. You turn the handle to see if the door is unlocked, but it does not move.

From the base of the lighthouse you get a great view of the surrounding area. As you look back in the direction from which you've come, you see that the tide is on its way in and the water is coming further and further up the beach with every minute that passes. You can also see a narrow path, paved with crushed shells on the other side of the sand spit. It looks like it leads back toward the village through the jungle.

It is time to make a decision. Do you:

Head back to the resort the way you came? **P20**

Or

Follow the shell covered path into the jungle? **P22**

You have decided to head back to the resort along the beach.

You climb down from the lighthouse platform and walk down to the beach. The tide is coming up so you are forced to walk higher to avoid getting wet. You wonder how much higher the water will come up before you get back to the resort. You can see piles of seaweed and small pieces of driftwood near the high tide mark.

You figure this is as high as the water will come up so you relax and get into your stride. You probably only have an hour or so before you will be expected back at the resort. You don't want to get into trouble because then you might not get to go out on your own to explore any more of the island.

As you walk along the high tide mark you watch the antics of the birds. Most of the time you're alerted by the parent birds whenever you get close to a nest.

When you look down the beach, the resort is a long way away. You didn't realize how far you'd walked, so you speed up a little in the hope of making up some time.

You hear a splash out in the water and turn to see what is going on. Now there are not one, but four sinister grey fins swimming back and forth along the beach. Only little fish are jumping out of the water at first, but then even bigger fish are leaping for their lives. When the seabirds dive in to feast on the sardines stirred up by the sharks, the ocean is turned into a battle ground for survival. Everything that moves is searching for a meal.

Walking so far has made you a little bit weary. You want to stop and take a break, but you also know your family will worry if you are late.

Not much further down the beach, you hear a frantic chirping. In front of you a mother bird is telling you off for getting too close to her nest. As you move inland a little to give the nest a wide berth you notice a small mound of stones. The stack looks like a marker of some sort. It certainly isn't a natural formation.

You walk towards the pile, curious to see what it is.

The cairn is nearly waist high. The stone on top is flat and has a compass rose engraved onto its surface. A needle on the rose points towards the jungle. You stand behind the cairn and look in the direction of the arrow. It points to a tall tree a couple of hundred paces into the jungle. The cairn has lichen growing on the shady sides, indicating to you that it has been there for quite some time. You scrabble around in the sand at the base of the cairn in case something is buried nearby but you find nothing. You're not quite sure what the arrow indicates, but you hope it could be a clue to finding some treasure. Is the arrow pointing to the big tree, or something else?

It's time for you to make a decision. Do you:

Follow the arrow, and head towards the big tree in the jungle? **P27**
Or
Follow the beach back to the resort? **P29**

You have decided to follow the shell covered path.

The shell covered path crunches underfoot as you walk. It is narrow but well maintained. You suspect it leads to the village and resort, but there are so many twists and turns that you're not completely sure. You hear animals moving around in the undergrowth.

Maybe this is a path that is used by the villagers when they go hunting or fishing. But then again, maybe it leads somewhere else altogether.

You know your parents will worry if you are away too long, so even though your legs are tired from walking, you start to jog along the path in an attempt to get back to the resort.

Every few minutes you slow down to a walk and have a bit of a breather. Your water is nearly gone. You hope there are signs of civilization soon. One time when you slow for a rest, you think you hear the sound of moving water in the distance. Then a few minutes later, you come around a bend in the path and see a small stream heading into a gully. The jungle is denser here because of the water. Huge ferns crowd the stream on both sides.

The stream at this point is barely a trickle. The sand is absorbing the water almost as quickly as it comes down the slope. You walk upstream for a while in the hopes of finding a pool deep enough to drink from.

After ten minutes or so you find a shallow pool between some moss-covered rocks. Bright red dragonflies hover over the pool, and funny mosquito-like insects skitter across the water's surface.

The water looks clean but how do you tell? If the stream were near the village you'd never drink out of it for fear of getting sick, but out here in the jungle, chances are it's okay.

You're very thirsty so you fill your bottle and take a little sip to test it. The water tastes wonderful and fresh. You drink your fill and then top up your water bottle. Who knows how long it will be before you find more?

After rejoining the path and walking for another fifteen minutes or so, you finally hear chickens clucking and the sound of children playing. Soon, the first of the village huts appears.

The villager's huts are simple, with four stout poles set into the ground and walls of corrugated iron. The top of the walls are left open to allow the cool breezes to blow through the hut. Above the walls a thatched roof made of palm leaves keeps off the rain. It's a warm climate, so most daily living is probably done outdoors, the huts are small and you've read they are used mainly for sleeping. You wonder whether the people living there would like things to be a little different though. The resort must seem like a palace to them.

Once you get to the village, you know your way back to the beach. As you pass the red and blue fishing boat you look for the boy you saw on the beach earlier but he is nowhere to be seen. A woman, who you assume is his mother, is outside stirring a pot set over a small fire. A man wearing sunglasses sits quietly nearby. The smell of spices wafts into your nostrils, and you realize how hungry you are.

Finally the resort comes into view. The gardens around the resort are full of red hibiscus flowers, fuchsia, and palms.

Down one end of the garden, a young woman is giving a demonstration on how to weave cane. Tourists are crowded around her taking pictures.

After a quick look around, you find your family in the cafe by the pool.

You apologize for being late and then tell them about your adventures. You reach into your pocket and feel the gold doubloon. It would be nice to tell the others about your find, but you decide to wait and see if you can find more before surprising them.

The food at the resort is mainly fish caught locally. You order fish, salad and freshly squeezed orange juice. Your stomach gurgles in anticipation.

Your family, and some other tourists they have befriended, have decided to take a bus into the island's main town further up the coast and ask if you want to come along.

You wonder if the town has a library. Maybe you could find some more information about the local history and pirate treasure before you go and see the village boy.

After your family finishes eating, everyone goes to change out of their bathing suits and grab their cameras, wallets and other things they want to take to town.

You transfer the gold doubloon into the pocket of your clean shorts without anyone seeing it, and grab some stationery and a pen from the desk drawer so you can take notes if you find out anything interesting.

The pale green bus is old and battered. There is no glass in the windows. Most of the people on board are locals from the village. One woman has a small metal cage with two chickens squashed inside. One chicken stares at you with its beady eyes as it cluck, cluck, clucks.

The road to town runs past a few huts. Up the hill to your right is the old fort. Then the road turns inland and enters the dense jungle. The road winds through a series of small hills and then drops back down to the coast. This northern part of the island isn't protected by a reef or sand spit so the waves pile in from the open ocean without obstruction.

At one point the bus stops to let off a couple of young men carrying surfboards. Ten minutes later you are bumping along through farm land and then the town finally comes into view.

A concrete breakwater protects the town's small harbor from the fury of the waves. A rusty small coastal trader is moored up to the wooden wharf. A steel crane standing high on rusted metal stilts lifts pallets from the deck of the ship onto a waiting flat-bed truck. A man in a fluro vest stands nearby with a clipboard, counting the goods as they come off the ship.

Just south of the wharf there is a big grassy area where locals have set up market stalls filled with fresh fruit and vegetables, crafts, cages of live chickens and fish of all descriptions.

Rather than look around the market, some tourists decide to check out the museum. You decide to tag along with them and see if you can find a library. Maybe it will have some book on the local history. If not, the museum might have an exhibit about pirates.

Everyone agrees to meet back at the bus stop in two hours.

On the way to the museum, you see a small stone building that looks like a library. You tell the others that you want to do some research and that you'll meet them at the museum or back at the bus stop depending on how long it takes.

After listening to a lecture about being careful and to make sure you are back at the bus stop on time, you set the alarm on your phone as a reminder and then head over and enter the library.

It's not as big as the library at home, and they don't have Wi-Fi so you can't check your email, but you soon locate the local history section and start leafing through the books and forget all about technology.

In one old book you find a picture of the lighthouse and accounts of all the ships lost on the reef before it was built. Historians estimate over twenty ships have gone down in the area. Some were rumored to be laden with gold, silver, and gemstones being transported from Mexico back to Spain.

You find fascinating tales of seamanship and bravery. Some of the wrecks were the result of bad navigation, others by hurricanes that sometimes affect the area. One story you read is of a ship that ran aground on the sand spit while trying to flee pirates. But no matter how hard you look, you can't find any reference to buried treasure.

You jump when your phone beeps. You can't believe that nearly two hours has passed. It's time to rush back to the bus.

Your family is waiting nervously when you come around the corner just as the bus is pulling up.

"Talk about cutting it fine," your mother says, giving the brim of your cap a tweak.

On the ride back to the resort you tell them all you've discovered about shipwrecks and the history of the lighthouse. Before long, the bus is dropping you off outside the resort.

You go up to your room and restock your pack with a couple of chocolate bars and another bottle of water. You grab a sweatshirt in case it gets cold and take the lighter that is sitting next to the gas stove in the kitchen and then head back to the beach.

You have a decision to make. Do you:

Go and meet the village boy? **P34**

Or

Use one of the resort's small dinghies and go for a sail? **P39**

You have decided to follow the arrow towards the tree in the jungle.

You look up at the big tree and then back at the lighthouse behind you to get your bearings. You know that once you enter the jungle you won't be able to see the tree or the lighthouse from the ground. You need to work out a way to keep walking straight and not end up going around in circles.

You find a smaller tree on the edge of the jungle that is in line with both the lighthouse and the big tree in the jungle and head for that. It is only a few hundred steps across scrub and low, grass covered dunes to the small tree. Once you get to the small tree, you look back across the dunes at the lighthouse and then pick another tree further into the jungle that is in line with the lighthouse and the smaller tree you first used as a landmark. By repeating this procedure you figure you can keep your direction straight enough to find the big tree.

The jungle is cool and shady. When you look up, only small patches of sky can be seen between the outstretched branches of the many trees and shrubs.

A small red headed, yellow breasted hummingbird hovers near a bright pink flower, sucking nectar with its long beak. The broad leafed plant reminds you of the lilies back home only much, much larger.

You stop and listen, amazed by all the unusual sounds. High in the canopy, you hear a loud squawking. It takes a moment for your eyes to adjust to the low light, but before long you see a toucan with its black and white body, yellow beak and bright blue eyes singing for a mate. Two bright green parrots sit on a branch nearby, plucking at red berries with their strong pink and grey beaks. The parrot's cheeks have a patch of red making it look as though they are blushing.

You would like to stay and watch, but you know that you need to get moving. You also need to focus, otherwise you might become disorientated and lose your way.

After repeating your technique for keeping your course straight a few times you finally come to the big tree. Its root system is like a swarm of giant snakes, twisting and turning as they wind around and then finally go underground. From this unusual root system a large trunk emerges covered in moss and lichen and small delicate ferns.

You raise your head and look up. The tree trunk seems to go on forever. Vines hang from above and colonies of other plants live in the tree's branches. You've never seen so many things growing on a single tree. Then you notice that some of the vines hanging from the tree have been woven into a ladder of sorts. Is this what the arrow on the rock was pointing you towards? Or are you imagining things? Maybe this is just how these particular vines grow?

Through some shrubs to your left you see a pathway covered in white shells that lead off into the jungle in the direction of the village.

You have a decision to make. Do you:

Have a go at climbing the big tree? **P31**

Or

Follow the shell covered path into the jungle? **P22**

You have decided to follow the beach back to the resort.

You decide to head back to the resort rather than go further into the jungle. Not that you are afraid, it's just that you'd like to go sailing out to the island off the other end of the beach.

You turn your back on the cairn of stones and carefully pick your way through the nesting birds back to the beach. Off in the distance, there is a family walking in your direction with two small children carrying buckets and shovels.

The family stops and lays out their beach towels and then puts up a brightly colored umbrella. The elder of the two children wanders down to the wet sand and starts digging, filling up the bucket with sand and then flipping it over to create the walls of a sandcastle.

The smaller child is five or six perhaps. His mother is covering him with sun block. After completing this important task, the mother and father lie on their towels and pull books out of their bag.

The smaller child joins his elder sister. He wants to help build the sandcastle, but it looks like the sister isn't that keen on his help. Maybe his building skills aren't quite up to scratch.

The sister waves her arm and the little boy decides to wander down and paddle in the water instead.

The water is calm enough, but you remember the grey fins you saw earlier and wonder where the sharks have gone. You can't see them at the moment, but you hope the little boy doesn't go any deeper.

You pick up your pace. You want to warn the parents of the sharks you saw earlier and are closing the gap between yourself and them quite quickly when a fin appears not far offshore. And it's heading straight for the young boy who is standing, chest deep in the water slapping the surface with his hands.

The shark must think the boy slapping the water is an injured fish. You shout a warning and start running.

The parents hear you yelling, and look up. They don't understand why you are running down the beach as fast as you can towards their children.

Then the father spots the fin and leaps to his feet. But he is too far away to reach his son in time.

You hit the water at a gallop and plough in, hooking your arm around the waist of the boy and drag him kicking and screaming through the water towards the beach.

The father arrives at your side and scoops up his son. You can see him trembling.

"My god that was close. Thank you so much!"

Your lungs are burning from your exertions. You gasp a quick "That's okay," and suck the warm air into your lungs. You are shaking too.

The young boy is oblivious to the close call he's just had. He's crying, not because of the shark, but at his shock at being dragged so abruptly from the water.

When his father puts him down, he heads straight back towards the water.

The father grabs his arm and tries to explain why he can't go back in the water. In the end the family decides it's probably safer to go back to the resort and the pool.

You wave goodbye, happy to have been the hero and stroll on down the beach past the village and onward to the resort.

It is time for you to make a decision. Do you:

Grab one of the resort's small sailboats? **P39**

Or

Go and meet the village boy? **P34**

Or

Go check in with your family? **P64**

You have decided to have a go at climbing up the tree.

The vines hanging down from the tree are about as thick as your thumb and strong enough to hold your weight when you pull down on them. Many of the vines have twisted around each other in such a way that there are plenty of footholds within reach. You have always been pretty good at climbing trees but you have never had a go at climbing one so large before.

The higher you climb, the more vines you have to hold on to. It is a long way up to the first branch. A couple of times during the climb, you stop to rest your aching legs.

When you finally reach the first branch you sit and look down. Everything below looks a long way away. Parrots squawk and zip past you on their way to the next bunch of berries. There is a bed of ferns in the crook of the tree that provides you with something soft to lean against.

You lay back and rest against the fern fronds. As you do so, you stare up into the higher branches. You are amazed at how much wildlife there is in the tree. You've counted six different birds so far, numerous butterflies, moths, flying insects of all sorts and even a small rodent of some sort.

You can see for miles from your vantage point. Then you notice something odd. There is a short piece of brass pipe lashed to one of the bigger branches with old hemp rope. The rope has been varnished to protect it from the elements. You are curious as to why anyone would put something like that up in the tree.

Holding onto a branch for support, you stand up and look more closely at the pipe. Then closing one eye, like you would when looking through a telescope, you peer through one end to see if it is pointing at something in particular.

The only thing you can see through the pipe is the top of the little island that sits offshore from the old fortress.

Is this a clue left by the pirates? Is the island the place you should be exploring if you want to find treasure?

You are lying in the crook of the tree again, thinking about this new development, when you notice one of the branches above you is moving. It is wriggling. Then you realize it isn't a branch at all, but a large python! The mottled pattern on the snake's back helps it blend in with the foliage so well, you nearly missed it altogether. The bad news is that the snake is heading down the tree towards you far quicker than you like.

The snake is big, maybe not big enough to swallow you whole, but it is certainly big enough to create a serious problem if it wrapped its strong muscular body around you. It could strangle you, or even make you fall out of the tree. You've read that python bites, although not poisonous, can cause serious infection because of the bacteria in their mouths.

You grab onto the vines again, ready to scoot back down, but then the snake turns off onto a higher branch and twists and turns its way out to the end where a nest made of twigs and moss has been built by a bird.

You admire how easily the snake makes it way out to the end of the branch. Then the snake's head disappears over the lip of the bird's nest only to return with an egg in its mouth. The snakes mouth hinges back to allow the egg to slide into its throat before it goes back for another. The lump in the snake's belly is easily visible. A mother bird sits on a branch nearby squawking in distress, helpless to save her babies.

There is a piece of broken branch lodged in the crook of the tree, and you feel sorry for the mother bird. You grab the branch and hurl it up towards the snake as hard as you can. The lump of wood barely clips the snake's tail before falling to the ground, but it is enough to give the snake a fright.

The problem is, now the snake is headed your way, and it's moving fast!

If you sit still, will the snake slither right on by you? Or, in its frightened state, will it give you a nasty bite and potentially ruin your holiday.

You have a decision to make. Do you:

Sit still and hope the snake passes you by? **P43**

Or

Grab the vine, slither back down the tree and keep following the shell covered path towards the village? **P22**

You have decided to go and meet the village boy.

You are keen to find the village boy you met on the beach and see if you can get more information. The stories that the village elders tell the children might contain clues about where to find more doubloons.

As you enter the village, you are surrounded by curious children, dogs, and even the odd chicken. You notice many of the dogs look similar. They are mainly tan in color, have short legs and long bodies. Some follow the children on the lookout for scraps they might drop, and some lie in the shade with their tongues hanging out.

As you head towards the beach, you keep an eye out for the red and blue boat the boy described. Then you see it pulled up on the beach.

In a hut nearest the boat, a woman who you assume is the boy's mother is outside stirring a large pot set on a metal stand over a small fire. A man wearing shorts and sunglasses, probably the boy's father, sits in a chair a few yards away.

You approach the woman and ask her if her son is around. She tells you that he has gone off to collect coconuts. She points towards a group of trees up the beach and you see a small figure up a coconut palm swinging a machete.

"Thank you," you say to the woman and trot off to speak to the boy.

When you reach the tree the boy has climbed, you watch out for falling coconuts. Five are already on the ground near your feet.

"Hello," you yell up to the boy.

He looks down and smiles. Then he chops down two more coconuts before walking down the tree trunk using only his hands and feet.

When the boy reaches the ground he picks up one of the coconuts and with skilful use of the machete chops off the fibrous outer husk until he gets to the hard shell of the nut itself.

With a quick chop he opens a small hole on one end of the coconut and hands it to you.

"Here, drink," he says.

You take the coconut and bring the hole to your lips and let the sweet milk flow into your mouth. It is the most refreshing thing you have ever tasted.

When you have finished drinking the milk, the boy takes the coconut and cracks it open with the blunt side of his machete. Then he levers a piece of white flesh off the brown shell and hands it to you.

You bite right in and chew the piece up. The boy takes a piece and does the same, all the while smiling with his eyes.

When you've both had your fill, he gathers up the other coconuts and puts them into a mesh bag and slings it over his shoulder. You walk beside him as he heads back to the village.

"Tell me a pirate story," you say.

"Okay. Just let me drop these off first."

His mother takes the mesh bag. "Okay you two, now get out from under me feet, I've work to do."

"Race you to the water," the boy says before taking off in a sprint.

You fling down your pack and follow as fast as you can.

The boy hits the water and after two long strides arches into a graceful dive and disappears under its glassy surface. You try to do the same, but your dive is more like a belly flop than a proper dive. Still, the water is cool and refreshing after your long walk.

After a quick swim you grab a towel out of your pack and the boy leads you to a patch of shade under a broad-leafed shrub and sits.

"So, you want to hear about pirate treasure do you?"

You nod eagerly. "Yes please."

"Okay," the boy says. "Here is one my grandmother tells about the last shots fired from the fortress."

"The year was 1726. A pirate and his crew of buccaneers were terrorizing the Spanish fleet in the waters of the Caribbean. The pirate was an ex British sailor who had talked the crew of a ship he was serving on at the time to mutiny."

"After taking over the ship, he installed himself as captain and started attacking the Spanish. Within a year he had four ships in his fleet. According to legend, he and his men were responsible for the loss of over twenty Spanish ships and a large amount of Spanish gold."

"Spain, you see, had taken to sending their treasure ships back home in convoys in an attempt to stop the pirates from looting their gold. But the pirates were fearless and sometimes just a little crazy."

You look at the boy and smile. You remember reading about such pirates online, but you weren't sure if the accounts were exaggerated or real.

"You see," the boy continues. "The pirate captain and his crew knew the waters in these parts far better than the Spanish, and they used all sorts of tricks to attack the gold laden ships heading back to Spain."

"One trick was pretending to attack the convoy with a single ship. Then, when the Spanish chased the pirates, the lightly loaded and much quicker pirate ship would escape by running through a narrow channel in a reef unknown to the Spanish. By the time the Spanish saw the danger ahead, it would be too late and their ship would be on the rocks."

"Before the other ships in the convoy could come to the damaged ship's aid, the rest of the pirate fleet would sail out of one of the many hidden coves and attack the floundering ship. Instead of risking further damage, the Spanish convoy would often leave the damaged ship to fend for itself and sail off."

"When given a choice of death or surrender, the crew of the floundering ship would sometimes murder the officers and join the pirates rather than be blown to pieces on the reef."

"Using the crew of the damaged ship as labor, the pirates would strip as many guns and gold off the Spanish ship before it sank. Then they sailed off to one of their hiding spots."

"One of these hiding spots was in the lee of the small island just offshore from where the old fortress sits now. It was a good anchorage protected from the fierce winds that blow around here at certain times of the year."

"But it didn't take long for the Spanish to get angry with the pirates stealing their gold. Using slave labor from the village, they built the fortress up on the cliffs. Once Spanish guns overlooked the calm waters between the little island and the shore, they could anchor in the bay without fear of attack from the pirate raiders."

"But the pirate captain had other ideas. He hated the Spanish almost as much as he loved gold. On a moonless night in the summer of 1726, he and his four ships sailed silently to the seaward side of the small island, hidden from the fortress. One crewman rowed a boat to shore and climbed to the top of the island where the pirates had secretly built a lookout tower. There, he acted as a spotter for the pirate gunners hidden from sight of the Spanish, and directed their fire towards the fort and the Spanish ship anchored in the bay."

"The pirate ships sat broadside to the fortress and aimed their cannon over the top of the island. When all four ships were ready, they fired the first volley before the Spanish even knew they were there."

"The pirate spotter on top of the island signaled the Spanish whereabouts to the gunners on board the ships and the pirates fired again. There were many casualties among the Spanish ships and at the fortress before the Spanish even figured out where the cannon fire was coming from."

"Another group of pirates had landed on the far side of the peninsula, and made their way through the jungle and up the hill under cover of darkness and were waiting to rush the fortress as soon the cannon fire from the pirate ships breached its walls."

"Meanwhile, the onshore wind didn't give the Spanish ships any chance to maneuvers. Most were burning before they even got their anchors up. One of the Spanish ships ran aground on the little island in its attempt to get away. The wreckage can still be seen on the rocks."

"The next day, the villagers praised the pirates for defeating the Spanish. You see, the Spanish had been stealing the villager's food and mistreating them. The pirate captain was treated like hero. It's even told he married the village chief's daughter."

"So what happened to all the Spanish gold?" you ask the boy.

"There are rumors that the pirates hid some of it around here somewhere, but apart from the odd coin that washes up, very little has ever been found."

"What about on the island?" you ask. "Do you think the treasure could be there?"

The boy shrugs his shoulder. "Could be anywhere I suppose. People have been looking for it for over a hundred years."

You are not encouraged by this information. Still, at least if there is a treasure, it is still out there somewhere.

The boy gets up. "I'd better get home. Mother will have more chores for me."

"Well thanks for the story," you say. "Maybe we can go searching for treasure together some time."

"Sure," the boy says. "Finding some gold would be great. I could pay to get my father's eyes fixed. Once his cataracts are removed he'll be able to go out fishing again."

You wave goodbye and think about what the boy said about his father. You hope you find some treasure, so you can share some with him.

As you walk down the beach towards the resort you have a decision to make. Do you:

Go out on one of the resort's small sailing boats? **P39**

Or

Go check in with your family? **P64**

You have decided to take out one of the resort's small sailing boats.

You are keen to get out to the small island. You figure it is an ideal place to find pirate treasure. Sailing is something you've enjoyed for quite a few years. Your local sea scouts group has regular lessons for cadets your age. You're not the best sailor in your corps but you are quite handy around small boats as long as the wind isn't blowing too hard.

A staff member from the resort gives you a lifejacket and a quick run-down on how to operate the boat's sail and tiller. The dinghy has a reasonably short mast and single sail, similar to the ones you've handled before. Rather than having a keel like bigger boats, the dinghy has a centerboard that you drop down through a slot in the bottom of the boat. This acts like a keel and helps keep the boat running in a straight line when you are sailing.

You place your pack into the waterproof compartment under the seat with the flares, spare rope and tiny anchor, push the boat out into the shallows and climb aboard.

After dropping the centreboard and raising the sail you settle down and turn the boat so the wind fills the sail. Instantly the breeze pushes you along through the water.

You keep close to the shore at first to get used to the boat's handling before heading out further into the bay. You find the dinghy reasonably stable and easy to sail. The wind is light and the waves are small. As long as you remember to duck when the boom swings around when tacking or jibing, it's pretty hard to make a mistake.

After a couple of trial runs back and forth along the beach, you point the boat towards the little island off the coast from the fortress. The onshore wind is the perfect angle for you to make it without having to do too much tacking.

As you sail, the boat tilts with the wind and you hear the water rushing along the hull.

A cheeky seagull comes to investigate the boat. He lands and then sits looking at you with his beady orange and black eyes from the stern of the boat. You can smell the bird's fish-breath from your position by the tiller, but it's nice to have some crew along for the ride.

"Ahoy ahoy," you say to the gull. "Now don't be pooping on the poop deck me hearty."

The seagull turns its head sideways and gives you a look as if to say, 'aye aye skipper' and then swivels its tail feathers over the side and drops a big white splat into the water. A moment later it squawks once and takes off to rejoin the other gulls fishing out towards the sand spit.

As you near the island, you get a good look at the fortress from the water. The cannon barrels pointing in your direction make you nervous, even though you know they are old and rusty. You can imagine how vulnerable those approaching the fortress from the sea must have felt many years ago.

Your sailing instructor taught you to check things out before landing your boat on an unknown beach in case there are hidden rocks that aren't obvious at first. The island isn't that big, so after making a quick pass of the beach, you decide to sail all the way around before landing on the tiny strip of sand.

The water is crystal clear. Even though it is quite deep, you can still see the bottom. The reef around the island is full of colorful fish.

You tack and turn to starboard ready to sail counter-clockwise around the island. When you reach the southernmost end of the island you tack back.

It's amazing how different the island is on the seaward side. It is steep and rocky, with vertical cliffs. They aren't as big as the cliffs on the mainland, but they still tower over the mast of your little boat.

Nesting in holes and cracks in the cliff are thousands of seabirds. As you sail closer the noise from the birds becomes louder and louder. Some of the bolder birds dive bomb your boat in an attempt to scare you away.

Further around past the cliffs, you see the wreckage of a ship on the rocky shore. The wreck looks like it has been there a long time.

Before you know it, you are back where you started having completed your circumnavigation of the island. You line up for your run onto the sandy strip of beach.

Landing will be tricky. You will need to pull the centerboard up out of its slot so it doesn't dig into the sand, and drop the sail at just the right time. Drop the sail too early and you won't have enough speed to reach the beach. Too late and you'll hit the beach hard and risk damaging yourself or the boat.

You are pleased you've done similar maneuvers a few times at home. After judging the speed of the boat and the depth of the water you get ready to lift the centerboard and tuck the halyard holding up the sail under you leg for quick access.

"Three, two, one," you count down.

Just as the water shallows, you pull up the centre board and drop the sail. The boat's momentum carries it onto the beach and the bow eases gently into the soft white sand.

You hop over the side into knee deep water and grab one side of the boat. With your feet digging into the sand, you drag the dinghy as far as you can up the beach to keep it from floating away. Then you take the bowline and loop the rope twice around a sturdy palm tree on the edge of the jungle before tying it off.

Happy the landing has gone so well, you put your hands on your hips and survey your surroundings.

The beach is small, only twenty paces wide. Lush green foliage grows right down to its edge. One end of the beach leads onto the rocks that go about half way around the island towards the shipwreck.

At the other end of the beach, the steep cliffs begin. Inland there are two hills of similar height, with a gully running up between them to the top of the island. You are keen to explore the island further and wonder which way you should go.

It is time for you to make a decision. Do you:

Walk around the rocks to where you saw the remains of a shipwreck? **P65**

Or

Go inland and explore the island? **P67**

You have decided to sit still and hope the snake passes you by.

The snake is moving quickly down the tree. You press your back into the bed of ferns and freeze, hoping it won't notice you.

The snake twists and turns along the branch until it is directly overhead. You want to turn your face up so you can see what it is doing, but you don't want to move and give yourself away.

The snake's scales feel incredibly smooth and cool as they slide over your shoulder and brush your neck. Is the snake about to coil itself around your windpipe and strangle you? Then you see its head moving further down and you feel the weight of the snake's body pressing on your legs.

The tail gives your neck a final flick as it passes and the snake disappears from view further down the tree. A drop of sweat runs down your cheek.

That was a little too close for comfort. Still, it was worth climbing the tree for the clue you've gained about needing to go to the island. Or is this just some game the locals play on the tourists to keep them coming back?

In either case you are keen to find out. You grab the vines and start your descent, but find that locating the footholds are much harder when climbing down. You wrap a vine around one ankle and search desperately with your other foot until you locate a place to stand. After resting your arms, you lower yourself down again and repeat the process.

Your hands and arms are tired from holding your weight and your hands are getting slippery with sweat. When you start to slip you manage to hook your arm through a loop to stop yourself from falling. Climbing down isn't as easy as you thought it would be.

Still you have no choice but to continue. You dry one hand at a time on your shirt then start your descent once more. But before long you are sliding down faster than you want. Your hands are burning from the friction. Luckily you are almost down when you let go and fall into the soft undergrowth. You roll as your feet hit the ground but still the wind is knocked out of you.

You lie on the ground and catch your breath. Two close calls in a row have given you the shakes.

After resting a minute you decide to head back towards the resort. You are keen to see if you can get out to the island and see if there really is treasure hidden there somewhere.

You also wonder if the boy from the village might have some useful information.

You go to the shell covered path and start walking. After walking for half an hour you come to a small stream and refill your water bottle. At little further on you finally you hear sound of chickens clucking and of the village children playing.

It is time for you to make a decision to make. Do you:

Go and meet the village boy? **P34**

Or

Go check in with your family? **P64**

You have decided to go inside the cave to investigate.

The cave's entrance is narrow but a faint light is coming from a crack high up in its ceiling. From somewhere deep in the cave's interior you hear a steady drip, drip, drip of water. The floor of the cave is damp and smooth and you are careful to watch where you step.

You wish you'd brought a flashlight with you, but thankfully there is just enough light from above to see where you are going.

The cave is narrow but the roof above is high. So high in fact, most of the ceiling is shrouded in darkness despite the narrow rays coming from above.

Enormously long stalactites hang from the cave's ceiling. Their paleness in the faint light make them look like icicles ready to drop down and spear anyone underneath them. As you get deeper in the cave, sharply pointed stalagmites grow up from the floor. Eventually the cave narrows and you come up against an almost sheer wall.

You can't go any further.

Before you walk back outside, you run your hand over one of the stalagmites and feel how cool and incredibly smooth it is. Tiny amounts of calcium from the surrounding limestone, dissolved in water and seeping though the ground from above, must have dripped inside this cave for thousands of years, gradually building up layer upon layer for these formations to occur.

You are so impressed you take your camera out of your pack to take a picture. It's pretty dark, but you're confident the flash will provide enough light to get a good shot.

For a brief second, as the camera's flash goes off, more of the interior of the cave comes into view.

It takes a few moments for your eyes to readjust again after the flash, but during that time you wonder if what you saw set into the cave's wall was real or just a trick of the light. You close your eyes and wait for your pupils to dilate again so you can see.

Carefully you walk toward the far wall of the cave with your arms extended. When you reach the smooth stone, you feel around for the narrow flight of steps you saw cut into the sheer rock face. The steps are smooth and very narrow. There is less light in this part of the cave so your exploration is as much by feel as it is by sight.

The first ten or so steps you can feel with your hands, they are only as wide as your foot and there is no handrail for safety. You put your back against the wall and take the first few steps sideways, keeping your back hard against the stone. Progress is slow. After half a dozen steps you wonder if this is a good idea. Still, it is lighter higher up towards the top of the caves.

Does this staircase lead all the way up to the fortress? Is it safe to climb?

You have a decision to make. Do you:

Keep climbing the stone steps? **P50**

Or

Go back and try to find another way up to the fortress? **P47**

You have decided to find another way up to the fortress.

Once out of the cave, you notice the tide is coming in and the waves are coming closer and closer to the rocky ledge you've been walking along. Spray is being whipped up by the onshore wind, making the rocks slippery.

Not wanting to hang around on the exposed ledge any longer than necessary, you hurriedly make your way back towards the tide pools. In the distance you see that the outer pools are already being swamped by the incoming tide.

Once off the ledge, you keep as far from the water as possible as you hop from rock to rock.

When you are nearly back to the beach, you see a pile of stones you hadn't noticed before, standing about as high as your waist on the edge of the jungle. The stones look to be a marker of some sort.

As you walk closer, you see the cairn is capped with a flat stone that has a compass rose and arrow engraved upon it. The arrow is pointing into the jungle. Is this marking an alternative route up to the fortress?

Pulling the branches aside, you make your way in the direction of the arrow. After about twenty steps you come across a path covered in white shells. The path is narrow and rutted. The jungle closes in on it from both sides. At one time it would have been wide enough for a horse and cart, or even a team of oxen to get up, but now the path is being reclaimed by the jungle and waist high weeds grow amongst the shells. At one point the path cuts across a narrow watercourse flowing directly down the side of the hill. The rocks in the watercourse are covered in a pale white mineral that looks similar to the surrounding limestone cliffs.

It is shady under the dense canopy of branches. You can imagine that travelling the path at night would be difficult. Even with a full moon shining, you can tell that little light would make its way through the trees above. You figure the shells were most likely put here to help guide the way in the dark, in much the same way that people paint the leading edges of concrete steps so they can see where to go at night.

The pathway is steep and follows the natural contours of the land as much as possible as it zigzags up the hillside. In some places large rocks have been used to bridge gullies or provide extra support for the path along the edge of the hill.

Eventually you arrive at a gate on the inland side of the fortress. Charred timbers are the only remnant of what would have been a solid barrier in its time.

You walk cautiously into the fortress. Most of the walls are still intact, but the central courtyard is a messy jumble of twisted timber and other wreckage. The fortress shows sign of a battle that must have taken place here many years ago. In some parts, sections of wall have been destroyed and blackened beams from buildings lay on the ground. Weeds grow between the flagstones. Along the front wall a set of stone steps lead up to a broad promenade along its top.

Three cannon sit along the top of the wall pointing out to sea. Each cannon sits on a cradle with wooden wheels sheathed in metal of some sort. The cradles are not in good order. One leans awkwardly to one side, a wheel collapsed.

You make your way across the courtyard and up the steps. The top of the wall is broad and paved with flat stones. There is a smaller defensive wall on its outward side to stop people, and the guns, from falling down to the rocks below. When you lean out and look down, you can see the ledge you walked along. From this vantage point it looks like a narrow ribbon of stone pressed hard against the cliff, barely a track at all.

The view from the wall is spectacular. Far off to your right you can see the bay, surrounded by the curve of the sand spit. The lighthouse looks like a toy in the distance. The resort and the village also look tiny. You can just make out the aquamarine water of the resort's biggest swimming pool. People on the beach look like insects scurrying around.

As you walk along the top of the wall, you look along the barrel of each cannon, trying to gauge what they'd been aiming at the last time they were fired.

Curiously, every cannon is pointing towards the small island off shore. Why would they be shooting at the island? If the fortress was under attack from pirates surely they would want to shoot at the pirate ships, not some speck of land?

You scratch your head as you think. The fortress is silent. All you can hear are the waves crashing below and the chatter of birds from the surrounding jungle. It looks as though nobody has been here for a long time.

As you walk along the wall towards the turret, you come to a statue. The statue is of a man with his arms outstretched as if he is preaching to people gathered in the courtyard below. His body almost forms a cross. In his hand is a book. The statue sits on a high plinth, but steps lead up to it. You remember the message in the cave that said 'embrace the saint' and wonder if the steps are there so you can climb up and hug the statue. Why else would there be steps?

You feel funny doing it, but you are willing to do anything that helps in your quest. After ascending the steps, you move into the statue's arms, as if to hug a parent. The statue's tunic is draped in such a way that it creates a groove in the stone for you to rest your chin along as you wrap your arms around the saint's torso. You close your eyes and feel the cool marble press against your chest.

When you open your eyes, your gaze is directed toward the little island offshore. Is that where the treasure is? Is this a clue to where the treasure has been hidden? Is the pirate treasure buried on the island?

It is time to make a decision. Do you

Go back to the resort and find a sailboat? **P39**

Or

Look around the fortress a little more? **P62**

You have decided to keep climbing the stone steps.

With your back hard against the stone wall, you slowly take one step after another. It is quite scary climbing in near darkness. You know that one slip will mean certain injury, if not death. Who would come to your rescue if you were to fall? A slight tremor makes your knees shake. Still you keep climbing.

You are pleased you can't see the floor of the cave below. It must be quite a long way down by now.

As you climb higher, the light from the crack in the cave roof gets a little brighter. You can see holes drilled into the wall further up the staircase. One of these holes has the remnants of a wooden torch stuck into it. You reach up and touch the torch as you pass, but the wood turns to dust in your hand. It makes you wonder how long it has been since someone has been up here.

When you reach the end of the stone steps, you are still quite some distance from the top of the cave. At least the light is much better here. The steps finish on a reasonably wide ledge. You look up.

The crack in the roof of the cave is wider than you first thought, about as wide as a bus and almost as long. It drips with creepers and vines. Some of the vines reach all the way down to the ledge. You go over to investigate.

The vines are about as thick as your thumb and twist around each other creating a natural ladder of sorts. You wonder if the vines will hold your weight and give them a strong tug. They seem pretty strong, so you jam your foot at the junction of two vines and step up. You bounce up and down to test their strength. They feel springy, but solid.

As you look up you see hundreds of butterflies hovering in a huge swarm near the cave's opening. They are beautiful. Their wings are framed in a reddish brown, but the main wing area is nearly clear, creating a stained glass window effect. They fly in circles that form a miniature butterfly tornado in the opening.

When you look along on the ledge again, you notice a couple of the butterflies have fallen and lay dead on the ledge. You pick one up and hold it up to the light. It is so delicate with two long thin antennae and a thin tongue, or proboscis, which curls back on itself and almost makes a complete circle. You take two of the beautiful creatures and put them in the front pocket or your pack, careful to fold the wings neatly against their bodies to keep them from getting damaged.

You legs are sore from the big climb up the steps, so you sit on the ledge and lean against the wall for a breather.

You are thinking about climbing the vine when you see something engraved into the smooth stone wall. You get up to investigate. The writing is in an old script but once you stand in a way that allows the maximum of sunlight to shine on it, you can read it.

Climb to the sky and embrace the Saint. Only then will you see your golden future.

You wonder what the inscription means by golden future. And how does one embrace the Saint?

You have a decision to make. Do you:

Climb the hanging vines to the top of the cave? **P52**

Or

Go back down and try to find another way up to the fortress? **P47**

You have decided to climb the hanging vines to the top of the cave.

Once again you place your foot at the junction of where two vines twist around each other and create a place for your foot. It's tricky to see each step because the vines are covered in glossy green heart-shaped leaves, but you find if you hold on with one hand you can pluck the leaves around each foothold as you go up.

After the first few steps you start to get the hang of vine climbing and make your way steadily up towards the roof of the cave. About halfway through the climb you reach the level of the butterflies. They are even prettier up close, with thin dividers between the sections that make up each of the wing panels.

It's a perfect spot for a breather. One of the butterflies lands on your forearm, giving you a closer look. It has six black legs and a narrow body. Its proboscis flicks in and out. When you are ready to start climbing again, you blow gently on the butterfly encouraging it to take off. With a flap of its transparent wings, it joins the others dancing in the sunlight.

Gradually you make your way up the top of the cave and pull yourself over the edge. The climb has taken a lot of energy and it takes a minute to catch your breath.

You sit up and look around. Lush foliage stretches in all directions and you wonder how many people have fallen down this hole by mistake. The jungle around the hole is foreign to you. Dense vegetation of every description crowds in. It makes you feel like you are the first person to stand here, but then you remember the steps painstakingly cut into the solid rock and laugh at your foolishness. Of course others have been here. Maybe this is where the pirates came to hide their treasure.

The jungle is so thick you have no idea which direction to head. You hope you can find a path somewhere. You walk around the hole, making sure not to trip and fall over the edge as you look for a path.

Then you see a flat stone with an arrow engraved in it wedged into the crook of a gnarled old tree. It points directly uphill along a very narrow and rocky watercourse.

You head up the watercourse thinking that if it leads nowhere at least you'll be able to find your way back to the hole and climb back down to the beach to get back to the resort.

The rocks in the stream have been rounded by the water running over them for so many years. Some of them are creamy white, and look to be coated in the same calcium material that the stalagmites were made of.

Finally after quite a steep climb, you reach the walls of the fortress. Rough blocks of stone tower high about you. There is no way to climb up here, so you turn inland hoping to find a gateway or a section of wall that has been breached so you can get into the fortress.

It is tough going. The jungle is growing right up to the old wall and often you need to work your way past a tangle of branches to keep moving. One tangle of branches is covered in thorns and red flowers making it difficult to pass, but then once you get through you see a section of wall that has partially fallen.

You scale the pile of tumbled down rocks and enter the deserted fortress. Many of the walls are still intact, but the central courtyard is a messy jumble of twisted timber and other wreckage. The fortress shows signs of the battle that must have taken place here many years ago. Parts of the wall have been destroyed and piles of charred beams lay on the ground. Tall weeds grow between the flagstones and a set of stone steps lead up to a broad promenade around the top of the wall. Three cannon sit on the promenade pointing out to sea. Each cannon sits on a carriage of timber that has wooden wheels sheathed in metal of some sort. The carriages are not in good order. One leans awkwardly to one side, its wheel collapsed.

You make your way across the courtyard and up the stone steps to the top of the wall. The top of the wall is broad. There is a smaller defensive wall on its outward side to stop people and the guns from falling down to the rocks below. When you lean out and look down, you can see the narrow ledge you walked along to get to the cave far below.

The view from the wall is spectacular. Far off to your right you can see the bay, surrounded by the curve of the sand spit. The lighthouse looks like a toy in the distance. The resort and the village also look tiny. You can just make out the aquamarine water of the resort's biggest swimming pool. People on the beach look like beetles scurrying around.

As you walk along the top of the wall, you look along the barrel of each cannon, trying to gauge what they'd been aiming at the last time they were fired.

Curiously, each cannon is pointing towards the small island off shore. Why would they be shooting at the island? If the fortress was under attack, surely they would want to shoot at the pirate ships?

The fortress is silent. All you can hear are the waves crashing below and the chatter of birds from the surrounding jungle. It looks as though nobody has been here for a long time.

You come to a statue just beside the turret on one end. The statue is of a man, his arms outstretched as if he is preaching to people gathered in the courtyard. In his hand is a book. It is an odd pose. The statue sits on a plinth, but steps lead up to it. You remember the message in the cave. It said, embrace the Saint.

You ascend the stairs and step into the statues outstretched arms. The statue's tunic is draped in such a way that it creates a groove for you to rest your chin in as you wrap your arms around the Saint's torso. You close your eyes and relax in the statue's cool embrace. Then you open your eyes and see the island offshore. Is that where the treasure is? Is the statue a clue to finding it? Could gold on the island be what a golden future means?

It is time to make a decision. Do you:

Go back to the hole at the top of the cave and climb back down to the beach and go back to the resort the way you came? **P56**

Or

Leave the fortress and try to find another way back to the resort? **P58**

You have decided to go back to the hole at the top of the cave.

You see a broken and charred gate on the far side of the fortress, but decide to go back over the collapsed wall the way you came in just to be sure you don't miss the track back down the hillside.

Going down is harder than climbing up because you can't reach forward and grab on to things so easily. A couple of times you slip on the smooth rocks as you descend. You slow down as you get close to the top of the hole, not wanting to slip over the edge.

The hole appears below you as a gaping crack in the earth. You work your way around the side and look for the vines that you climbed up. It's hard to tell which vines are which from this angle. You regret not marking the right ones.

When you're pretty sure you've found the place to descend, you lie on your belly clutching the vines and lower yourself feet first over the ledge.

It is hot and your hands are sweaty. You twist your head around searching for a foothold. You finally jam your foot over a twist in two vines and are able to take the pressure off your arms.

This isn't as easy as you thought it would be.

Finding the next foothold is just as hard. You arms strain as you try to find a place to rest your foot. This is so much harder than climbing up, when you could easily see where to put your foot as you climbed.

Your arms are aching as you look for a step. Your feet are flailing around desperately. You feel your hands slipping on the vines as your strength starts to go. You try to grip harder, but you can't. You are slipping! The friction burns your hands. The pain is too much and you fall through the darkness.

Unfortunately, this part of your story is now over. You made an unwise decision in trying to climb down the vine. Remember it's often harder climbing down than climbing up, especially when you can't see where to put your feet. Pity you didn't think of that.

But not to worry, you can start over.

It is time for you to make a decision. Do you:

Go back to the very beginning of the story? **P7**

Or

Go back to your previous decision and decide to leave the fortress and try to find another way back to the resort. **P58**

You have decided to try to find another way back to the resort.

The most obvious way to leave the fortress is through a charred gate on the far side of the courtyard. You step over the massive burnt timbers lying on the ground and step outside the compound where there is an overgrown pathway covered with white shells twisting down the hillside.

After the first sharp corner, the pathway disappears under the canopy into the jungle. Being unused like it is, the jungle has taken back much of the path. Deep ruts have been cut across it during the rains and the footing is tricky in places.

As you are jumping over one such channel cut into the pathway you notice a huge centipede crawling down its centre. You can't believe the size of it. You remember reading about the giant centipedes that live here in the Caribbean, but you never dreamed you'd see one!

It is longer than your foot. You stop for a quick look, and then remember that it is also extremely poisonous and feeds on birds, lizards, tarantula spiders, and even bats! Then you remember it is also supposed to be very fast on its many, many feet.

You move down the hill, looking back once or twice to make sure the nasty looking beast isn't following you. This is not an insect you want to mess around with.

About half way down the hill, near the edge of the path, you see a huge spider's web strung between two trees. You move a little closer to have a look. The spider is bright yellow with black stripes on its legs. You've read about this spider too. It's a banana spider, also known as the Brazilian wandering spider, one of the most lethal in the world! Suddenly the jungle feels like a dangerous place.

Your walk becomes more of a trot as you scrunch down the shelled path. You look right and left, wondering what other lethal creatures are lurking in the jungle ready to leap out and ruin your holiday.

At the bottom of the path you pass a stone cairn. On top of the cairn is a flat stone with a compass rose and an arrow engraved into it pointing back up the hill in the direction from which you've come. You are relieved to be back on the beach.

You pull your water bottle out and drain the last of it into your parched mouth. You try to forget about spiders and centipedes and think about more pleasant things like gold doubloons and pirate treasure. You wipe your mouth with the back of your hand and put your water bottle back in your pack.

There are a few boats out in the bay, but none are sailing near the island. After another half an hour's walk you are back at the resort.

It is time to make a decision. Do you:

Go check in with your family? **P64**

Or

Go and take one of the sailboats out to the island? **P39**

You have decided to go deeper into the underground chamber.

There is very little light as you head down the next flight of steps into the underground chamber. Your hand touches the cool stone of the wall as you descend step by step; more feeling your way than seeing. Dark is closing in on you and the walls are damp with moisture.

It smells musty down here, like dirt and pee and dead animals.

When you reach the bottom of the staircase, you can barely see your hand in front of your face. The ground under your feet is slippery and sloping steeply off into the darkness.

You are beginning to think this was a bad idea when you hear screeching above your head and you realize that what you smell are bats.

And if bats are hanging on the ceiling, it means the slipperiness under your feet is most likely bat droppings.

You turn to go back up, but in the process you slip onto one knee. You don't want to put your hand down in the bat poo so you try to get up without using your hands.

As you lurch to your feet you lose your balance and twist around, both feet slip out from under you and you fall backwards. You reach out to steady yourself, but there is nothing to hold on to. Your shoulder hits the ground with a thud and you find yourself sliding further down the slope.

The further you slide, the steeper the floor becomes, until it is so steep you couldn't get to your feet even if you wanted too. After sliding for ages, you smack hard into a stone wall at the bottom of the ramp.

You are wet, bruised and covered in muck. A faint light shines back at the top of the slope but the slime covered ramp is impossible for you to climb no matter how hard you try. You are stuck in the bowels of the fortress. With luck someone will find you before you die of thirst.

Unfortunately, this part of your story is over. You made a bad decision to go deeper when you didn't have enough light to see properly. Hidden dangers lurked in the darkness.

Luckily you can have another go at getting it right.

It is time to make a decision. Do you:

Go back to the very beginning of the story? **P7**

Or

Make that last choice differently? **P62**

You have decided to look around the fortress a little more.

You turn your back on the statue and walk back along the top of the wall towards the steps leading down into the courtyard. There are a couple of inner doors built into the fortress walls you want to investigate.

Bolted to the wall beside one door is an iron basket filled with the remnants of a fire. The burned wood doesn't look as old as the other charred remains scattered around the courtyard. It makes you wonder if someone else has been up here recently.

The doorway is a wide arch of stones fitted perfectly into the wall without the need for mortar. Two large hinges are set into the wall, but you can't see a door anywhere. You take a step into the passage and turn right. The passage leads to some steps that take you down below ground level.

By the time you are halfway down the steps, the light is fading fast. Then you see a faint light in front of you as you carefully feel you way down the remainder of the steps. A narrow slit in the seaward wall provides you with just enough light to see that you are in a hollowed out chamber below the courtyard, held up with massive stone columns. More iron baskets are attached to the walls, along with a series of iron rings linked together with rusted chain. You shiver when you realize this must have been where the Spanish held their captives.

You poke your head into another doorway and see another flight of steps leading even deeper into the fortress. How many levels are there?

Leaning on its side against one wall is an iron gate. The gate has bars running from top to bottom. On the end of each bar is a sharp spike. This must be the gate from the doorway above, but why has it been taken off its hinges and dragged downstairs?

Then you see that there is a narrow ledge in the wall above the gate. Light from a narrow slit in the ledge is pouring into the underground chamber. Whoever leaned the gate against the wall must have used it as a ladder to climb up to the ledge, but why?

You cross the chamber and test the bars on the old gate. They are rusty, but will still support your weight. Carefully you climb the eight or so bars up to the ledge.

What you see nearly makes you fall, because lying on the ledge is a skeleton.

You scurry back down and try to control your shaking. An image of the skeleton flashes in your mind. There is something not quite right about this picture. Once you stop shaking, you grab onto to the gate and start climbing once more.

As you peer over the edge of the ledge, the skeleton comes back into view. Its bones are white and perfectly laid out, as if a person had climbed up onto the ledge, laid down on their back, and gone to sleep. But that couldn't be what happened. Where are the skeleton's clothes? If the person had died down in this chamber, surely they would have had on rags at least. But there is no sign of any clothing.

Could this skeleton be someone trying to scare other treasure hunters off?

You look out of the narrow window inset into the wall above the ledge. The wall on this part of the fortress is very thick and the window gets smaller and smaller as it goes through the stone. By the time it gets to the opening on the outside of the wall, the opening is only the width of your hand, far too small for a person to fit through.

But it is the view out the window that interests you most. Surely this can't be by chance.

Framed perfectly by the window, across the narrow stretch of water, is the small island.

It is time for you to make a decision. Do you:

Head back to the resort, get a boat and sail out to the island? **P39**
Or

Go down the steps deeper into the underground chamber? **P60**

You have decided to go check in with your family.

Your family are pleased to see you. They yell for you to jump into the pool and join them, so you strip down to your swimsuit and dive in. The water is cool and refreshing after your long walk. You lie on your back and float as your sore muscles relax.

As you float, you watch the birds flit around the flowering shrubs planted around the pool area. They are a noisy lot, and not at all scared by the people. Some birds pick at crumbs dropped on the ground in the outdoor eating area.

For a few minutes you dive and swim and splash the others, but before long you get restless. What you really want to do is go exploring again.

You tell your family that if you find treasure, you'll buy them each something special. After learning this they seem keen for you to go off again.

You go up to your room for some more supplies. You take a couple of chocolate bars and a bottle of water from the mini bar. You also grab a sweatshirt in case it is cold later on as the sun goes down and put them in your pack. You spot a lighter next to the gas stove in the kitchen and slip it into your pocket, thinking it might come in handy too.

After zipping up your pack, you head down the steps to the reception area, walk through the lobby and head out the front door towards the beach.

It is time to make a decision: Do you:

Go and take one of the resort's sailboats out to the island. **P39**

Or

Go left towards the old fortress? **P12**

Or

Go right towards the lighthouse? **P8**

You have decided to walk around the rocks towards the shipwreck.

You take your pack from the watertight compartment in the sailing dinghy and slip it over your shoulders. The plan is to walk around the rocks to the shipwreck you saw when sailing around the island. There could be all sorts of interesting things to find.

The tide is on its way out. As the minutes pass, more and more rocks are exposed. Hundreds of black mussel shells are attached to those recently exposed, a feast just there for the taking. Maybe you'll gather some of the shellfish on your way back to the beach and steam them open over a small fire.

Getting around the rocks isn't quite as easy as it looked like it would be when you sailed past in the dinghy. In a number of places, deep channels, too wide to jump, run from the ocean right up to the rocky shore making it tricky and a little dangerous. Luckily the waves are small and you are able to negotiate your way by hugging the cliff and using vines hanging from above as handholds as you work your way around towards the wreck.

When the ship comes into view, you are amazed how big it is. Huge ribs curve up and out from the massive timber keel. Few of the hull planks remain, most having been washed away over years by the many storms that frequent these parts.

Below the bowsprit, attached to the solid prow of the boat, is the wooden figure of a woman. Her back is attached to the ship, her chin is up, chest thrust forward, arms calmly down by her sides. She looks as if she is surrendering herself to the sea, passive yet strong and ready for whatever the sea may throw at her. Then you notice the carved figure has the body of a fish. The figurehead is a mermaid.

The ship has been wedged high on the rocks by the sea, pushed further and further onto land by each subsequent storm. Only the sturdiest of timbers remain intact. The deck has holes in it and the mast is only a stump. Where the rest of it has gone is a mystery.

You walk around the ship, studying it from every angle. You wonder how many gold coins were spilled into the sea when it came ashore. How many unfound coins remain somewhere nearby today?

Maybe you should go for a snorkel and see if you can find any that have been missed by other treasure hunters over the years. Storms would constantly churn up the sand on the seabed, who knows what treasure might have been uncovered in the last big blow.

You strip down to your bathing suit and grab your snorkel. But then as you reach the seaward side of the wreck and look back at the island, you notice a ladder made from two long wooden poles leaning against the cliff. Smaller branches are lashed to the main supports with vines to create steps. You like the idea of diving for coins, but you also wonder where the ladder leads.

It is time for you to make a decision. Do you:

Go snorkeling by the shipwreck? **P69**

Or

Go back to the beach and explore the islands interior? **P67**

You have decided to go inland and explore the island.

The plan is to explore the interior of the island. Maybe you can even get to the summit. There could be all sorts of interesting things to find along the way.

When you reach the top of the beach, you pull back a palm frond and step into the jungle. You stop for a moment and listen. You wonder what creatures live here. You can hear parrots squawking and the whoop, whoop, whoop, of some larger bird flying through the canopy high above. You look around trying to decide which way to go.

There is a natural path leading slightly uphill towards the centre of the island. The path looks like it acts as a watercourse when the heavy tropical rains come. The ground has been washed clean of dirt, and you find yourself walking on a layer of pebbles, occasionally stepping around large boulders that block your way as you go.

Some of the pebbles are almost clear. Quartz you figure. Then others appear that are amber in color. Then a glassy looking stone of pink appears. You reach down to pick it up and hold it up to the light. You can see right through it. You remember reading about rose quartz, but you've never seen a piece so large or so perfectly round before.

You pop the rock into your daypack and dig around with the toe of your shoe to see if you can unearth any more. Each time you rake the pebbles in the watercourse over, more colored stones appear. All of them have glittering quartz in them. Some are a smoky grey and have a stripe of white running down their centers. Others are a pale green. You select a few of each color and tuck them away for safe keeping.

Then you see two fist-sized chalky white rocks similar to ones you've seen before. You pick them up and hold them together. You rub them together as fast as you can. Sure enough, little sparks of light are generated by the friction. You remember the name of this cool phenomenon. Triboluminescence.

You put the two white stones together with the others you've collected into your daypack and start walking uphill again. Before you go very far, you come across a large pile of rocks. On top of the cairn is a flat rock with a compass rose and an arrow engraved on it. The arrow points away from the natural pebble path and towards two large trees up the slope to your right.

Why the arrow is pointing you to steeper ground you're not quite sure. It is a far more difficult route to the top of the island than following the watercourse.

It is time for you to make a decision. Do you:

Carry on up the watercourse? **P74**

Or

Follow the arrow and go up between the two trees? **P76**

You have decided to go snorkeling by the shipwreck.

You walk down to the water's edge and strip down to your bathing suit. You leave your pack sitting on the rocks and look for a safe place to enter the water. There is a wide channel with a sandy bottom between the rocks that you think might be a good place to start your search. After finding a good spot you put on your snorkel and ease yourself into the water.

The water is nice and refreshing after your walk around the rocks. Visibility is excellent and you can see many small fish darting back and forth. Rock walls hem you in on either side. From a big crack in the rocks, an orange lobster looks back at you. Its beady eyes follow you nervously as you glide past.

Every hole and crevice seems to be home to some creature or other. Urchins with sharp red spines are scattered across the bottom.

You take a deep breath and head down to the bottom, looking back and forth for anything interesting as you go. When your lungs begin to burn, you make for the surface to catch your breath.

With each dive you move further away from the island. After a number of unsuccessful dives, you decide to turn and head back towards shore. You are almost back to where you started, when something catches your eye.

You take a deep breath and head down once more. Then you see it again, wedged into a crack in the rock. It looks like a handle of some sort.

You grab on to the handle and pull. As you kick towards the surface, a short, slightly curved steel blade slides out of the narrow crack in the rock. You realize you've found a pirate's cutlass or machete as they are called here in the Caribbean.

It is a beautiful sword. Inset into its silver handle are a number of gemstones. One glistens green, another red, and yet another amber. Holding tight to your find, you kick towards shore, eager to have a good look at your discovery.

After climbing back onto the rocks, you inspect the blade a little closer. It is remarkably clean. It's strange that something that had been submerged under the water for any length of time is so new looking, especially here in the tropics where the marine life grows so quickly. You would have thought it would have been encrusted with barnacles, algae and other sea life.

You hold the blade up to the sun. Beams of light reflect off the shining steel. Then you feel the cutlass begin to hum. When you tighten your grip on the handle, the blade vibrates even more. The hum turns to a high-pitched ringing as the blade vibrates faster and faster.

A big spark flashes from the end of the blade and you are knocked to the ground as the cutlass clatters onto the rocks.

"Ouch!" you say, rubbing your hand. What sort of strange cutlass is this?

You have seen pictures of similar swords in pirate books you've read, but you've never heard of one giving someone an electric shock before!

"That was so random," you mumble.

Afraid to pick up the cutlass with your bare hand, you dig into your pack and pull out your sweatshirt. Using it as insulation you carefully pick up the blade and wrap it up in the sweatshirt before placing it inside your pack for safekeeping.

The treasure hunting is going well so far, even if what you are finding is a little odd. If you want to do more exploring, it is time for you to make a decision. Do you:

Go back to the beach where you landed and go inland to explore more of the island? **P67**

Or

Climb the pole ladder? **P71**

You have decided to climb up the pole ladder.

Upon closer inspection the ladder looks quite sturdy. It is made from two long wooden poles with stout branches lashed between as steps. Just to be safe you take the first few steps carefully, not sure if the old lashings will hold your weight, but after the first couple of steps you are quite confident that it is safe.

When you are about half way up the ladder, you hear what sounds like men singing. You wonder where they could have come from. When you turn your head around to see who it is making all the noise, you are so shocked at what you see you nearly fall.

On the deck of the wrecked ship are a group of men dressed in long black shorts and striped shirts of varying colors. A few of the men have scarves tied around their heads.

One of the men wears white pants, high black boots and a jacket with tails. He has a black hat on his head and holds a cutlass in his hand like the one you found. Many of the men hold tankards in their hands and are drinking and singing.

You can't believe your eyes. What are these men doing here? Are they ghosts? You wonder if the vibrating cutlass has caused you to go through a time-warp somehow. Why are the men dressed so strangely? Nobody dresses like that anymore, except people going to a costume party.

Unsure of what is happening, you climb the ladder as quickly as you can, hoping the men don't see you. When you reach the top of the ladder you hide behind a bush and watch.

Once the men finish their tankards, a couple of them bring a chest up from the ship's hold. The man with the cutlass is yelling orders. You hear the sailors yell.

"Aye aye Captain!"

The wrecked ship doesn't look as damaged for some reason. And it's only just on the rocks, not way up like it was before. The mast is back too, and from it flies a Spanish flag of red and gold. You shake your head and wonder what is going on here. This can't be happening!

Then you see the gold and red flag drop to the deck and a black and white skull and crossbones go up in its place. The pirates have taken the ship. But how? All this happened years ago!

Six of the men lower a wooden rowboat over the side of the ship and climb down some rope netting into it. The other men then carefully lower the trunk down to them. Once the trunk is safely stowed in the bottom of the boat and the oars readied, the men in the boat row off around the island.

Where are they going? Is there treasure in that trunk?

When a loud boom sounds, you look back towards the mainland and see smoke coming from the walls of the fortress. Someone is shooting the old cannon on the wall. How can it be? You notice the tower on one end of the fortress is still intact. But that's impossible!

Then a series of massive booms sound behind you. They must be coming from the far side of the island. Seconds later, part of the fortress wall is smashed in by cannon balls smacking against it. Men in the fortress are running around like busy ants behind the walls.

There is another BOOM and two Spanish ships at anchorage in the calm waters below the fort burst into flames. Spanish sailors are jumping into the sea to escape the fire.

You don't know how it is possible, but somehow you've ended up in the middle of a battle.

Is the cutlass you found magic? You look again at the cutlass in the hand of the captain on the wrecked ship. The handle glitters green, red and amber just like the one you found.

More flashes appear on the fortress walls and you hear the scream of a cannonball overhead. One cannonball crashes into the trees nearby, breaking branches and sending a flock of birds squawking as they fly off in alarm. Another flurry of shots from the fortress smash into the deck of the wrecked ship and some of the pirates go flying.

It is time for you to make a decision. Do you:

Walk around the island and continue to watch the pirates in the row boat? **P89**

Or

Stay where you are and keep watching the pirates? **P93**

You have decided to carry on up the watercourse.

You have decided to ignore the arrow pointing you up towards the steeper part of the slope and continue along the easier and less steep watercourse that leads up the centre of the valley. You've been making good time and can't see any reason to change your strategy. The watercourse is easy to climb apart from when you need to work your way around the occasional large rock blocking your way.

The creatures on the little island don't seem afraid of you as you go along. Maybe they haven't seen many people before. One little bird is flitting quite close by, almost following your footsteps. The bird has a fat body and a tail shaped like a fan. It nips around with remarkable speed nabbing tasty morsels. Then you realize the bird is hunting all the insects that you have disturbed.

As you progress further up the path, the ground starts to rise sharply and more big rocks start to block your path, making the climb more difficult.

As you move around one of the boulders in your way a sound further up the hillside attracts your attention. You stop walking and listen. The noise is getting closer.

A large cracking sound startles you. Whatever it is coming down the hill towards you is moving fast. Could it be an animal of some sort, or is it something else? You crouch down, dropping to one knee and try to see under the branches blocking your view.

When you see the tumbling boulder, it is too late for you to move out of its way.

It is coming right at you. You scream. In the split second before it hits, you have the sudden realization that the arrow on the cairn was trying to warn you of rock falls!

Unfortunately this part of your story is over.

You decided to continue up the watercourse. Those boulders

blocking the path further down the hillside, should have given you a clue that this is an unstable area. Avalanches and rock falls often run down the centre of gullies like this one.

It is time for you to make a decision. Do you:

Make that last decision differently? **P76**

Or

Go back to the very beginning of the story? **P7**

You have decided to follow the arrow and go up between the two trees.

Whoever bothered to build this cairn of stones probably did so for a reason, so you decide to head up between the two large trees and see where it takes you. You're not very far up the slope when you hear a crashing sound flying down the hillside from above.

You crouch down and try to see under the branches. What is making all the noise? Then you realize it's a rock slide. A big rock from higher up has been dislodged and is coming down the hillside along the path of the dry watercourse.

A flash of grey the size of a car zips past you. The sound of branches breaking and the rumble of smaller rocks being loosened fill the small valley.

Had you decided to continue on up the watercourse, you would have been squashed like a bug.

You are shaking a little. That was too close for comfort. You sit down with your feet tucked under you and listen to the sounds crashing further down the valley.

Determined to get to the top of the island, you get up and move off. The slope is steeper here, but at least there isn't quite as much undergrowth and you've got tree branches to pull yourself up with.

Before long you reach a grassy patch of level ground. Growing in the middle of the meadow is a huge tree dripping with oranges. You can't believe your eyes. Never before have you seen such a big tree laden with so much fruit.

You pluck an orange from a low-hanging branch and start peeling off the skin. Then you break the orange into sections and pop one in your mouth. When you bite into it, juice runs down your chin and the orange flavor bursts into your mouth. This has got to be the tastiest orange you've ever eaten.

You wonder why it is here on the island, and why it is the only tree in the little meadow. You also wonder how anything could taste so delicious. Did pirates plant the tree here so they could pick the fruit to prevent scurvy from a lack of vitamin C? The tree looks old, but could it be that old? Maybe one of the villagers put it here. You must remember to ask the village boy when you get back to the mainland.

After finishing the orange and picking two more and putting them into your backpack for later, you look around wondering which way to go from here. You remember your math teacher telling you that the shortest distance between two points is a straight line, so you point your nose towards the top of the hill and start walking.

Once you've left the meadow, the ground gets steep quite quickly. Loose stones underfoot mean you have to pick where to step carefully. Sometimes your foot slips so you have to move quickly to regain your balance.

Finally the ground becomes less steep and you have the feeling the top is just over the next rise. Then you hear the sound of hundreds of birds. You must be close now.

After climbing up one last slope, you see the ocean. When you look out at the endless expanse of ocean it feels like you've come to the edge of the world.

Birds swarm in the sky. There are so many of them you wonder how they manage not to have mid-air collisions. A couple swoop down to check you out, screeching at you for invading their territory. Others are diving into the sea below, catching fish for their young ones back in their nests in the cliffs.

The ocean sparkles with a million pinpoints of light. A small patch of cloud far out to sea billows up like cotton wool but its underside is dark and flat. Rain falls in streaks from its grey bottom, but the rest of the sky is clear and sunny.

You are up high enough to see the slight curvature of the earth on the horizon as it stretches off in both directions. Seeing this curve reminds you that you are standing on a sphere that orbits around a sun in a solar system that is in a tiny part of the much larger Milky Way galaxy. It makes you feel incredibly small in one way, yet up here so high, you also feel like a giant looking down on everything as far as your eye can see.

You are about to sit down and rest for a moment, but before you do, you want to check out the strange looking structure that sits a few paces back from the edge of the cliff on the highest point of ground. It looks as though it has been here for quite some time.

The structure is a three-legged tower. The legs of the tower are spaced wide at the bottom and joined together at the top like a Native American tepee. Timber poles are lashed between each of its legs adding stability to the structure. A narrow ladder goes from the ground to a small lookout platform about three quarters of the way up.

A pair of old wood and iron pulleys hang from chains looped around the timbers. A rope runs from one pulley through to the other and then its end disappears over the edge of the cliff.

You are surprised you didn't see the tower from the water when you sailed around the island, but then the tower is set back from the edge a little, leaving only the length of rope to be spotted from below.

You walk around the structure looking at the placement of the pulleys. They look like they are for lifting things up from the water below. Like a primitive crane of sorts, but why here?

You walk towards where the rope is hanging over the edge of the cliff to check it out. A few paces away from the edge you get down on to your hands and knees and crawl carefully forward. As you near the edge you lay on your belly and inch forward and peer over the edge.

The view straight down makes your stomach lurch. There is nothing below but water.

Looking straight down from such a height makes you a little dizzy. The clearness and depth of the water makes the distance to the surface look even greater than it is. You grab onto the rope for security, just in case.

It is just as well, because the ground under you is rumbling.

"Earthquake!" you yell out as you push yourself back from the edge. But it is already too late. The edge of the cliff is breaking away. You twist the rope around your wrist and hang on as tight as you can, hoping that the rope will be strong enough to hold your weight.

As the edge of the cliff cracks way, the old rope creaks a little but thankfully, it doesn't look in any danger of breaking. Before you know it, you are hanging over the water far below.

You wrap one leg around the rope to ease the stress on your arm and hang on for dear life as the breeze swings you back and forth. Gradually the swinging stops and you try to pull yourself up a little at a time. It is hard work, and before long your arms are getting tired.

You are considering letting go and taking the plunge into the sea when you feel the rope begin to rise. You look up and hold on even tighter.

Then you hear a voice from above. "Hang on."

Slowly you start to rise. When your head reaches the top of the cliff, you see a boy from the village over by the tower pulling on the rope.

Before you know it, you are over the edge and back on firm ground. The boy ties the rope around part of the wooden frame and comes over to where you are lying on the ground.

You sit up, shake your aching arms, and look up at the boy. "Wow that was close. What are you doing out here?"

"When I saw you sailing towards the island I decided to take my father's boat out and join you. I thought you might like a friend to help you look for treasure."

"That would be great," you say. "After my close calls today, I think it will be a lot safer exploring with someone else."

"Calls?" the boy asks. "You mean this isn't the first trouble you've been in today?"

You tell him about the rock fall.

The boy smiles at you. "Sounds like you need a minder."

The two of you have a good laugh and then the boy reaches his hand out and helps pull you to your feet.

"You're probably right," you say still holding his hand. "What's your name?"

"It's Kai," says the boy and you solemnly shake as you swap names.

"So what should we do?" asks Kai.

"I don't know. Maybe we should climb up the tower and see if we can spot something interesting from up there?"

"Or, we could go back down to the beach and go exploring around the island in my father's boat," Kai says.

It is time for you to make a decision. Do you:

Climb the tower? **P81**

Or

Go exploring in Kai's father's boat? **P94**

You have decided to climb the tower.

After walking over to the tower, you approach the narrow ladder that leads up to the observation platform. You should both get an excellent view of the island and surrounding ocean from way up there.

Kai runs over and starts climbing. He's quick. You figure it's probably all the practice he's had climbing coconut trees. You take the climb a little slower, preferring to get there in one piece rather than rush.

After the climb, the two of you find yourselves standing on the platform looking out over the surrounding jungle and ocean. The ocean breeze blows through your hair.

As you suspected, the view from up here is amazing. Over the treetops, and across the short stretch of water, you can see the walls of the old fortress. White spray crashes into the rocks below its crumbling walls.

Further to the left, the resort buildings nestle close together in a big U-shape around the aqua blue of the biggest swimming pool.

Then you see the thatched huts of the village. They blend into their surroundings and are much smaller and harder to spot. The villagers' fishing boats are little more than brightly colored dots on the beach.

The lighthouse looks small from this high up. Its red and white stripes make it look like a piece of Christmas candy.

"I can see a lot, but no obvious spot to hide treasure," you say.

"Me neither."

"So maybe you're right. Maybe this tower was just for the pirates to use when they were attacking the fortress."

You are about to climb down when you notice something lying in the long grass ten or so paces from the tower. The area is so overgrown that you almost missed it.

"What's that?" you say, pointing to a metal grid of some sort.

"I don't know, let's go down and take a look," Kai says as he swings his leg down and starts descending.

By the time you get down, he is pulling weeds from around the object.

"It's a metal basket of some sort," Kai yells.

You help him clear the rest of the weeds around the basket and then the two of you sit it upright.

The basket is made from strips of metal woven together and attached to a slightly heavier iron rim. The diameter of the rim is a little bigger than your outstretched arms and comes up to your waist. Three lengths of chain are attached around the rim of the basket at one end and joined together with a big iron ring at the other.

"I bet the pirates used this to move things up and down the cliff," you say. "See how it works? You tie a rope around this big ring at the top here, and then raise and lower it using the pulleys attached to the tower."

"Wouldn't you need a lot of men to do that?" Kai asks.

"No, you see the pulleys make it easy. Just like when you were pulling me up. The good thing is you only need one person if the rope is long enough because you can operate the pulleys while you are in the basket."

"How?" Kai asks.

"You just climb in the basket and slowly let out the rope," you say. "The rope is attached to the top of the basket. Then it goes around the pulleys which take all the weight. Then it comes back to you in the basket."

"I see," Kai says, studying the apparatus. "And then when you want to come up again you just pull on the rope and up you come. Right?"

"Right," you say. "Tie the loose end of the rope onto the basket whenever you want to stop, and you just hang there."

"Wow," the village boy says. "That sounds like fun!"

"It could be dangerous," you tell him.

Kai looks at you and smiles. "We could always go exploring in my father's boat if you're afraid."

You're not sure if you are afraid or excited.

It is time for you to make a decision. Do you:

Lower yourselves over the cliff? **P84**

Or

Go exploring more of the island in Kai's father's boat instead? **P94**

You have decided to lower yourselves over the cliff.

After getting all the grass out of the metal basket, you and Kai roll it to the edge of the cliff nearest the tower. You run the thick rope through the big iron ring and tie a couple of knots to secure it. Then you tie an extra knot just to be safe.

The rope now runs from the top of the basket through two pulleys and then runs back to where you are standing. There is lots of rope left over so there should be enough to get you all the way down the cliff.

"Let's test it first okay? We'll lower the basket on its own before we try it with us in there."

The two of you maneuver the basket as close to the edge as possible.

The boy lets out a little more rope and you push the bottom of the basket over the edge. After a couple of minutes, you yell out. "Okay, that's enough. Let's see how hard it is to pull it back up again."

Kai starts pulling in the rope. "Hey it's easy, just like you said," he says. "Hardly heavy at all."

You grab onto the rope and help pull. The basket comes up surprisingly fast with both of you pulling. Before you know it, the rim of the basket is level with the edge of the cliff.

"Our turn," Kai says with a big grin.

You both take hold of the rope and creep forward on your backsides until your legs are dangling into the basket. Then with a quick look at each other, you both hop into the basket. It sways a little but because you are both holding onto the rope it doesn't drop at all.

"Don't look down," you say. "And not too fast, it isn't a race okay."

Letting a little rope out at a time, the two of you lower yourselves down the side of the cliff. As you do, you pass by the nesting birds. The parent birds squawk in alarm as you pass, but refuse to leave their nests while you are there.

About a third of the way down the cliff you pass a narrow opening in the rock wall.

"Stop," you say. "I think I see something at the back of this hole."

You loop the rope around a big hook on the side of the basket and lean into the recess. The opening is narrow and covered in bird droppings, but it is big enough for you to crawl through.

"I wish we had a flashlight," Kai says.

Then you remember the lighter in your pocket and have an idea. You grab some dried grass and small twigs from a deserted bird's nest and squash it into a ball. Holding the lighter below the ball you flick the lighter. The ball catches fire immediately. Before long it is well alight.

You toss the ball into the opening. The light from the flame allows you to see a small chest hard up against the back wall of the tiny cave.

"Wow!" you say. "Look at that!"

Kai is speechless. His mouth is hanging open and his eyes are huge.

After double checking that the rope is well tied off, you climb over the rim of the basket across a narrow ledge and into the opening. You crawl past the burning ball towards the chest.

A solid clasp holds the lid of the chest closed, but there is no lock. You release the clasp and lift the lid.

When you see what is inside the chest your mouth opens wide too. You reach in and grab a handful of gold doubloons and hold them out for Kai to see.

"We've found it!" you cry out. "Look!"

"Yippee!" Kai yells. "But what now? How do we get it back to the mainland? It looks heavy."

You both think for a moment.

"I have an idea," you say. "Help me get the chest into the basket. Then we can both pull us up to the top. Then you get out and go down and get your father's boat and bring it around to this side of the island and wait below while I lower myself and the chest down into your boat."

Kai grins. "Aye aye, captain!"

The chest is pretty heavy, but the two of you manage to slide it out of the cave and down into the basket. Then the job of pulling the basket back up starts. The added weight of the chest has made the job harder, but with the two of you it only takes about ten minutes to get back to the top and tie off the rope.

"Right, I'll be back as soon as I can," Kai says as he climbs out.

While he's gone, you sit in the basket and enjoy the view. After a while the birds forget you are there. When you hear the steady putt-putt of a motor you look off to your left and see the boat coming around the headland.

You untie the rope and start your way down. Going down is a lot easier than it was going up. You are nearly down at water level by the time the boat is below you.

As Kai cuts the engine, he reaches up and grabs the basket to hold to boat in place while you pay out the last of the rope. The boat sinks a little deeper in the water as it takes the additional weight of the chest.

After getting the chest out of the basket Kai grabs a rope and ties the chest down so it won't move about on the trip back to the village. Then he turns to you. "Alright, let's pick up your sailboat and I'll give you a tow back in. It will be much quicker."

"Wait. It might be better for me to take the basket back up and hide it at the top," you say. "We may not want people to know what we've discovered quite yet."

Kai nods. "Okay I'll meet you back on the beach by your sailboat."

You jump back into the basket and start pulling. Without the weight of the trunk, you make pretty quick progress. "See you soon," you yell down as the village boy motors off.

Once you're at the top, you untie the basket and roll it under some bushes. You pull the rope off the pulleys and hide that too. Then you head back down the way you came to the beach.

Kai is waiting for you when you arrive. You tie the bowline from your sailboat onto the back of his boat and jump aboard with him for the ride back to the mainland.

"So what are you going to do with your share of the treasure?" you ask.

"I'm going to get my father his operation to fix his eyes, and then depending how much money there is left over, maybe the people of the village can buy the resort from its owners so that they can run it as a business and afford to set up a school for the children."

"Buying the resort might take a lot of money," you say.

As you sail back, you think about the villagers and the lack of jobs and education compared to how much you and your family have.

"Hey I have an idea," you tell Kai. "Why don't you take all the treasure to make sure you have enough to buy the resort?"

"But what about your share?"

You lift the lid and take a couple of coins from the top of the pile. "This will do me. I just need enough to buy my family a present each. Oh, there's just one condition."

"What's that?" Kai asks.

"You have to write me a postcard and keep me up to date, until I can talk my family into coming back for another holiday."

"If I have anything to do with it, next time, your family's holiday will be free!" Kai says with a big grin.

You put the coins into your pocket. "Sounds like a good deal to me."

"Oh, and I want you to have this." The boy smiles and lifts the string of shells from around his neck. "These are cowry shells. In the old days my people used them instead of money. I want you to have them."

You take the necklace and place it around your neck. "Looks like we've found two sorts of treasure today," you say.

Kai nods his agreement. "You're right. Treasure is great, but friendship is the best treasure of all."

Congratulations! You've found the pirates treasure. This part of your story has come to an end.

It is time to make a decision. Would you like to:

Go back to the very beginning of the story? **P7**

Or

Go to the list of choices and start reading from a different part of the story? **P318**

You have decided to watch the men in the row boat.

You realize you are too close to the pirates raiding the Spanish ship. The men at the fortress have seen the pirates on deck and have turned one of their guns on them. You need to get out of the way before you get hit by a stray shot. You move behind a huge rock and wait for the Spanish to shoot again. Then, when they are reloading you can leave your shelter. When you hear three more booms, you make a run for it.

You run as fast as you can from one rock to the next. Each time the Spanish shoot, you move a bit further around, finding a place to shelter before the next barrage. By staying near the shoreline you can see the rowboat with the pirates and the chest as it makes its way around the little island.

The ground level is climbing as you go. The shoreline cliffs are getting steeper. At one point you have to use vines and branches to help put yourself up the hillside.

Before you know it, you're nearing the top of the island. You can see three pirate ships sitting behind the island firing their cannon over the hill towards the fort. At the top of the island, a man stands on a wooden tower waving flags, directing the pirate ships where to fire.

The pirates are faster at reloading their cannon than the Spanish and much more accurate. The pirates also have bigger targets. Both the Spanish ships and the fortress are larger than the quicker but smaller pirate raiders.

You've had to move inland a little and can no longer see the fortress between the trees. Nonetheless it is easy to hear the booms coming from both sides of the battle. Not many shots are coming from the fortress any more.

Near the top of the hill the jungle thins and the ground starts to level out. You can see the ocean through the trees again. The pirates in the rowing boat are making good speed. They've almost reached the headland. A few of the shots from the fortress come close to the rowboat, but then the pirates round the headland and gain protection from the island. When the spray settles, the men are pulling strongly on their oars. After the rowboat rounds the headland it disappears from view under the cliff.

Then suddenly the gun fire stops. It is so quiet, you can hear the birds and the slap of the waves on the hull of the pirate ships far below. It is dead quiet for nearly a minute. Then the pirates begin to cheer. The fortress has stopped firing. The pirates have won the battle.

The man in the tower is jumping up and down with glee. After a moment's celebration, he climbs down from his lookout post, grabs onto a rope and climbs into a metal basket hanging over the edge of the cliff. Using pulleys attached to the tower's strong timbers, he lowers himself towards the water below

You still can't see the rowboat and wonder why it hasn't reappeared near the ships further out to sea.

You creep to the edge of the cliff on your hands and knees and peer over the edge. The basket is hanging just above the water. The pirates in the rowboat are lifting the trunk they took from the Spanish ship into the basket.

You wonder what they are doing. Then the man in the basket is joined by another from the boat and they start hauling on the rope, pulling the basket up again.

Should you run? Why are they bringing the trunk up to the top of the island?

Then you notice the basket has stopped rising. Instead, it hangs beside the sheer cliff. You see the two men lift the trunk out of the basket and push it into the side of the hill.

You wonder if when you get home to the future, there is any chance that the trunk will still be there. But to find that out, first you have to get back to the right time, back to your family and not this crazy place you've found yourself in, but how?

You think hard about your situation. You're pretty sure that the cutlass you found by the wrecked ship has something to do with it.

You are a bit scared, but you are determined to get back to your family. You take off your pack and take out the cutlass and lay it on the ground.

Carefully you fold back the sweatshirt exposing the sword. You stand back, but nothing happens. Maybe the magic only works when someone is holding the cutlass up?

Your hand trembles a little when you pick up the cutlass. Last time you held it you were knocked off your feet. A little afraid, you hold the sword as far from your face as possible.

The vibration starts as a quiet hum. Slowly it gains speed. Before long the cutlass is moving back and forth so fast it is only a blur and a high-pitched sound surrounds you. But before the cutlass knocks you down, you throw it as hard as you can over the cliff.

The sword is halfway to the water when there is a blinding flash. When you are able to see again, the pirate ships are gone.

You walk towards the edge of the cliff to where the rope is hanging over the side, get down on to your hands and knees and crawl carefully forward. As you near the edge you lay on your belly and inch forward.

The view down makes your stomach lurch. All you see is a dangling rope running down the sheer cliff. Where have the men gone? Are you back in the present?

The clearness and depth of the water, makes the distance to its surface look even greater than it is. The height makes you a little dizzy. As you look down you grab onto the rope for security, just in case.

It is just as well you did because the ground under you has been weakened by recent rain. Suddenly you feel the earth beneath you start to rumble. You push yourself back from the edge but it is already too late. The edge of the cliff is breaking away. You twist the rope around your wrist and hang on tight, hoping that it will be strong enough to hold your weight.

As the ground gives way, the rope creaks and stretches, but doesn't break. You swing back and forth over the edge in the slight breeze.

You wrap one leg around the rope to ease the stress on your arm and hang on for dear life as you dangle over the water far below. Gradually the swinging stops and you try to pull yourself up a little at a time, but it is hard work, and your arms are getting tired.

You are considering letting go and taking the plunge into the sea when you feel the rope begin to rise. You hold on even tighter.

Then you hear a voice from above. 'Hang on!'

Slowly you start to rise. When your head reaches the top of the cliff, you see the village boy standing by the tower, pulling the rope through a series of pulleys.

Before you know it, you are back on safe ground. The boy hooks the rope around a cleat on the frame of the tower and comes over to where you are lying on the ground.

You sit up and look up at the boy. "Wow that was close. What are you doing out here?"

"When I saw you sailing towards the island I decided to take my father's boat out and join you. I thought you might like a friend to help you look for treasure."

"That would be great," you say. "I think it will be a lot safer exploring with someone else."

The boy smiles. "You're probably right. So where should we look first?"

"I don't know. Maybe we should climb up the tower and see if we can spot something interesting from up there?" you say.

"Or we could go back to the beach and go exploring in my father's boat," the boy says. "My name's Kai by the way."

It is time for you to make a decision. Do you:

Climb the tower? **P81**

Or

Go exploring in Kai's father's boat? **P94**

You have decided to stay where you are and keep watching the pirates.

The battle is raging. The fortress is firing their cannon as quickly as they can reload, but the Spanish are fighting a losing battle.

One of the pirate's shots hits the top of the turret on one end of the fortress wall, taking off its roof. Others smack into the various walls breaching them.

The fortress is beginning to crumble from the vicious attack. One of the Spanish ships is sinking. Its mast is broken and men are swimming for shore. When the fire reaches the powder kegs, the ship explodes sending flames and splintered timbers shooting off in every direction. The burning timbers hiss as they sink below the water.

You see more puffs of smoke from the fortress wall. The Spanish are still fighting despite the odds being against them. It has taken the men in the fortress a while to figure out where the pirate ships are shooting from.

Some of the Spanish turn their guns on the pirates looting the ship on the rocks just below your position. The old guns aren't very accurate, and unfortunately as the gunners on the fort take one of their last shots, you are in the wrong place at the wrong time.

You never see the cannonball coming.

Unfortunately you've been hit by a cannonball and this part of your story is over.

It is time for you to make a decision. Do you:

Go back to the very beginning of the story? **P7**

Or

Make that last choice differently. **P89**

You have decided to go exploring in Kai's father's boat.

You and Kai have taken the safe option. You have decided to go back down to the beach and take his father's boat out exploring around the island a little more.

The two of you have lots of fun diving at different spots around the little island, but unfortunately you don't find any more treasure. This is a real shame because the boy and his family could really do with the money that finding the treasure would bring.

The boy explains how his father is unable to fish because of the cataracts on his eyes, and the only thing the family has to live on is the fish he can catch, the vegetables his mother grows, and a few dollars his aunty makes working at the resort.

"How much would it cost to fix your father's eyes?" you ask him.

"More than we'll ever have," the boy replies.

You think about this as the two of you sail back to the mainland. Kai's story makes you realize how much you have compared to him. After all, your family can afford to take overseas holidays to exotic places and eat fancy food and swim in fancy pools. Kai's family is struggling just to put food on the table.

When you get back to the beach by the resort, you are about to say goodbye to your new friend. Then you have an idea. You reach into your pocket and then hold out your palm towards the village boy. In the middle of your hand sits a gold doubloon.

"Here you go. I found this near your village. You should take it and use the money for your father's operation. It only seems fair."

The boy's eyes light up when he sees the coin. "But that's gold. It must be worth ..."

"Please take it," you insist. "I only ask one thing in return."

"Sure," Kai says. "Anything."

"Send me a postcard from time to time ... until I can talk my family into coming here on holiday again at least."

The boy smiles and lifts the string of shells from around his neck. "These are cowry shells. In the old days my people used them instead of money. I want you to have them."

You take the necklace and place it around your neck, then drop the coin into the boy's hand. "Looks like we've both found treasure after all," you say.

Congratulations! You've found some treasure. But is there more if you take another path?

This part of your story has come to an end. It is time to make a decision. Do you want to:

Go back and try a different path? **P7**

Or

Go back and find out what happens if you lower yourself over the cliff? **P84**

Or

Go and read a different story? **P5**

In The Magician's House

In your turret.

You can't remember a time when you didn't live and work in the Magician's house. It is cloaked in mystery and you explore it every day.

There are many rooms inside the Magician's house, but you have to catch them while you can.

You find the kitchen easily most mornings. You just follow the lovely smells and don't think too hard about it. Perhaps your recent dreams help you get to breakfast without much trouble. More likely it's because the Magician wants his breakfast - why would he hide a place he wants you to go to?

You can find a lot of places in the house, even rooms you've never been to before and for this reason you're often asked to fetch things by the others who work in the house. They get lost more often than you do. You sometimes find other servants in the corners of rooms and give them a friendly pat to bring them out of a 'drawing room dream'. That is what the cook, Mrs Noogles, calls them. Dreams swirl around in the Magician's house just like dust does in the corners of other houses. Little stories get stuck in the crannies. Just for a moment, while you are sweeping a corner, you can find yourself running across a green field, speaking to a great crowd, steering an iron horse through twisty roads, or picking ripe strawberries in a bright warm field. Those are the dreams and they are quickly over, but other times you are transported to different places. So you watch where you step.

It is very early in the morning, and you wake up in your turret. It is your own tower above the house with a winding staircase that connects you to the house.

There is something cold against your cheek. You put your hand out and feel a smooth hard object. It's that red frog again.

You open your eyes and see the red frog staring at you. You lift it from the pillow and place it on a shelf. The shelf contains treasures and oddities that you've picked up, and some, like the frog, that have followed you home. The frog sits perfectly still and turns to stone, but you know it is likely to change back and follow you like a naughty puppy. No matter – it's harmless and has never gotten you into trouble. You just hope you don't tread on it by accident one day when it isn't a stone.

The sky is dark purple, with one last star valiantly blinking as the rising sun starts to turn your corner of the world into day. You love looking out of your tower window and catching the day starting like this – in this moment the whole world is magic, not just the place you live.

Down the spiral staircase, on the next floor, you wash the sleep from your eyes and put on fresh clothes. A sound like a marble falling down the stairs becomes the sound of a rubber ball until the red frog appears with a final splat. He takes a quick dip in the big jug of water you keep for him there. When he jumps out he doesn't leave any wet marks on the flagstone floor. He seems to absorb moisture. The jug is now only half full and you top it up.

By the window, a row of ants are marching across the floor. The frog jumps over to the row of insects, and whips out his tongue to catch ant after ant until the column is gone. If only getting *your* breakfast was that easy.

From the window you can see the buildings of London- St Paul's cathedral is a beautiful dome by the river Thames. You see horses and carts making their deliveries down the twisty lanes. Much of London is still sleeping but servants are stirring to light the fires and make their master's breakfasts. You must tend to your master too.

As you move further down the turret you wonder which room it will join with today. Sometimes it will deliver you to a hallway which easily gets you to the servant's staircase and down to the kitchen but often there is another destination at the foot of the stairs. Things are seldom as they appear. You have learned to be cautious in case you step in a lily pond in the wide conservatory or walk into the shiny suit of armor which appears in different places each day.

The stairs wind down until you meet up with the rest of the house. Here is where you are usually faced with your first choice for the day. This morning a wide corridor stretches off to the left and right. The ceilings are high and arched. Embroidered tapestries hang along the oak paneled walls.

To your left, the corridor ends abruptly. A suit of armor stands at the dead end, its bright metallic form is leaning slightly forward, its gloved hand is holding up the edge of the last tapestry. Behind the tapestry, you can see the corner of what looks like a small door.

In the corridor to your right is an impassable hole in the floor with a ladder poking out. The carpet is ripped and torn around the hole as though a bomb has gone off in the night. That's weird, you think, you didn't hear an explosion.

You have never seen this hole or the secret door behind the tapestry before.

It's time to make your first decision for the day. Do you:

Go down the ladder into the hole? **P123**

Or

Take the secret door behind the suit of armor? **P100**

You have decided to take the secret door behind the suit of armor.

The magician doesn't leave notes, but he does leave signs. The door behind the tapestry is like an invitation and you've decided to take it. You take a good look at the tapestry before you go behind it. You know this way might not be here tomorrow so you want to remember the picture so you can recognize it again. It is just a forest scene. The suit of armor is over six feet tall and brilliantly polished. It has a helmet with a full visor and armor underneath that would cover a person's whole body – there are even covers for the feet and gauntlets for the hands.

The armor moves about the Magician's house all the time. You bumped into it last week when you were carrying a large flower display and spilled water all over yourself. Another time you found it in the garden looking up at a tree. Maybe the armor moves itself or perhaps it still contains a trace of the adventures its wearer had.

Just as you are ducking under the arm to enter the door you notice a leather pouch swinging from one hand. You take a look inside the pouch and find a jar. It reminds you of the jars the cook, Mrs Noogles, lined the pantry with after she made jam from the plums you picked from the three trees in the garden. This jar doesn't have any jam in it, but there is a faint yellow swirl inside – perhaps a gas of some sort. It is warm in your hand and there is a faded handwritten label on one side. The label simply reads *sunshine*. You decide to take the jar with you. Now you examine the door.

The door behind the tapestry is made of wood and is set flush with the wall so when the cloth hanging covered it, there were no bumps that would have made you think something was behind it. The tapestry isn't one of the most interesting in the Magician's house – many are embroidered with scenes of fantastic creatures but this picture only shows a dense forest and a tower peeking out of it. The door creaks as it opens stiffly inwards. Inside there is a dark passage. It probably travels between other rooms in the house and was designed as a servant's passage – big old houses have them so guests can move about in the grand spaces and servants can bustle about without disturbing them. Who knows, maybe you have found a speedier way to the kitchen.

You take a step inside. As you do, you hear a plop. The red frog lands in front of you.

"Hmm," you say. "Coming along to explore, are you?"

The red frog looks up at you with its big eyes. It can probably see quite well in the dark, but you can't.

Fearing you will tread on the little amphibian, you bend and scoop it up. It feels warm in your hand. It makes a couple of leaps up your arm and then snuggles itself on your shoulder. Together you begin to step down the hidden passage.

You treat a new part of the Magician's house like you're walking on thin ice. You keep your back foot ready to take your weight should reality give way. The Magician's house swirls with dreams that pool in corners of rooms and cluster on carpets like other houses attract dust. It's not the usual way for a house to behave.

Behind you the door clicks shut and it is suddenly dark. You hear clanking as the suit of armor resumes its position in front of the tapestry, and drops the tapestry back over the doorway. . . Oh well, it isn't as if anyone would come looking for you anyway. You shudder when you think about being trapped in here forever. Don't be stupid, you remind yourself. You know better than to get frightened in this passage. You might as well feel like that in the whole house!

Now, where are we going?

As your eyes try to make sense of the darkness, your feet slowly feel their way forward. You can smell dust in the air, but there doesn't seem to be anything to trip on. The leather pouch, slung over your shoulder, feels warm. You take another peek inside the pouch and realize the jar is quite visible. Sunshine, eh? You take out the jar and unscrew the lid a tiny bit. Soft yellow light swirls out like smoke. As the light spreads you can see more and more of the passage. Not knowing how much light you have, or how much you'll need, you put the lid back on. Now you can see quite well and resume your cautious exploration.

A cool draft to your right draws your eye to a part of the wall where the paneling is different. At eye level is a piece of board about the size of a large book with a hinge at one end. It's a little window of some sort. You open it and find yourself staring into a room you've seen before. It's the Magician's drawing room and has high ceilings and long portraits hanging from every wall.

It is time to make a decision. Do you:

Investigate the Magician's drawing room? **P103**

Or

Go down the secret passage? **P106**

You have decided to investigate the Magician's drawing room.

The drawing room is octagonal. It has a carved door in one wall and paintings on all the rest. The paintings are all of the Magician. The one closest to the door shows him performing in a theatre. He is dressed in purple robes and a pointy hat and is making a great glass orb float in the air. The next painting shows the Magician sawing a long box in half – there is a person's head at one end and their feet at the other. Another painting shows the Magician making potions and in another he wears shiny armor and stands next to a dragon.

The pictures are bemusing. Although you recognize the Magician in each picture, you can't recall what he looks like when you look away. You're never able to remember exactly what the Magician looks like even though you have breakfast with him most mornings. It's the same with these paintings. You can remember details like the clothes he is wearing and other people and things in the picture, but when you look away you can't bring the Magician's face to your mind.

The red frog climbs up from your shoulder and jumps on your head. It is looking through too.

There is a table in the center of the room. On top of the table is a round woven basket, shaped almost like a ball. The basket has a woven lid. As you watch it, the basket gives an almost imperceptible shudder. You wonder what is inside. The frog on your head gives a little twitch, wanting you to move on. Then the basket gives a little twitch too. What is in there?

By the light of the sunshine jar, you see a catch in the wall. You lift the catch and a panel swings open. You step inside the room with the basket, curious about what is inside it.

You cross the room and take a quick peek out of the far door. You smile. The kitchen door is only a short distance down the hallway. You put the frog down and leave the door open so the kitchen will be more likely to stay put. You'll only be a minute and then you can get straight to breakfast.

You turn back to the table in the middle of the room. There is something fascinating about the basket sitting on it.

The basket twitches again as you get closer. You pick it up. It's surprisingly heavy. It shudders and shakes a moment, and then remains perfectly still. You put it back on the table and place your hands on the lid. You ready yourself to open and shut the lid fast to see what is inside. You'll be really fast.

You count out loud: "One, two, three!"

The snake in the basket is faster. Before you blink it has sunk its fangs into your wrist and then disappeared back into the basket. You replace the lid as a cold heaviness spreads up your arm. You watch as your hand and arm turn to stone as the poison spreads further. Before you can run to the door, your whole body becomes heavy and everything slows down.

Staring across the room you see another picture of the Magician. He has a flute and he is charming a snake out of a basket, the same basket that is on the table, the same snake that bit you. The Magician's eyes are laughing.

Sometime later, you hear people coming into the room. Being a statue, you can't turn to see who is there and the voices are muffled. The snake's bite has dulled your senses. Eventually the gardeners arrive and tip you up into a wheel barrow. They move you outside by the topiary and fountains. You watch the moon getting full and then turning into a small crescent again. Some nights strange creatures come into the Magician's garden. If you ever change back you'd like to find out more about them. From time to time the red frog comes and sits beside you.

You finally come back to life during a lightning storm. Wet and cold, you head back indoors and gingerly head back to your room in the turret. Maybe someone else will have moved in? To your relief it still looks like your room. In the morning you are incredibly hungry and vow to yourself NOT to get distracted on the way to breakfast in the future.

At breakfast everyone greats you like a long lost friend and asks what it was like to be turned to stone.

After breakfast you go out to see where you had been standing in the garden and see that your footprints are still clearly visible on the ground. You must have been standing there for months.

It is time to make a decision. Do you

Return to your room in the turret and start over again? **P97**

Or

Keep going down the secret passage? **P109**

You have decided to go down the secret passage.

A faint breeze alerts you to the possibility of another door in the passage. On one side of the hall the wall is made of blackboard canvas with upside down writing and numbers on it and some sort of map. Why is the writing upside down? Hang on – some of this writing is familiar. This is the back of the big roller blackboard in the Magician's classroom.

The schoolroom must be on the other side of the wall. When the board is rolled forward the writing on this side will be upside down.

Yesterday in the school room you were asking how long it took to sail to the other side of the world. Miss Eleanor Spurlock, the teacher, drew a quick map of Australia as she answered the question. You remember her drawing the southern continent now. That island you are looking at is Australia. Hmmm, you didn't recognize it at all round the wrong way.

The giant blackboard takes up half of one of the schoolroom walls. There is a rope and pulley to turn the blackboard – when you pull the rope the whole board rotates like a giant flat wheel revealing a new expanse of board for Miss Spurlock to draw on. Sometimes she asks you or one of your classmates to turn the board. Turning the crank is fun, but what is also interesting are the pictures which are sometimes revealed in a new stretch of blackboard canvas.

Once, a large portrait of a tiger appeared and nobody had the heart to erase it, so everything was written around it that day. Later, when you looked for the tiger again, it wasn't there.

Another time a large sailing ship was revealed with a sailor leaning over the side to see a mermaid. Again, everyone agreed to leave the picture and next time it came around you saw that the ship was leaving. The man now had a tail and he was swimming off with the mermaid.

Further down the secret passage you hear someone crying through the walls. You recognize the back of a large painting with a spy hole within it. You open the sunshine jar a tiny bit so you have more light. This section of the passage is quite different from the rest. It is all made of wood and parts almost look as if it has grown here rather than been built.

The back of the picture seems very organic. It has a glossy wooden frame which is odd considering this is the back of the picture and nobody would be viewing it from this side.

When you slide the panel open you are looking into a circular room a little bigger than your own turret. There is a wooden bed with blue and green embroidered sheets and coverlet. The bed has roots growing into the floor as if it had grown there.

A girl is thumping the pillows on the bed. A mirror leaning against one wall reflects the picture you stand behind. It is a picture of Medusa – the woman who had snakes instead of hair.

You have seen her in a book about mythology. The rest of the room contains a chest and small book case and a table and chair. There is an ornate window with a seat built under it and some sort of weaving frame.

The crying girl rolls across the bed and then pushes herself up and over to the dressing table. She is wearing a green velvet dress. Her long black hair is arranged in raven ringlets. She angrily wipes her eyes and reaches for a book.

You see she has a stack of them. You love books and you peer to see what kind they are, but the next thing you see is that she hurls the top one against the window. You brace yourself, thinking the window will smash, but the book just bounces off it and slaps to the floor. She sighs and opens another one up and starts reading.

She seems so despondent.

You let more sunshine out of the jar to see the picture you stand behind. You see it is in fact a door set into the wall. There is wooden handle on the picture and, just like the bed, the handle seems to have grown there like a branch.

Should you open the door or continue down the passage?
It is time to make a decision. Do you:
Continue down the secret passage? **P109**
Or
Open the door? **P113**

You have decided to continue down the passageway.

You have a nagging feeling you missed out on something but breakfast is the most important thing on your mind. You head on down the corridor and soon there is another little door just like the first one you entered. Hopefully the kitchen is on the other side.

The passage door opens into a large pot cupboard and with a clatter you crawl out through pans and tins into the kitchen. As you open the door, you smell reassuring breakfast smells. Your homing instincts have done it again.

The kitchen is the anchor of the whole house. It is more solid and reliable and, of course, it is where the food is. To call it simply 'the kitchen' just doesn't do it justice. It is a vast area with three different fireplaces, multiple ovens, and work tables. Over to the right are two wooden doors which lead to the pantries and the herbarium. They are always there – they don't move around. Over to the left a door takes you to the sun room and on to the cook's quarters. The sun room looks out to the garden and even when it's night time it looks like day through its windows. The gardeners sit there in the evenings sometimes to look for slugs.

The floor is made of flagstones. They are great grey slabs of stone sunk into the ground. They were once flat but over time they have acquired slight dips where they have been smoothed by many feet. The passage of time has served to form comforting paths which ease the way for someone burdened by a tray of empty glasses or piping hot pies.

The kitchen is a deep room – the walls either side of the cupboard you crawled out of are covered in shelves and more cupboards containing plates and pots and saucepans of burnished copper.

The other side of the kitchen is set with benches running from one end to the other. The wall immediately above the benches is set with a crazy collection of different tiles – yellow and cerulean and violet and black and white with blue pictures. Above those are wide windows which go to the ceiling. From wherever you are in the kitchens you can look out to the gardens. Above your head hang strings of onions, herbs and plaits of garlic. There are hooks holding jugs and copper pots.

The room is warm, even when snow is covering the garden outside and it is cool when summer is at its height. At the stove your friend Henry is frying bacon and sausages. Mrs Noogles turns to you and smiles.

"You've made good time this morning – come and help with these potato cakes."

You make haste to help her at the griddle and when they are all cooked and piled in a golden pyramid you take them to the table. The rest of the household are arriving now – some arrive through doors and others in stranger ways than you arrived. Scarlet, the house maid, suddenly marched up from some steps which materialize from a large flag stone in the floor. Last to arrive is the Magician. He folds himself into the room and smiles at everyone in morning greeting. The gardeners lift their caps at him and Scarlet makes a quick bob. You are putting the last of the cutlery on the table so you nod and he nods right back.

"Get yourselves seated!" commands Mrs Noogles and everybody does. You know that in most great houses the master would eat on his own – never with the servants and never in the kitchen. But the Magician is not like most masters.

Everyone makes quick work of breakfast. You eat heartily and like most of your colleagues you put a few snacks aside for later. If you have trouble finding the kitchen you won't go hungry.

Henry, your friend, has found a strange boy called Charlie in the house. Mrs Noogles cleaned him up and invited him to breakfast and the Magician seems to have taken a shine to him. He invites him to join you all. You're pleased – Charlie seems like fun. He's heading out to grab his gear and asks if you want to go with him. You're considering whether you will when Mrs Noogles says you only have two options:

Do a few tasks in the herb room and then get to school, or polish the suit of armor – which might take a while.

It is time to make a decision. Do you:

Help with the herbs? **P134**

Or

Polish the armor? **P112**

You have decided to polish the armor.

Mrs Noogles shows you to the armory. You had no idea there was one. She taps on a flagstone and it rumbles open. Down forty or so steps you find a large bench set up with clothes and oil and screw drivers and hammers. There is not one but three suits of armor waiting patiently by the bench as if they were queuing to get their library books issued, or to buy something in a shop. So that's why you see the suit of armor everywhere, there is more than one!

"Goodness! It's been a while since we did some polishing. Looks like the job has been piling up," says Mrs Noogles.

She points out what needs to be done. Each suit must be dismantled and each piece polished and oiled. You'll be lucky to be out of here by dinner. Oh well, you think, better get started, it's not always an exciting day in the Magician's house.

You have just finished the first one when you look up and find a fourth has arrived. This could be a really long day.

It's time to make a decision. Do you:

See Mrs Noogles about another task instead? **P134**

Or

Start at the beginning of the story and try another path? **P97**

You have decided to open the door.

The picture door creaks open stiffly. As you step into the room you smell clean fresh air and the scent of pine trees. The girl whirls towards you in surprise. She grabs a book as if she will throw it at you and you duck in case she does. Then she puts down the book and smiles as she works out you aren't a threat.

You introduce yourself. As you do the red frog jumps down to the floor with a plop.

"Nice frog. Is it enchanted? What can it do?"

Now that she mentions it, you suppose the frog probably *is* enchanted in some way but you explain you have never seen it do anything useful or even interesting. It's just a frog.

"Have you tried kissing it? They do that in stories you know."

You both look at the frog, but neither of you think this is a good time to try kissing it. The girl introduces herself as Devorah. You decide to ask what the problem is – you explain how you accidentally ended up spying on her on your way to breakfast.

"It wasn't on purpose – I was on my way to the kitchen and I found the secret passage and then…"

Devorah cuts your apology off:

"It's perfectly fine – I am so happy to have someone to talk to! This may mean I can get out of the passage too!"

While she's talking you look around the room. You see you are high up in a wooden tower. It is much bigger than your own bedroom turret. There is no staircase, so you wonder how Devorah gets outside. Her home is less like a building and more like being inside a giant tree. Near the picture doorway you entered is a balcony which looks to be the only other possible way out. Looking out from there you find that the view is completely different from your bedroom - instead of seeing London, a great forest stretches out as far as you can see. It's clear you've stepped through a portal to somewhere far from the Magician's house. At the foot of the tower, great roots anchor it to the forest floor as though it grew there. It's a long way down and the surrounding trees are not close enough to jump to. You can see a rough road starts at the foot of the tower and disappears into the forest. Here and there, the road appears again on the hills off in the distance. At the top of one hill you see a small thatched hut. Other than that, the tower is alone in a sea of trees.

Devorah calls you back into the room.

"Be careful out there – she might see you!"

"Who?"

"The witch, Baba Yaga."

You tell Devorah you've never heard of Baba Yaga.

"How can you not know her? She torments the country."

You tell her you may not be from her country. Devorah nods, understanding what you are just realizing. The Magician's house has connected to a very different part of the world. You have stepped into a room that isn't part of his house at all.

Devorah explains she has been imprisoned in this tower for months.

"It was winter time when I came here and now it's nearly winter again. My father the King stood up to Baba Yaga. She arrived in her house that moves on chicken feet and she took me away. I thought she would eat me but she locked me up here. I suppose my father will do what she wants with me imprisoned. And worse, when she visits me she talks about her son all the time. I think she wants me to marry him."

"I've been trying to steal a little of her magic each time she visits – just a tiny amount when she climbs in the window and won't notice. Her magic is very strong. I'm using it to try to escape."

Devorah has only recently been able to come through the picture doorway but hasn't yet been able to cross over to the Magician's house.

You ask why the witch climbs in the window and doesn't use the door.

"There is no door. This is an enchanted tower." Devorah looks at you like you don't know anything. You don't know much but this story is reminding you of another story about a girl with long, long hair. Maybe that's where this witch Baba Yaga got the idea from.

"How do you steal her magic?" you ask.

Devorah looks ashamed. "I know it's not very safe or nice to use other people's magic, but I need to get out of here. I thought if I made a magical door I might be able to escape. "

Devorah says that every time the witch visits she steals magic by plucking a hair from her as she helps haul her in the window. "I learned a little magic from my great-great-aunt who lives outside my father's castle. She taught me how to weave rogue magic a little and that's what I've done."

Devorah shows you a fine thread of plaited hair surrounding the picture. In this way she's charmed the picture to become a portal. You tell her you think she has been very clever.

"I've added some charms of protection as you would to a door. I was hoping it would start to act like a door and it has! I just felt for other magic and tried to connect to it. So far I've only managed to get a little way down the passage. You coming through might have helped strengthen the connection, I'm sure, but I think I'm going to need a little more magic to get myself through."

Devorah is keen to try to get through the passage again and into the safety of the Magician's house. You both step through the picture door and close it behind you. Back inside the corridor you open the sunshine jar again. You head to the door you thought would take you to the kitchen.

At the end of the passage there is a door exactly like the one you entered this morning – you have travelled in a circle and are back where you started. When you open the door the suit of armor stands there holding the tapestry up. You walk through alright, but something is wrong, Devorah can't come through — it's as though there is a wall for her that you can't see.

"My spell isn't strong enough. I can't get through the door. You've been able to visit me but I need a bit more magic to get through. I'll have to wait for the witch and risk taking a tiny bit more of her power."

You are nervous of Devorah getting caught by the witch stealing more magic. Maybe you could do something to help.

"Have you tried signaling to that hut you can see from your tower?" you ask.

Devorah looks alarmed.

"Hut? You saw a hut? But that's her! She travels in a hut on chicken legs. There isn't anyone else on that road and no other dwelling. That means she's coming. I have to get back before she finds what I've been doing."

Devorah hastens back down the passage to her prison. What should you do?

It is time to make a decision. Do you:

Go for help? **P121**

Or

Return with Devorah to her tower? **P117**

You have decided to return with Devorah to her tower.

You head back down the passage behind her. Behind you the door shuts and now the passage is in near darkness. The sunshine jar is empty.

Now the tower must be close by on your right. You bump into Devorah who must be searching too and then retch as you smell something rotten like dead meat. Devorah is trembling - she leans close and holds a finger to your lips. You don't need her to tell you that the witch is here.

The sound of the witch's voice makes your blood run cold.

"That's right, my pretty, keep quiet and let me listen to your heart, beating fast like a trapped little bird. Two trapped birds. Mmmmm, someone smells delicious. It seems you've found yourself some tasty company."

The witch is very close. You step backwards softly, wishing frantically that the Magician's house would play a trick on her so you can escape. You put your hand out to feel the wall, but instead you feel trees! Underfoot the ground is suddenly rough and you realize the witch has transported you both back to her forest. It is dark and terrifying.

The red frog tickles at your neck. You didn't even know it was still with you. You carefully gather it and crouch down to feel for a safe place on the ground for it to sit. You might be going to meet a sticky end but there's no need for the frog to join you. It feels very warm, perhaps trying to give you a little courage. When you stand up again Devorah feels for your hand. You stand still and listen for the witch's approach. You can't run because you would just hit a tree in the thick forest.

Just then Devorah taps you, and you wonder why. Then you see a red glow on the ground that is steadily getting bigger and brighter. The frog is giving off light and getting larger! It is now the size of a cat. As the light gets brighter, you start to see the shapes of trees and the forest floor – ahead you see the looming form of the tower that Devorah has spent so many months trapped inside. At the base of the tower stands Baba Yaga. She is a black malevolent shape that reeks of carrion. Perhaps the frog wants help so you can make a run for it?

Baba Yaga steps forward.

"What's this? You've found a new pet."

She looks at the frog as it quietly glows and grows. She appears about to kick your little friend, so you throw the empty jar of sunshine at her. Maybe something good will have an impact on a creature that seems all evil. The witch doesn't flinch but she doesn't hurt the frog. Instead she turns her gaze and looks at you. Her eyes are black and merciless, and the light from the jar shows a strangely distorted face with a wide mouth and sharp, pointed teeth.

She licks her lips and her face twists into a horrible smile. Then she says, "Let's get the oven stoked."

Out of her mouth comes a cackling bird call. There is a scrabbling and creaking sound as her enchanted hut comes into the clearing. It moves on four giant chicken legs with a drunken gait like weird dancing. The hut turns so the front door is facing you. The door opens and you see an oven with a raging fire inside.

"Crebbit!"

The frog makes the first sound you have ever heard from it. It is now the size of a lion. It jumps between you and the house as if to say "Don't try it."

The witch laughs and then several things happen at once. She raises her hands to throw a spell and the frog opens its mouth. She opens her own mouth but nothing comes out because the frog's long tongue has shot out and wrapped around her, and she is being dragged into its mouth. There is a gulp from the frog and then its stomach glows an especially bright red like a furnace. You imagine you can hear the witch screaming but you aren't sure because there is suddenly so much more noise. The witch's house is disintegrating and four normal-looking chickens are suddenly freed from the spell that has made them carry her home. They head off into the night squawking and flying about erratically into the forest. The tower, Devorah's prison, begins to creak and change too. The witch's magic is fading rapidly.

The picture of Medusa, which Devorah made into a door, lands near you with a thud. It is propped against the trunk of what was once the tower but now is a very tall, but ordinary looking tree. Light is now coming from the sky and you can see the forest around you.

Devorah walks toward the painting. After meeting the witch, the picture of Medusa with snakes for hair doesn't seem too bad. You catch yourself thinking she might have been a very lonely person if everyone she met turned to stone. Devorah tries the door, luckily it is still working.

"Quick! You had better return before the magic is gone," she says.

You try to convince her to come with you but she shakes her head and points up the dirt road. There in the distance, you see horses and riders approaching. Devorah waves to them.

"It's my father's men – they will take me home. This place has been hidden to them by magic but now they've found me." The riders carry banners and wear old-fashioned chainmail and leather helms. Large dogs run alongside the horses. You are glad they are apparently friends of hers.

Devorah throws her arms around you in a hug and then pushes you through the painting door with the red frog following. It shuts with a clang and you know it will never open again. You start to fumble your way along in the passage. There is a loud plopping sound and then you see a slight red glow ahead at your feet. The red frog is still glowing and it helps you find a door.

You fall out of the passage and crash into the suit of armor which crashes to the floor of the kitchen. Most of the Magician's staff are at the large kitchen table having a meal. Mrs Noogles, the cook, gets up and tells you that you can clean up that suit of armor as soon as you've had something to eat. Then she notices the red frog. It is the size of a very large dog.

"What have you been feeding that frog?"

You reflect that in a normal house people might have been asking where you have been all this time, but this is the Magician's house and people know bizarre things happen. You bet your weird morning was one of the oddest though. The red frog hops over to the door to the garden and looks up at the door knob. You open the door and watch it hop off toward the water fountain. You wonder if you will find it back in your tower tomorrow.

Mrs Noogles calls you to the table and you realize you are famished. You sit down and listen to the others talking. The Magician looks over to you and smiles and you grin back.

You have reached the end of this part of the story.

Now you have another decision to make. Do you:

Start the story over again and try another path? **P97**

Or

Go to the list of choices and choose somewhere else to start reading from? **P319**

You have decided to go for help.

You watch Devorah run back to her prison. There must be something you can do. You don't think the hole in the ground will help. You need to find the Magician or someone else who knows magic. You look behind another tapestry and find a door which leads you to a balcony. There is a clanking beside you and you turn to see the suit of armor now standing to attention at the start of an ornate flight of stairs.

You know these stairs very well. If you run down the middle you'll take twice as long to get down them as it would if you skip down the sides. There is a party in the middle of the stairs – or the house is keeping the memory of one. If you go down the centre all you'll do is end up saying "excuse me" and "pardon me" and "it's just down the hall" to a host of tittering ladies and mustachioed men and avoiding waiters carrying trays with precariously balanced glasses.

You want to go down fast. You leap down the stairs hugging the wall and then hear banging and crashing in a nearby room but you can't spare time to investigate. It can't be Devorah because she can't get through. At last you see the kitchen door.

You burst through and find most of the household sitting eating their breakfast. The Magician is sitting there too making short work of a plate of sausages and other good breakfast fare. The cook, Mrs Noogles, starts to tell you off for being so late. It's your job to help. At the same time you are blurting your story to everyone and repeating the message that there is a girl trapped in a tower by a witch.

"Interesting," says the Magician.

"Appalling," says Mrs Noogles. One of the garden boys hesitantly asks whether Devorah is good looking. You scowl at him and yell in frustration:

"I need some help here!"

There is silence after you yell and then you hear a croaking from a pot cupboard. Mrs Noogles opens the cupboard door and out squeezes the red frog. Everyone stares. It is now the size of a large dog. It's also giving off heat and belching. The smell is not pleasant. The frog looks at you and then hops to the garden door. It looks up at the door knob expectantly. You start to let it out when the Magician calls out "Wait!" He crosses over and takes a good look at the frog. He opens its mouth and peers in. It doesn't smell good.

The Magician announces the frog has recently eaten something or someone particularly malevolent.

"Was the frog with you at this tree tower?"

You nod yes.

"Well I suspect your new friend won't be having any more trouble from her witch. This frog is attracted to bad and it's had a bellyful today."

The Magician turns to the cheeky gardener.

"You'd better fetch a shovel. What goes in must come out and we'll need a pit digging for this lot. Still, it might be just the thing to start a nice crop of rhubarb."

The Magician lets the frog outside and together you head back to the tapestry where you found the passage. There is no door anymore and the tapestry has changed.

You look at the new scene depicted on the fabric. Between the forest's trees is a road. A group of riders is heading off down its path. All but one of the riders wears armor. She has long raven hair, and has half turned back on her horse and waves at you. It is Devorah. She is going home.

You have reached the end of this part of the story. Do you:

Return to the beginning of this story and try another path? **P97**

Or

Go to the list of choices and choose somewhere else to start reading from? **P319**

You have decided to go down the ladder into the hole.

You hold onto the smooth wooden ends of the ladder that poke out above the floor and swing yourself onto its rungs. You clamber downwards hoping you'll soon smell frying bacon.

You want to go to the kitchen but you know that you can't always predict where things will be in the Magician's house. The kitchen could be found upstairs or down. There is no sense to it. In fact most people who live in the Magician's house keep a sandwich or an apple in their pocket in case they don't see the kitchen for a while. As you think about food your stomach growls, anticipating one of Mrs Noogles' breakfasts.

Mrs Noogles is the cook in the house and she never wanders far from her domain, partly because she is always busy concocting food and partly because she says she has lost patience with the rest of the house. Her quarters are at the back of the kitchen. She has a sunny room with a view of the garden, a fire place and an easy chair. You have never seen her in the chair, as she is usually bustling about. You wonder what she might be making or what she might have left out for you to eat if she is having one of her rare days off. It is your job to help with the breakfast for the household staff and anyone staying at the house.

The ladder is sturdy and well secured so it doesn't wobble. As you climb downward, the hole in the floor above recedes. Tiny glow worms give enough light for you to make out what sort of a hole you've entered. You put out your hand and touch smooth cold rock and moss. In one place there are so many glow worms that you can make out mushrooms growing on a ledge beside a cave. The cave would be great to explore one day, when you've done your work, had breakfast. That's assuming you ever see it again. There are places you don't see very often in the Magician's house.

As you climb further down the hole the light gets dimmer. Your eyes are open wide and straining to see between the rungs of the ladder. Suddenly, another pair of eyes opens right in front of you.

You freeze and grip the ladder tightly. The eyes look at you and you look at the eyes. You hear your heart thump loudly and then, even louder, you hear the noise of your rumbling stomach. The rumble echoes through the hole. The owner of the eyes lets out a deep chuckle and you relax at once. You are just about to ask the owner of the eyes if they think the kitchen is near when they surprise you again. Whoever it is reaches between the rungs of the ladder and pushes you off! You lose your grip

and

fall.

You flail uselessly but can't grip on to anything to stop your fall. But as you reach about you realize you aren't falling that fast. It is like falling through treacle or custard. The air is thicker than usual. You relax a little and enjoy falling for a while, there isn't anything you can really do about it and at this speed you don't think you'll get hurt.

Just as you are starting to really enjoy the ride it changes: you fall faster and light rushes up underneath you. Before you can panic you arrive with a thump which knocks the breath out of you. When you come to your senses you see you are back on your bed in your turret room. Above, you can see a hole in the arched ceiling, except instead of seeing the morning sun through the hole, you just see darkness. You hear that chuckle again and a face pushes into your room as if parting black clouds. You recognize the eyes, bright green and very large. The rest of its face is a velvety black so it is hard to see a mouth or nose or eyebrows but it is shaped like a very large shaggy cat. It grins to show an impressive amount of teeth.

"Hey – why did you push me?" you ask the cat creature. It grins again and then replies:

"To get you where you were going faster!"

The cat face disappears but then pops back a moment later.

"Don't suppose you could throw a few mice in the hole sometime? I'm getting bored with catching bats."

You stare at the hole a bit longer but the creature has gone.

A plunking noise alerts you to the red frog. It is springing up the wall. Its little suckered feet allow it to stick where gravity wouldn't usually allow, but it's a difficult task. It hurls itself toward the hole in the ceiling but with each jump, gravity takes its toll and twice it falls, morphing into something made of rubber which sends it bouncing a little higher up the wall to try again. Finally it lands just next to the hole and catches one side of it with a foot, before losing its grip and landing beside you. You stare at the hole – part of it has come away from the ceiling rather like a pancake you once flipped too high. The frog hurls itself up the wall again and pulls another section of the hole away.

You get up and look at it – where the hole has been torn back by the frog your bedroom ceiling is just as before. The frog has one more try at removing the hole – this time it manages to wriggle underneath. Before long the hole falls lightly from above and covers most of your bed. The frog sits on top of it. The other side of the hole isn't a hole at all. You touch it cautiously. One side is soft but solid and like a big black piece of silk. The other side is a hole. You fold it up so the hole is on the inside and soon it's not much bigger than a handkerchief. Thinking this hole might come in handy; you carefully put it in your pocket before you and the frog head back down the stairs.

This time when you head down the stairs the hole has gone because it's in your pocket. You can still go behind the tapestry which the suit of armor is showing you, or you can head down a green carpeted hallway.

Which way should you go?

It is time to make a decision. Do you:

Go down the hallway? **P126**

Or

Go through the secret door behind the suit of armor? **P100**

You have decided to go down the hallway.

You step carefully hoping to find your way to breakfast. You treat the ground as if it is an icy surface – keeping your back foot ready to take your weight should reality slip away.

The Magician's house swirls with dreams that pool in corners of rooms and cluster on carpets like other houses attract dust. Although you can't remember living any other way you know it's not a usual way for a house to behave.

Mrs Noogles has had quite enough of the rest of the house. She is the cook and she never wanders far from her kitchen domain – partly that's because she is always busy concocting food and partly because she long ago lost patience with the rest of the house. She has burnt the dinner too many times being caught out in a 'drawing room dream' as she calls it. She can reliably find her quarters through a door at the back of the kitchen – a large sunny room with a view of the garden, a fire place and an easy chair. She also has an area of the garden where she directs the growing of herbs and vegetables and fruit and a room where she dries herbs and stores her preserves and jams.

Actually you quite like some of the dreams you have found in the house – but you have learned to watch your footing so you don't have to see a dream through if you don't want to. They aren't all pleasant. Finding your way through the dreams doesn't seem to be something everyone in the house can do. Mrs Noogles looked at you strangely when you once described your 'back-foot' technique to her.

The grand staircase appears and you nimbly miss the third step down. Treading on the third step transforms the quiet house to a crowded party with a ball going on and a host of masked people leaping about making noise and clinking glasses and talking about ridiculous things. It was good the first few times you experienced it, but it makes going down the stairs very slow because of all the times you need to say "excuse me" as you pass people and "no thank you" as you are offered drinks and "just down the hall on the left" for the people looking for a powder room. If you do go down through the party it all disappears when you hit the last stair.

If you are really hungry you can pick up little pies from the silver trays as they are offered around. Unfortunately it is the sort of party where all the food is very small and you are expected to take only one thing from a tray at a time, so really it is better to push on and look for the kitchen.

You slide down the last half of the banister, feeling pretty pleased with your start to the day. Ahead, the kitchen door is open at the end of the corridor and there are pleasant cooking smells wafting toward you. You veer to the left to avoid a dream of walking through a summer field after a sun shower. It is always annoying to get wet feet and again it slows your progress enormously. You are just passing a last door when you hear a huge thump and somebody cries out.

Oh no! You are so close to breakfast!

What do you do? Do you;

Find out what made the noise behind the door? **P128**

Or

Ignore the noise and head down the passageway for breakfast? **P109**

You have decided to find out what made the noise behind the door.

You open the door cautiously and immediately let out a sneeze. The room is swirling with soot from the chimney. Sitting not far from the hearth is a small person rubbing their head. They are so covered in soot that they are almost completely black – except for the whites of their eyes which look up at you in fear. It's a chimney sweep. You have seen them before on London's streets making their way through the city. You've never seen one up close before though.

"Please, I lost my way and I'm in ever so much trouble. I didn't mean to cause a mess."

The sweep looks scared and you wonder if he's hurt. You can't imagine how he could have been cleaning in the Magician's chimneys. You know for a fact the Magician sends a pair of enchanted squirrels through there every second Wednesday so he doesn't need a sweep.

"Cheer up, you aren't in trouble," you say. "I was just about to get some breakfast – are you peckish? If you want to eat, come with me. I can help you find the front door after that if you like."

The sweep smiles and nods. He looks down at himself and is clearly wondering how he should proceed because with every step he will make a sooty outline.

"Don't worry", you say, "there's a lot of cleaners here." You don't mention you haven't seen them yourself, but someone or something straightens up round here all the time. "We'll get you seen to."

You step back in the hall and he follows. You have just shut the door when the sweep suddenly exclaims:

"My brush!"

He opens the door again and stops stock still. The room is completely clean – the only evidence he has ever been there is his brush sitting at attention by the fireplace.

"See," you say, "they are very fast. Now let's make haste before we miss breakfast."

The sweep is astounded that a sooty room with no other door has been cleaned so fast and he enters the room cautiously to collect his brush. As he leaves he bends to look under the furniture as if maids with dusters and brooms might be hiding there. You take his hand and carefully negotiate the last few steps to the kitchen.

The kitchen is like the anchor of the whole house. Somehow it is more solid and reliable and, of course, it is where the food is. To call it simply the kitchen just doesn't do it justice. It is a vast area with three different fireplaces, multiple ovens, and work tables. To the right, are two wooden doors which lead to the pantries and cool store and the herbarium. To the left, a door takes you to the sun room and on to Mrs Noogles' quarters. The sun room is sunny and you can see the garden as if its day even when its night through its windows.

The kitchen floor is made of flagstones, great squares of stone that remind you of a giant's chess board. They were once probably flat but over time they have acquired slight dips and been smoothed by many feet. Rather than tripping you up, the passage of time has served to form comforting paths barely perceptible to the kitchen traveler but a surface which eases the passage of someone burdened by a tray of empty glasses or piping hot pies. The walls on either side of the door where you entered are covered in shelves containing plates and pots and saucepans of burnished copper. The other side of the kitchen has a bench running from one end to the other. The wall above the bench is set with a crazy collection of different tiles – yellow and cerulean and violet and black and white with blue pictures. Above the rows of tiles are wide windows which go all the way to the ceiling. From wherever you are in the kitchens you can look out to the gardens. From racks above your head hang strings of onions and herbs and plaits of garlic and hooks holding jugs and more pots. There are all manner of things that might help feed everyone in the Magician's house.

The room is warm, even when snow is covering the garden and it is cool when summer is at its height. At the stove, your friend Henry is frying bacon and sausages. He grins at you and nods to the sweep and then gets back to his task.

"What manner of mess do we have here?" Mrs Noogles says as she emerges from the store room carrying eggs and potatoes. She sets the food on one of the big preparation tables and smoothes down her capacious apron. She fetches a bowl and a grater and points.

Mmmm, potato cakes, you think. You know what to do and set to grating the potatoes. Mrs Noogles meanwhile takes charge of the sweep.

"Hmmm, we'll need hot water and soap." From above her head she reaches for a large tin tub. At that moment Scarlet, the housemaid, comes into the room. She is yawning and stretching and about to start her day too. Mrs Noogles sends her up to the servant's wardrobe to find some clothes for the sweep and then sets the tub into an alcove. She bustles about fetching kettles of hot water, and raps on the window to attract the attention of a passing gardener. He comes in with more water from the pump which she adds to the steaming bath. The sweep stands about surveying the kitchen and being careful not to let soot fall in the way. He eyes the bath warily but is clearly interested in the food you are preparing. Lastly Mrs Noogles directs you to fetch a screen from the store room and then she and the sweep disappear behind it and there is a splashing sound as the sweep is immersed in water and given a good soaping. Mrs Noogles lets out a steady stream of instructions to you and Henry from behind the screen.

You put the potato cakes onto the griddle and start making the toast.

"I won't half be in trouble, Mrs Noogles, if I don't get out and find my boss." The sweep is resisting his transformation a little half-heartedly you think. He is probably relishing the chance to get clean and looking forward to the prospect of a hot breakfast.

Scarlet returns with towels, britches, a shirt and some shoes. There are all sorts in the store rooms including fancy dress. You are fairly sure Scarlett was wearing a different pair of shoes earlier. Mrs Noogles comes from behind the screen and gathers them up and then leaves the sweep to get dressed. She plunges herself into plating up bacon and sausages and the potato cakes you and Henry have prepared. You have buttered the toast, and now you set about wiping down the table and setting out places for everyone in the household.

"I think Himself will be coming down for his breakfast this morning, so let's lay a few extra places."

How Mrs Noogles knows this, you can't guess. 'Himself' is the name she uses for the Magician. You know from talking to servants in the alley that it isn't usual for a master to eat with the household staff, but the Magician isn't usual and neither is the house. It isn't usual for the staff to go to school but a schoolroom presents itself from time to time and no matter how much you've tried to avoid it the doors all open onto lessons in a determined way.

The sweep rounds the screen, and looks a perfectly ordinary person now he is not covered in soot. You are about to usher him to the table when every door to the kitchen opens at once – two gardeners enter from outside, stamping their feet to avoid dirt coming onto the floor, Murphy the butler arrives from another door, and the teacher comes through a cupboard door. The Magician just arrives at the table without the need of a door. One moment he wasn't there and the next he sort of folds himself into the space.

"A particularly fine morning, Mrs Noogles," says the Magician. He nods to the sweep and points him to a seat at the long wooden bench table. The gardeners don't need telling, and sit themselves on a bench as fast as if they were playing musical chairs. Soon everyone except Mrs Noogles and yourself are watching as you plunk down plates and knives and forks and toast before helping to carry over platters of potato cakes and bacon and a great dish of scrambled eggs and fried tomatoes. As soon as the Magician raises a fork to his mouth everyone else follows.

"I think we'd like to know your name, young man," states the Magician.

"I'm Charlie," says the sweep.

"He came down the chimney," you add, though you suspect the Magician knows this already. He knows most things that happen in the house.

The Magician nods and continues to ask Charlie questions. Charlie explains that his father earned less money than his family spent.

"The result of earning *more* than you spend is happiness but the result of earning *less* than you spend is ruin. Well, that's what my muvver said when they were taking all our furniture away."

Now Charlie's family are in debtor's prison and he had been sent to work in a blacking factory.

"I was gluing the labels on the pots. Night times I stay in an attic, with other boys like me. One of them told me about sweeping. I thought it might be better than gluing. It's not though. I got turned around in the dark and lost and I fell and I heard them on the roof tops looking for me. I called out and the guv'ner said I was lost too far down and just to leave me. And that's what they did."

You shudder at the cruelty of leaving Charlie like that.

"What are you going to do now?" you ask.

"Tomorrow I'm going back to the blacking factory. It pays my way. Maybe soon my father will be out of prison and I can go back to school."

"You like school?" The Magician perks up. You aren't so excited by this topic. You were hoping the events of this morning might delay school.

"Charlie," says the Magician, "how would you like to work for me for a while? I could use another assistant at the theatre where I work. You can room here with the other staff and, if you'd like, you can attend the school room with the others."

Charlie grins and nods and thanks the Magician for his offer. He turns and grins at you.

"Thank you so much for bringing me here!"

You are a little embarrassed because you have only brought him a few doors down the corridor but you can see your actions have changed his life for the better, and that makes you feel really good.

Charlie will be fun to have around and maybe you'll get to go with him to the theatre. You've been once or twice helping to deliver the Magician's equipment and guarding it from prying eyes. Charlie needs to go and get his things from the attic where he stays. He asks if you want to tag along.

It is time to make a decision. Do you:

Go with Charlie to collect his things? **P146**

Or

Don't go with Charlie? **P134**

Suddenly Mrs Noogles is calling. She wants you to clean up after breakfast.

You take the scraps out to the hen house and when you return Henry is whistling as he washes the dishes. You join him drying the plates and then Mrs Noogles gets you to work on her herbs. This is something you really like doing. Mrs Noogles has all sorts of dried plants which she uses for cooking and medicine. You are gradually learning a lot about the process. This morning there are several herbs to bind up to dry and others to take down. Sometimes your job is wrapping muslin over flower heads to collect the seeds. Every job has a different smell to it. You package up mustard seeds set aside from the other day and offer to take them back into the storeroom before you head to the library.

The storeroom is one of your favorite rooms. It smells of thyme and cumin and paprika and other good things for cooking. At the back of the room, are shelves of jams and pickles and once you found a whole tin of jam tarts, and you went back to the kitchen with one less in the tin. You look at the shelves now and notice a little tube with writing on it. *Hope* it says. Curious, you pick it up and look at it before putting it back and then stacking the shelves. You have to reach high up to store the mustard seeds and unbeknownst to you the little tube falls in your pocket.

The library is another of your favorite rooms and it's where you left your homework yesterday. You've discovered a pretty good way to get there – carry a book. You learned the trick from Hannah, one of the librarians, who you noticed takes a book with her whenever she returns there. It isn't unusual for a librarian to carry a book but the way she carried it was unusual. It was like an explorer with a compass. The rooms of the house are never short of books. The kitchen has cookery books of course, but you wouldn't want to take one of those and get Mrs Noogles annoyed. But over at the end of the benches is a room between the kitchen and the greenhouse. It is a small sunny space where the gardeners sometimes meet and talk. Mrs Noogles can pass them a plate of biscuits and they can hand over bunches of carrots or new potatoes without taking off their boots. It's called the mud room because it's often filled with muddy boots but that's only one side. There's also a wooden table and old comfy chairs and, the thing you've come for, a book shelf.

You don't need to read the book but you can't help scanning the titles. There is one about the history of roses – hmm, clearly a gardener's choice and so are many of the others, but this one seems out of place: *A Baroness Instructs the Genteel Art of Dance*. Huh! Nobody is going to miss that. You pull it out and cross through the kitchen. You don't think too hard about the library but step out into the corridor holding the book out a little ahead and let it make the choices about the direction you take.

The first room you enter is the ballroom. You step round a corner and there it is and when you turn back the corridor is gone. In fact you are now standing in the middle of the ballroom. Arriving like this makes some people dizzy, but you've had it happen before so you stay on your feet.

The last time you were in here you were helping at the Magician's winter solstice ball. It was a strange and wonderful affair. Guests were arriving for days and the Magician erected a series of towers in the garden for them to stay in – rather like some people would erect a marquee or tents. It was hard to know the difference between guests and entertainers, as many of the Magician's friends are also entertainers.

There were jugglers and lion tamers and trapeze artists and illusionists. There were also a couple from America who were crack shots with pistols and a number of fortune tellers and musicians. The days before they arrived were spent dusting the dreams from the house – Scarlet, Henry and yourself were set to work using brooms with pillow cases tied onto their ends herding them into wardrobes and placing signs on their doors such as 'do not enter' – but still some people did. Some went inside for fun (the picking strawberries dream in winter was quite entertaining) others went in because they did not seem to think the signs applied to them.

The pistol shooting man was one of these. His name was Bill and he strode into a cupboard on the first day he arrived and did not come out again for three days. His partner didn't seem to mind and spent most of her time with a snake charmer who could tell the most entertaining stories. When the pistol shooter returned she had already developed a new act with snakes. She claimed they were good to work with because they were deaf, and were not spooked by the noise of pistol shots and whip cracks.

The last night of the get together was solstice night – the longest night of winter. The Magician said it was the night winter cracked and spring got in under ice and snow and began to send out green shoots and warmth under the earth. There was feasting and merriment and lots of dancing. The Magician had walked out onto the ballroom floor first and had invited out Mrs Noogles to be his partner. She had been wearing a dress with the colors of autumn leaves and as she danced the dress became the colors of spring.

The ballroom is deserted now after the hectic days and nights of the solstice ball, and your feet echo as you cross the parquet floor made from small blocks of wood laid in an intricate scene. Without people all over it you can see it is a mosaic of a forest with trees all around the outside of the room and in the middle there is a party going on with tall regal people and other creatures – half men and half goats – dancing and playing flutes. There are a group of girls dancing in a circle with the goat men. At the edge of the party, looking quite out of place, you see what looks like one of the young gardeners who works for the Magician. Come to think of it, you haven't seen him since the solstice party. You stare at the picture on the floor. Is the gardener trapped in the mosaic? Is the picture somehow real?

In your hand the book gently tugs at you and you remember you were heading to the library. You feel strange walking over the floor. It's like the feeling you have in a graveyard where you don't need to be told to keep to the path. You take care not to tread on the animals and people as you make your way across the room. There are several doors in the far wall — all big and imposing. The book tugs you toward the one on the left. The suit of armor is standing beside it. Was it there before? You were quite busy looking at the floor so you can't say for sure. You open the door and have a moment of pride. The book has acted like a compass steering you toward the mass of books and manuscripts the Magician has stored. On the other side of the door is the library. It is a cavernous expanse of tables and shelves and cabinets with treasures from the Magician's travels.

"Don't shut that door!" a voice calls out from behind stacks of books on a table.

Then out from behind the stack comes Hannah, the librarian.

"From the sound of your footsteps, you were on a flat wooden floor. Leave the door open so I can move some of these books out to be sorted. That door has opened straight onto a flight of stairs for two days which was absolutely useless for sorting!"

You hold open the door as the librarian bustles over and wedges a wooden triangle underneath it. Then she pulls a velvet curtain rope from her pocket and secures the door handle to a hook at the end of a shelf for good measure.

Looking up she explains. "I wouldn't want to lose my new stock somewhere in the house if the door shut. You never know when the house is going to shuffle around."

You nod in agreement and are about to go and grab your homework when you wonder if Hannah will know whether the gardener is in any trouble. You offer to push the trolley of books she is now loading up from the table. When you get closer you notice they smell vaguely of smoke and one or two are singed at the edges.

Hannah sees you pick one up and sniff it and offers up an explanation: "Fire rescue. There are some rare volumes here. I want to air them out and check them over for my catalogue."

Hannah goes back for more books. She returns pushing another trolley. The smell of smoke is profound even in the large ball room. You look down at the floor to find the gardener – he isn't where you remember him. The others are all there but you can't be sure they are where they were before. There is still a party scene with music and dancing and strange creatures, half goats and half men. Hannah notices you staring at the floor and comes over to take a look.

"Those are satyrs," she says.

"The picture on the floor has changed," you tell her. You explain how earlier you saw the gardener and now you don't.

Hannah is instantly interested. She studies the floor more intently and, like you, takes care not to walk on the creatures beneath your feet.

Suddenly she calls out. "Is this your man?"

"It could be," you reply.

It's hard to tell now because the gardener appears to have climbed a tree. As you walk toward the gardener's new position in the floor you notice something else. A wolf. You are sure you didn't see it before and it is approaching the reveling group. A long tongue lolls from its mouth and it appears to be very large.

You explain that the floor's picture has changed and you think that the lad in the tree is the gardener.

Hannah springs into action and races back inside the library declaring: "We must rescue him at once!"

She returns wearing a cape with a hood and carrying a sort of basket.

"Well," she says, "are you coming?"

You wonder just how you'll enter the floor scene and how you'll rescue the gardener but you nod to Hannah as she begins a circuitous sort of half dance, gesturing to you to do the same. As you follow her path it begins to make some sense. Her footsteps wind between the trees and other motifs that are set into the floor. In time, the ballroom floor softens between your feet and then you begin to scuff up dirt, then leaves and small twigs. Looking up you see that the ballroom walls are now decorated with a forest scene on the wallpaper. The smell of burnt books gradually fades and is replaced by the pleasant smell of damp earth after it has rained.

Before long you duck to avoid a branch and when you look around there is no sign of the ballroom at all. Hannah moves along stealthily. From her basket she draws a dagger and tucks it into her belt. She also brings out a bar of chocolate and breaks a piece off.

"While we are down here it would be best if you don't eat anything from this forest – do you understand? This type of enchantment often works by binding you with food and drink."

You nod and start to think back on the breakfast chats where the librarians have been describing their acquisition activities. You'd assumed they would be (you blush a little) boring. But the way Hannah has jumped into this mission makes you think you have completely underrated her job. Just then you hear a howl in the distance. Hannah slows and cocks her head to listen. She signals for you to hold still. Slowly she takes off her cloak and turns it around – inside it is the color of blood.

"I'm going to scout ahead. Walk toward the sound of music and keep out of sight. See if you can find the gardener. You'll see my cloak when I want you to."

"But won't the wolf see you?"

"Wolves are color blind, but they smell and hear better than we do. Anyway, I'm not convinced that the wolf is our greatest enemy here. I'll be back soon."

She flips the hood of her cloak over her head and vanishes, apart from her basket, which winks out of sight as it disappears under the folds of the cloak.

You head on through the woods, scrunching leaves underfoot as you move between the trees. You aren't sure if you are following a path or just places where the trees are not too close together. You come to a clearing and notice a strange thing. Over to your right, a tree is bursting into pink and white spring buds, but the path by which you entered the glade is covered in orange, brown and red fallen leaves. There are patches of snow to your left, but ahead the trees hold ripe summer fruit. This place has all the seasons going on at once. You walk across the clearing to a peach tree laden with perfect golden fruit. The air, as you get closer, is heavy with the sweet fruity scent. You are about to reach out and pick one when a voice from above calls out.

"I wouldn't if I were you!"

Up in another tree is the gardener. His smile broadens in recognition when he sees you, and he jumps down to clap your back and jump around.

"You've come from the Magician's house!"

You tell him how you saw him in the floor and followed a path till it turned into the forest. You ask his name and he tells you he is Ted. As soon as Ted speaks his name you remember him clearly, which makes you worry there might be some sort of forgetting spell involved in this adventure.

"How long have I been down here?" Ted asks, "Is the solstice party still going?"

You explain it's been quite a while since the Magician's annual party. And then you wonder:

"Have you eaten anything?" Ted shakes his head.

"I'm not sure but places like this usually have enchanted food. Look around, its summer and winter and spring all at once. Whatever grows here is grown with the aid of magic. The Magician has rules for us gardeners: we grow things in season and there's only a little magic around the edges – keeping the bugs away and helping plants find the light and grow deep roots, but the food we eat is nourished by the land and not magic. This here is something different."

Then the gardener looks at you expectantly. "I don't suppose you brought any food did you?"

In fact you do have something you saved from breakfast – everyone keeps a snack in their pocket if they work in the Magician's house. You pull out a crumbling piece of toast and the gardener looks at it as though it is a three course meal on silver trays. He is about to take a corner before asking:

"Do you know how to get out of here?"

You tell him you don't know, but before he can be too disappointed you tell him about the librarian. "She'll know what to do or else there will be three of us missing and surely the Magician will come looking with three staff lost in the house!"

Ted nods his head. Just then a howl sounds very close by and Ted invites you to climb up into the tree he came down from. You find he has made a platform up there – a number of slender branches and stems have been woven across some central ones to form something like a large hammock. He has other things up there too, and he's also woven a set of stairs to a higher platform.

You have only just climbed up when you hear paws padding into the glade and you know the wolf is below. There is a sniffing and snuffling under your tree. The wolf must have followed your scent. You wonder if it will leave or stay and what has happened to Hannah.

Just then a whistle sounds and the wolf crashes off. There is another whistle, closer this time and then the wolf comes racing back to sniff at your tree and then tears back off across the glen in another direction. Someone else enters the clearing and you and Ted look at each other trying to work out if you should call out or not. Hannah's voice interrupts your silent debate:

"Well, is anyone going to invite me into the tree?"

Ted lowers down his hand and Hannah, ignoring it, climbs up like a monkey. You think of all those ladders in the library and wonder if that is how she got to be such a climber.

"Right," she says, very business-like. "Looks like we've got ourselves a typical enchanted forest situation. A few ways in but, as yet, no discernible way out. A fly trap of sorts. There's a big doggie out there with sharp teeth but, he likes to play fetch. Not really a problem." She looks at Ted. "You been here long?"

Ted tells Hannah his story. Blushing, he tells her that there were some beautiful girls he'd seen heading off each night, as if to a ball, and he'd wanted to dance with one of them. He'd followed them the first night and had seen them enter the ballroom and start dancing. Before long they had disappeared from sight and he'd felt sure if he knew the steps, he could dance his way into the heart of the last dancer.

"Hmmm," says Hannah. "So you weren't meant to land in this trap – you've just come in the back door. I was hoping we wouldn't have to go talk to the satyrs, but we may need to find out how to get back to the house from them. They aren't always friendly. Still, we might have something we can trade."

The drumming of hooves can be heard in the distance – you look down below in time to see the wolf, who had been curled up at the foot of the tree, prick his ears and listen intently. He wags his tail and retreats into denser forest a short distance away. You can see him crouching. It isn't long before three brown pigs appear. They have long tusks and are covered in shaggy hair. They begin to root about under the peach tree. One of them runs at the tree and bangs it with his head. A few ripe peaches fall to the floor and the pigs begin to snarl and fight over them. While they are battling for the peaches the wolf leaps out and rushes toward them. The pigs race off and the wolf gives chase.

"I think we should join the party," says Hannah. She climbs down from the tree and starts walking. Ted follows and you climb cautiously down too. As you walk you ask Ted if he's spoken to the satyrs before.

"Oh yes. After I was lost here I asked them if they knew the way for me to get back home but they answered me in riddles and taunted me. The librarian is right, they aren't very nice. The pigs are their pets and they aren't very nice either. "

You head on through the trees which seem to go on forever. This world looked small from above on the tiled floor of the ballroom, but it is so much bigger here. The librarian produces another round of chocolate from her basket and Ted's eyes light up.

"Have you got a lot of food in that basket?" he asks.

"I've got one or two goodies."

She smiles at Ted, but you think she isn't quite as confident as she was at first. The terrain around you is changing. The trees are thinning out and the seasonal changes that could be seen from a short distance – ice and snow in patches among summer greens are less evident. The wood gives way to scrub, and then the dirt starts to kick up dryly as you tread. It is desolate.

"If I had to guess I'd say someone doesn't want us to come this way," says Hannah.

"I haven't seen this part of the woods before," says Ted.

He sounds uncertain. You wish you could do something to help. You put your hands in your pockets and check to see if there's anything useful. There's the hole – but you can't imagine that would be useful right now. And what's this? You pull out the tube you'd seen earlier today in the store room.

"What's that?" asks Hannah.

You hand her the tube marked 'hope' and she smiles broadly.

"I'd say this is very handy."

She breaks off the end and you see that the tube contains a series of doughnut shaped lozenges. Hannah hands them around and pops one in her mouth. Ted, as always, is eager for any 'real' food.

You put the hope into your mouth and feel a rush of zingy citrus. "Lemon!" you say just as Ted calls out "Strawberry!"

"Mine is raspberry," says Hannah. "Hope must taste differently to different people. Huh? Did anyone see that building there before?"

Not too far away a large wooden building stands on its own. It has large windows at the front and a double width door. Above the door is a sign which clearly states 'Library'.

"Well that's just dandy," exclaims Hannah, "now we just need to enquire about returns."

She sets off again and you and Ted follow, looking at one another and laughing. You can't believe things seemed so grim before. You head towards the building. As you do, the ground changes, becoming a little flatter and with a tile here and there, a wooden one. Around the building the ground is different, and it starts to change underfoot as you near it. Before long the floor resembles that of the ballroom floor earlier this morning except instead of seeing a forest floor and satyrs and wolves and trees you see some of the people who live in the Magician's house and even the Magician himself standing with his hands on his hips looking up at you.

Just as you are about to get to the library there is the sound of angry squealing in the distance and the pigs race up in a cloud of dust. The satyrs are close behind and they laugh at you menacingly. The pigs start to blow at the library and the building begins to buckle and sway. You pick up speed to try and get to it before it disappears. Hannah lets out a whistle and the wolf appears and starts snarling and snapping at the pigs. They stop blowing as the wolf harasses them. The library is within reach. Ted opens the door and holds out his hand to you and tosses you inside. Then he reaches for Hannah who is still encouraging the wolf. The satyrs have begun to angrily kick at the wolf, which dodges them as it continues to keep the pigs from destroying the library.

At last Ted grabs on to Hannah and pulls her into the library. He is about to slam the door when Hannah grabs it and lets out a low whistle. The wolf leaps inside too as she slams the door on the angry pigs and satyrs outside. The library begins to move as if it has been picked up by a tornado. Books explode from shelves and whirl around. The wolf leans into Hannah and whines in fear. Ted steadies Hannah but she doesn't need any help that you can see. At last the wind dies down. Hannah opens the door with the wolf beside her. She steps out and you see you are entering the magician's library.

Across the room you see the door Hannah propped open earlier and beyond that... a great big hole in the ballroom floor. The Magician is standing next to it as though he is preparing to cast a spell. He waves and doesn't seem concerned about the mess.

You are the last person to step out of the strange library. The building melts back into the library wall leaving a door that is framed with intricate carvings of leaves and vines and little pigs and satyrs.

Congratulations you've reached the end of this part of your story. What would you like to do now? Do you:

Go back to the beginning of this story? **P97**

Or

Go to the list of choices and pick another place to start reading from? **P319**

Or

Read a different story? **P5**

You have decided to go with Charlie to get his things.

It is still pretty early in the morning. Along the road deliveries are being made in the neighborhood, bread and vegetables and meat and coal. As you round the corner of your street Charlie exclaims and says "But that's the house we were cleaning over there. How did I end up in your master's roof? How very strange!"

If Charlie is going to be living at the Magician's house he'll learn pretty quickly that 'strange' is an everyday event – but he's had a frightening time lately and you don't want him scared. Instead you ask him about his family. Charlie chats about growing up outside of London in the country, the school he went to and the books he read. He might like the Magician's school room – people turn up and teach and the lessons have a way of coming in handy later on but each time you stumble upon the school room it seems entirely accidental.

As you talk the streets narrow and get busier. Charlie points at a large stone building.

"That's where my family are."

A sign outside reads *King's Bench*.

"Do you think the Magician would let me take them some scraps sometimes? They have poor food there. It's a bleak house."

You nod. Mrs Noogles often gives away food to people who come around the back. No doubt she will find some food for Charlie's family. It does strike you as odd that someone should be imprisoned for not paying their debts – how would they ever get out? How could they work? Charlie explains that often relations pool together to pay debts. He is hopeful a family cousin will help them.

Down a small alleyway you come to the house of the bailiff who has taken in the sons of the debtors. It is one of a string of rickety houses built into the side of the prison's brick wall - which is the only straight part of the buildings.

The bailiff's house is four rickety stories high, and patched up here and there like a quilt with spare boards. Like the rest of the street there is an air of dilapidation and squalor. You follow Charlie through a faded red door. Inside, the building smells of boiled cabbage and sweaty socks.

"The first floor is the bailiff's rooms." says Charlie.

As he starts up the stairs, a woman with a baby steps into the hallway and waves to him. "Home early Charlie? Everything alright?"

"Yes Mrs Winch – everything's roses! I've found a man's going to put me up and give me a job and he has a school room! I'm going back to school! I'm just getting my things."

Mrs Winch reminds him about the rent that is due and Charlie says he will be back to pay the balance. He springs up the stairs beckoning you to follow. The next floor is rented out by the room to families and couples and smells of double cabbage and socks. You wonder what the next floor will smell like as you start up the next set of stairs. Unlike the Magician's house you don't have to be careful of slipping into dreams but there is a real danger of slipping through the floorboards, as they are buckling and broken and patched.

The last floor is a converted attic. You needn't have worried about the smell because the draught carries it all away. It is cold and grim.

Charlie moves to a small pile of rags and boxes in the corner, and gathers his few things. You see his treasures are books and papers and his coat and hat. Here and there in the attic are other piles of belongings that must correspond to other boys. Charlie explains they are all children of debtors and the bailiff's family are very good to keep them. They are able to pay a small rent and also make some payment toward their family's debt. Suddenly Charlie looks stricken.

"Do you think the Magician will pay me?"

Charlie glances around the attic and you know he is thinking that if he can't be paid he really should stay in the grim position he was just happily leaving. You reassure him that the Magician is a strange fellow but also a fair one and if he needs money you are sure it will be provided, especially if Charlie is helping at the theater, because this is how the Magician earns his living. Charlie grins and looks very happy.

At the bottom of the stairs the bailiff's wife is waiting with a baby on her hip. She puts a finger up to her lips to tell you to keep quiet. She points to her front room and then retreats to the back of the house. At her warning you both slow down and hear gruff voices.

"You owe me a boy! That latest one didn't show this morning. I heard he was doing chimneys. I pay you good money to find me kids for the factory. Pay me back or give me another boy!"

Charlie's eyes go wide – there's obviously some arrangement about his job at the blacking factory. You both try to make your way cautiously outside to the street. Just as you are at the front door there is a banging at it. You and Charlie scarper back up the stairs and crouch down to listen from the first floor. Charlie whispers that when the coast is clear you should both run out.

Heavy steps are heard in the front passage and someone opens the front door. Peering round the banister you see the back of a big man with a heavy belt and a set of large keys filling the doorway – this must be Mr Winch the bailiff. He is talking to another man who sounds just as angry as the one in the front parlor. It is the chimney sweep and he is complaining that he lost the new sweep straight off and he wants some money back.

It seems the bailiff isn't quite so kind after all. He is organizing children of debtors to be used as factory workers and chimney sweeps. He is taking money from the other men and he is getting rent from the children.

"Now see here!" He is telling the chimney sweep, "It's not my problem if you lose your workers down chimneys – you got to train them proper! I might find you another boy for the same arrangement, but I don't owe you nothing!"

"You owe me something though, Winch," It is the man from the factory.

"You guaranteed me that boy for nine months of gluing. Assured me you did! Then he's hopped off to the sweep and he's lost him! You lost me my worker and he was a good one too – he could read! He never glued the labels upside down!"

The three men continue to argue. You feel a squeeze from Charlie and look at him. He is signaling you to follow him down the hall and holding his fingers to his lips to say to keep quiet.

Singing in a room off the hallway draws your attention to a doorway. Perhaps it would be a good idea to ask one of the people living on this floor to shelter you for a while? On the other hand, you and Charlie have done nothing wrong. The bailiff might be making money from other people's misfortune but he has made his own trouble, he really doesn't own you. Maybe you should both just head through their argument and step out the front door?

It is time to make a decision. Do you:

Ask the singer if you can shelter with them? **P150**

Or

Try and run out of the house? **P161**

You have decided to ask the singers if you can shelter with them.

You decide to wait it out until the men have gone from downstairs. Charlie knocks gently on the door next to you in the hallway. The singing stops and a woman's voice can be heard asking who is there. Charlie opens the door and steps inside with you following closely. If the person inside gives you up you will be trapped.

The room inside faces the sun. The brightness momentarily blinds you after the dark dinginess of the rest of the house. You also notice with relief that you have stepped out of the smell of cabbage and dampness that overpowers the rest of the house. Instead the air is filled with a very pleasant mix of flowers and perfumes. In the middle of the room, a long worktable sits on rows of shelves holding all sorts of jars and bottles. Closer to the window there are potted leafy plants with pink and white and purple flowers. You recognize a mortar and pestle on a work bench along with many more little bottles. This room seems like a place you might find in the Magician's house, not a poor London tenement building.

"What do you two want?" the voice is old and delicate like lace and has a French accent. In amongst bottles and beakers you finally discern the room's occupant. She is an old woman with a grey smock over her voluminous skirts. She is carefully pouring liquid from a large container into several small bottles.

"Pardon Madame, je suis Charles."

Charlie introduces himself in French and asks if you can both shelter for a short while. Surely he must be the only French speaking chimney sweep in London! The little old woman is impressed too. She asks him questions and then, realizing you are not following the conversation, continues in English.

She laughs wryly when she hears that Charlie's labor has been sold to both the blacking factory and the sweep.

"That rogue! You were right to be careful, Charlie. He won't want you knowing what he's up to. He may lose his job at the prison if it's known he is profiteering. You must wait here until it is safe to leave."

Just then you hear heavy footsteps out in the corridor as the three men head up to the attic. There is a splintering sound and loud cursing. One of your pursuers has met with a rotten step. You wonder if the bailiff will notice that Charlie's things are gone. You don't have to wonder for long – his voice belts out to his wife through the house.

"Myra! You seen that Charlie today? His things ain't here!"

Mrs Winch yells back that the boy came earlier with another kid to fetch his things – she says she reminded him about the rent. The bailiff's footsteps come back down He is telling the sweep and the blacking factory manager not to worry, now there's two kids, one for each of them...as soon as he finds them.

"I'll let that Charlie know there'll be trouble for his family if he doesn't get back to work, that'll fix him. The other one's probably a stray you can put down your chimneys and nobody will miss them."

Footsteps on the landing are coming closer. There is a knock on the door and the door knob begins to turn.

You shudder to think of going down a small dark chimney and look pleadingly at your host, hoping she will not give you away. She looks very angry at what she is hearing and beckons you both to step inside a wardrobe in one corner of her room by her bed. Would that be a good place to hide?

Quick! Make a decision! Where are you and Charlie are going to hide? Do you:

Hide in the wardrobe? **P157**

Or

Dive under the bed? **P152**

You have decided to dive under the bed.

The bailiff's feet appear on the floor just inches from you. He asks your host if she has seen two kids.

"No, Monsieur."

"Well you won't mind me having a little look around then will you?"

His feet return to the bed and in seconds he has grabbed both you and Charlie and is dragging you out. He hauls you both down the stairs and triumphantly presents you to the sweep and the factory manager.

"There you go, one for each of you. You'll have to lock 'em up when you aren't using them. This one knows it's a longer lag for his dad if he don't work and no doubt this one can be convinced to do their duty too. A bit of hunger will work wonders."

The sweep looks at you with disgust. "This one doesn't seem small enough for chimneys, but since Charlie managed to wiggle out before, I'll take him again."

The blacking factory owner grabs you by the back of your shirt. "This one doesn't cough. I lose them to the black lung after six months of stirring the pots. Maybe this one is built of stronger stuff. Give me a rope."

While the bailiff goes for a rope you struggle to get free of the factory manager's arms. Meanwhile Charlie's face is twisted in anguish. He looks terrified to be going back to the dark chimneys. His predicament might be worse than your own.

You have an idea and look at the sweep. "My master sent me back here to get your name. You left your boy in his chimney and he wants you to pay for the damage he caused."

The sweep looks cautious. "Now steady on here – a boy getting stuck isn't my fault."

The greedy factory manager recognizes an opportunity and turns to the sweep. "Tell you what, since you can't have him running around ruining your good name, how about you give that one to me as well and I'll keep him secure."

The sweep nods and starts deliberating about money with the bailiff, he feels he has paid for something he didn't get. Mr Winch ends up agreeing to give him some coins and then fetches with rope to tie up you and Charlie.

Charlie doesn't look much happier but you think if you're both together you might be able to find a way back to the Magician's house. You try to give him a reassuring look as you are both bundled down the stairs.

The blacking factory man whistles out the front door to where another man in a horse and cart is waiting. He jumps down from his seat and comes inside to help your captor. You think about running, but the two men overpower you, tie your legs and toss you on the back of the cart with a rag tied over your mouth to keep you from yelling out. In this part of London you doubt anyone would come to your aide anyway. A smelly tarpaulin is thrown over you. There is just enough light to see Charlie's frightened eyes as the cart starts moving down the lane.

You judge that you have only travelled a few streets before the cart stops once more. There are voices. Then the tarp is moved and you are hoisted over the back of a man and taken inside a building you guess must be the blacking factory. You are taken down some stairs and dumped in a pile of sacks. Charlie lands with a woof of dust beside you. The manager addresses him:

"Well Charlie, you've lost me a good day's work, if not more. The rest of the boys have probably been slacking off while I've been out chasing you. It's not good for business, boy. From now on you'll be staying here with your friend and we can take what you owe me out of your wages. I've half a mind to beat you black and blue but that will probably just make you slower. Starting tomorrow I want you two working. Tonight you'll sleep down here with the rats – that will give you a taste of what it's like to cross me. It's just a taste mind. You don't want to go doing that regular."

He picks up a stick and tosses it towards you both. "This should give you a fighting chance against being bitten. With any luck you'll clear a few rats out for me."

With that he loosens the ropes around Charlie's arms and leaves. You hear a deadbolt slide home and lock you both in. There is faint light coming from under the door and a little more shows between the floorboards over your head. You hear Charlie moving around getting untied. He isn't the only one rustling. Rats are coming out of the corners to see what might be worth picking over.

Once Charlie has freed himself, he helps you too. The two of you stand up rubbing the places where the ropes had rubbed at your wrists and look at your prison.

"I've lost my books," says Charlie, and a few tears start to leak from his grimy face.

You look at him and laugh: "Charlie, we're locked in a cellar with the light fading and a horde of rats about to bite us and *you* are crying about a book."

Charlie smiles and awkwardly wipes the tears away. He starts apologizing to you for the trouble you are in. You hush him quiet and are about to tell him not to worry when a rat makes a dash across Charlie's boot and bites at his shoe lace. He shoes the rat away by stamping and picks up the stick.

"I have an idea about the rats," you say.

"Did you happen to put anything from breakfast in your pocket?"

Shamefacedly, Charlie nods. From his trouser pocket he pulls a rather mangled piece of toast, and from your own pocket you pull out the hole you folded up and tucked away this morning. Charlie watches, astonished, as you lay it out on the floor like a carpet. As soon as the hole is laid down the ladder appears – inviting you in.

"Are we going down there?" asks Charlie.

"I'm not sure," you say, "but hopefully the rats are."

You sprinkle a line of crumbs close to the hole and carefully sprinkle some more down the sides. You both stand back to watch.

Before long the boldest rats are scampering toward the hole and munching on the crumbs, others follow not wanting to miss out. Thinking there is a feast inside they swarm down the sides – you count at least fifty. You hope the creature inside enjoys them as much as mice.

Now that the rat problem is over, you look around the cellar to see if there is any way out. It's built of stone blocks and the walls are very solid. You walk to the back behind barrels of foul-smelling stuff and more piles of sacks, but find the cellar has no other way out.

Charlie has been searching too. He comes down the cellar stairs from where he has been checking the door and peers into the hole. "Where does that go?"

"I don't know." You explain that you think there will be an opening down the ladder but you have no idea where.

Charlie asks if he has heard correctly and that when you first explored the hole its bottom was on the ceiling. You nod. Charlie looks around and finds half a brick. He leans over the hole and drops it in. You both listen. Splash! Wherever the hole ends up it's a wet ending. Then you hear a yell and Charlie says he thinks it's a boy who works stirring the blacking pot upstairs. The hole might come out right over the boiling cauldron. You certainly don't want to end up in that.

A big cat face emerges from the hole. "Thanks for the rats, my friend, but luckily I missed the brick." It looks around. "This isn't the Magician's house is it? "

"Sorry about the brick," Charlie stammers, "We are attempting to escape from this cellar and I was trying to determine where the hole would lead us."

The black cat eyes him and evidently decides to forgive him for chucking the brick down its hole. "Then I suggest the hole be repositioned somewhere which would allow you both an alternative exit. "

After the cat disappears you pick up the portable hole and think about where it might be best to put it next.

Charlie though, is way ahead of you. "If we put it on the floor and it comes out in the ceiling of the room above, it might follow that if we put it against the far wall we might get out of the front door!"

He's really quite clever and completely wasted putting labels on jars, you think. The two of you take hold of the hole and then cast it like a fishing net at the back wall of the cellar hoping it will form a tunnel rather than a hole. It works.

When it lands this time, there is no ladder and you can just walk inside. Near the entrance of the hole there are glow worms to light the path, but just as before they soon give way to darkness. You are out in front and before long your foot finds the end of the path and a custardy nothing beyond it.

"Jump, kittens!" You hear the cat say. So taking each other's hands you both leap. The two of you fall in slow motion. Eventually, you land on a heap of sacks by the front door of the factory. Behind you, a large black hole has been blasted into the brick wall of the factory.

Quickly, you roll up the hole and stuff it back in your pocket. In moments you are both running towards the Magician's house and clapping each other on the back congratulating each other on your escape.

You have reached the end of this part of the story.
It is time to make another decision. Do you:
Start at the beginning of this story and try another path? **P97**
Or
Go to the list of choices and read from another place? **P319**

You have decided to hide in the wardrobe.

Just as the wardrobe door is shut, the bailiff enters the room.

Through the keyhole you see a barrel-chested man with long greasy hair tied up at his neck. A leather belt stretches around his waist from which jangles a bundle of large keys. He asks the French lady if she has seen two runaway kids.

"Their parents are debtors."

She says she hasn't seen you but he strides into the room and looks around anyway. She asks him to leave saying he will damage her things but he ignores her. He crouches low and looks under the bed you nearly hid under. He takes another look around and then leaves. The lady puts her fingers to her lips and gestures for you to stay put. Next to you Charlie is fidgeting.

"Is he gone?" he whispers.

"Shhhhhh ...," you hiss.

Soon you hear the bailiff's feet treading back down the stairs. There is muttering and talking from the three men. There is one, then two, and a short while later, a third bang of the front door. All this time the lady has been patiently working with her bottles. When the last man leaves she gets up and beckons you both out of the wardrobe. You both thank her for hiding you. Your rescuer introduces herself as Mignette. "I'm happy to have helped, children. I know what it's like to be hunted. I escaped from Paris during the revolution. You never knew if you would be next to be imprisoned or worse. So I packed what I could of my business and came by boat to London."

"What is your business, Madame Mignette?" you ask.

"Why perfume of course! All the rich ladies need perfume so they do not have to smell the filth of the streets and to make the men think they are like flowers themselves!"

Mignette points to the row of little bottles she is filling and offers you a sniff. The delicate scent of flowers waft from each small vial.

You watch Mignette place a small cork stopper in each and then melt wax around the cork to keep it secure. Lastly she reaches for glue and labels but Charlie stops her:

"I know the drill, Madame," he declares and deftly adds a label to each perfume while Mignette goes on to fill another batch. Having watched the process you help with the corks and wax and the three of you complete her work.

After a while Mignette suggests you are both probably safe to leave, "If they were watching the building they have probably gone." She hands you both a small bottle of perfume as thanks for the morning's work. You thank her again and warily head out of her apartment.

Outside you keep a sharp eye out as you head back to the Magician's house. Before long you are entering the servant's entrance and looking at the disapproving face of Mrs Noogles. You realize you have been away all morning and haven't been any help in the kitchen. Lunch looks to be almost prepared. Charlie hands her his bottle of perfume and says you both stopped to earn a gift for her. Mrs Noogles breaks into a grin and tells you that you deserved some time off. "Now get your young selves off to the school room and I'll see you when it's time to eat again."

With a sinking feeling you realize you haven't done your homework. Maybe a new pupil will distract Miss Spurlock. You glance at Charlie and see he is giddy with excitement at the prospect of schooling. You have to smile yourself – school can be a chore but it is interesting and you know it would beat working in the blacking factory or cleaning chimneys any day. You show him to the door which you hope will lead you to the school room. As you head down the corridor you resume your careful walking and explain to Charlie that this house has its own equivalent of faulty floorboards. Charlie looks disbelieving but then you both wander into a patch of carpet which acts like sand and causes you to drag your feet and hear gulls in the distance. You take his hand and guide him to the wall where your footing is surer, and before long you are entering the school room.

Miss Spurlock looks up from a book she is reading the class as you both enter the classroom. She smiles at Charlie and says she has been expecting a new student today. She asks Charlie about his education and he chatters about books he has read.

"You like stories, Charlie?"

"Very much, Miss."

Miss Spurlock says she'd like him to write her a story so she can get an idea of his education so far. She hands him paper and ink. Then she hands you a list of mathematical problems to practice.

The thing about Miss Spurlock is she always comes up with fascinating math problems. The first one is about calculating how many cream cakes you would have to eat if you were trapped in a pile of them and the way out was a trap door in the floor. Her instructions always say *show your workings*. Miss Spurlock says the workings are more important than the answer when you are learning to reckon. You know there may not be a perfect answer but it is fun to consider. You sit down and think about what you know and soon your mind is deep in numbers and their logic. Charlie scrawls furiously beside you. When Miss Spurlock sends you out to help with lunch he is still scribbling.

Back in the kitchen with Mrs Noogles you set out the dinner plates and she again tells you the Magician will join you all for the meal. You are slicing tomatoes for the salad when everyone else arrives to eat. Miss Spurlock is looking very happy. When the Magician arrives she suggests to him that Charlie reads his story to everybody. The gardeners look a little uncomfortable at this and you can tell they think the story will be boring and might interfere with the Victoria sponge cake Mrs Noogles has ready for dessert.

Charlie looks nervous but the Magician says it is a magnificent idea and he would love to hear it. So Charlie stands up and begins his tale.

You can't believe it! He has taken your adventures this morning and dressed them up. He describes Mignette and her escape from

France with so much more detail. The maids gasp and worry if she will make it to safety. Then Charlie describes fisticuffs between the bailiff and the chimney sweep and finally the hero – Charlie Dickens – is saved with his friend (You!) and is able to attend a fine classroom and eat first-rate food. Everybody cheers at the end and Miss Spurlock tells him he has a talent for telling stories and he should keep it up.

You have reached the end of this part of your story. Do you:
Start over at the beginning and try another path? **P97**
Or
Go to the list of choices and start reading from another place?
P319

You have decided to try and run out of the house.

Halfway down the stairs Mr Winch steps out above you and the factory manager steps out below.

You both try to get to the door but it's useless, the two men overpower you and truss you up like a chicken for the roasting pan. You are gagged and put into big sacks and thrown on the back of a cart. In no time you are carried into the blacking factory where Charlie worked before he became a chimney sweep.

The factory manager throws you both into a room with jars and labels and says just three words,

"Get to work!"

He closes the door and you hear a bolt being slid on the other side, locking you in.

"I'm so sorry," says Charlie. A tear escapes down his cheek.

"Don't worry," you say.

Then you remember the hole in your pocket. Charlie watches as you place it on the floor. The ladder appears and Charlie follows you down.

"Where does this go?" asks Charlie. You have to tell him you don't know but it seems like a good way to get out of the factory. After a while you hear the voice of the factory manager above, he's discovered the hole and it sounds as if he's following you down.

"Jump," you tell Charlie and you pull him loose from the ladder. Your fall is slow, like moving through custard. When you land you recognize the foot of the grand stairs – you are back in the Magician's house.

"Step exactly where I step," you tell Charlie and head up the stairs. About half way up, there is a bit of a trap for the unwary traveler. If you head up the middle you'll end up in the middle of party, crowded with people. You know how to avoid it though, by skipping up the side. Charlie follows and you are nearly at the top of the stairs when the factory manager comes out of the hole. He is only slightly surprised to find himself in a grand house and immediately leaps up the stairs to catch you both.

Charlie moves as if to run but you tell him to wait. As you expected, the manager disappears into a crowd of people, he's now trapped in the party. You and Charlie slide down the banister and nearly bump into the magician.

"Have you been bringing vermin into the house?" he asks you.

"Sorry Sir, we had to, we were being chased," says Charlie.

"Don't worry lad," says the magician and he snaps his fingers. On the stairs appears a fat black rat. It seems a bit confused about how it got there, sees the hole in the ground and runs down it.

A few seconds later there is a squeak and a purring voice from the hole speaks up, "Delicious!"

"Right you two, off to the schoolroom," says the Magician.

You have reached the end of this part of the story. Do you:

Go back to the beginning of this story and start over? **P97**

Or

Go to the List of book and try another story? **P5**

Lost In Lion Country

Left Behind.

You only jumped out of the Land Rover for a second to take a photo. How did the rest of your tour group not notice? You were standing right beside the vehicle taking photos of a giraffe. It's not like you walked off somewhere.

The next thing you know, dust is flying and you are breathing exhaust fumes as the Land Rover races off after the pride of lions your group has been following all morning.

"Wait for me!" you scream as loud as you can. "Wait for me!"

Unfortunately, the sound of the revving diesel engine drowns out your cries. Surely one of your family members on the safari will notice you are missing. Maybe that nice teacher lady from Chicago you were chatting to earlier will wonder where you are. Won't the driver realize he's one person short?

You smack yourself on the forehead. This will teach you for sitting alone in the back row while the others on the safari sat up front to hear the driver's commentary.

"This is not good," you say to yourself.

What are you going to do now? It's just as well you packed a few emergency supplies in your daypack before boarding the tour. You have bottled water, a couple of sandwiches, a chocolate bar, your pocket knife and your trusty camera. But these things won't help you if you are seen by hungry lions, leopards, cheetah or one of the other predators that stalk the savannah.

With the vehicle now only a puff of dust in the distance, you notice something else much closer, a pack of hyenas. These scavengers weren't a problem when you were in the vehicle, but now you are on foot and the hyenas are heading your way!

You know from all the books on African wildlife you've read, these dog-like animals can be vicious and have been known to work as a team to bring down much larger animals. They would have no problem making short work of you if they wanted to.

If they find you out here all alone in the Serengeti National Park, you'll be in big trouble.

You look around. What should you do? You know that normally the thing to do when you get lost is to stay put so others can find you when they come looking, but the hyenas make that impossible.

Off to your right is a large acacia tree that you might be able to climb, while on your left is a dried up creek bed.

With the hyenas getting closer you have to move.

You need to make a decision. Do you:

Run over and climb up the large acacia tree? **P165**

Or

Climb down into the dried up creek bed so you are out of view? **P168**

You have decided to run over and climb up the large acacia tree.

The giraffe has moved off to look for more tasty leaves. As you head towards the acacia tree, you keep looking over your shoulder at the pack of hyenas to see if they have spotted you. Luckily, the pack is upwind so their keen noses may have not picked up your scent yet, especially with all the wildebeest and zebra in the area. Still, they are covering the ground faster than you are.

The hyenas are funny looking animals. Unlike dogs, their front legs are slightly longer than their back legs, causing them to slope up towards their head. The members of this pack have light brown bodies with black spots, black faces, and funny rounded ears. If you weren't so afraid of getting eaten by them, you'd stop and take photos.

You are nearly at the tree when one of the hyenas perks up its ears and yips to the others. Suddenly the whole pack is running as fast as they can right at you!

There is no time to waste. You run towards the tree and start looking for a way up. Luckily, you can just reach one of the lower branches. You pull yourself up by clamping your legs around the trunk and grabbing every hand hold the tree offers. Once you are up on the first limb, the climbing gets easier.

The hyenas are under the tree now, eagerly yipping to each other. A couple of scrawny looking ones take a run at the tree and jump, snapping at your legs. You pull your legs up, and climb a little higher. They circle the tree and stare up at you with their black beady eyes. You are trapped.

You take off your daypack and slip out your camera. No point in missing a great photo opportunity just because you're in a spot of danger. After taking a couple shots you pull out your water bottle and have a little sip. You don't want to drink too much because you're not sure when you'll find more. The grasses on the savannah are turning brown, so you doubt there has been much rain recently. You can see down into the creek from here and it looks bone dry.

Some of the hyenas lay down in the shade of the tree. Their tongues hang out of their mouths. Are they going to wait you out? Do they think you will fall?

You remember reading that hyenas hunt mainly at night. Are they going to hang around in the shade until sundown? How will your family find you if you have to stay up here?

It could be a long wait so you try to make yourself comfortable. After wedging your backside in between two branches and hooking your elbow around another, you start to think about what to do to get out of this situation.

It is pretty obvious that climbing down and running for it would be a really bad idea. The pack of hyena would have you for lunch before you could get five steps. Maybe when they realize they can't get to you, the pack will move on. Or maybe they will see something that is more likely to provide them with an easy meal.

Just as you are about to lose hope, you see a dust cloud in the distance. It is getting bigger. Is the dust cloud being caused by animals, or is it the Land Rover coming back?

You stand up and look through the leaves and shimmering haze rising from the grassy plain. Further out on the savannah thousands of wildebeest are on the move.

Surely the cloud is moving too fast to be animals. Then you see the black and white Land Rover owned by the safari tour company. But will they see you? The track is quite some distance away from the tree you are in. You didn't realize you'd come so far.

You scold yourself for not leaving something in the road to mark your position. You yell and wave and wish you'd worn bright clothing so the others could see you through the spindly leaves, but the Land Rover isn't stopping. It drives right past your position and races off in the other direction.

"Come back!" you yell.

You sit down again and think. What can you do? It looks like you are on your own, for now at least.

Then you remember the sandwiches in your daypack. Maybe the hyenas would leave you alone if you gave them some food? But then what happens if they don't leave and you're stuck up the tree for a long time and get hungry?

A pair of vultures land in the bleached branches of a dead tree not far away. Do they know something you don't?

It is time to make a decision. Do you:

Throw the hyenas your sandwiches and hope they will eat them and leave? **P172**

Or

Keep your food for later and prepare for a long wait? **P175**

You have decided to climb down into the dry creek bed.

You slide in the loose dust and pebbles as you climb down into the dry creek bed. Hopefully you'll be less visible to predators down here. When you reach the bottom, you turn to the north and walk in the direction of the last village your tour passed through.

Unfortunately the creek bed does not run straight and after a few twists and turns, you are not that sure which direction you are heading. You don't want to stick your head up above the top of the bank any more than necessary, just in case some hungry animal spots you and decides you would make a tasty lunch.

Then you remember a trick taught to you by your scout leader. You can use your watch as a compass. First you draw a clock face on the ground with the 12 o'clock position pointing towards the horizon nearest sun. Then you imagine an arrow running out to the horizon between the hour hand, which at the moment is on the two, and the 12 o'clock position. Because you are in the southern hemisphere, this imaginary arrow, which points towards one o'clock, should show you where north is. If you were in the northern hemisphere it would be the opposite and point south. You know this method is not exact, but it's better than nothing.

Using this method, you calculate you are still heading in the roughly the right direction.

In a couple of spots along the bottom of the creek bed, the mud looks damp, but there is no running water. You know drinking plenty of water is essential in a hot climate so finding some is important if you are going to survive.

As the creek has dried up, deep cracks have formed in the ground, turning the creek bed into a crazy paving of dried mud. Insects buzz and the hot sun beats down on you. You pull your water bottle out of your daypack and have a small sip. You would like to drink more, but until you find another source of water, you want to make sure what you have will last as long as possible.

Lots of acacia trees grow along the creek. Along the branch of one tree sit ten or so brightly colored birds. They are cute little things with light green bodies, yellow chests, orange faces and red beaks. The whites around their beady black eyes give them a slightly startled look. You think they might be Fischer's Love Birds, but you've left your bird identification book on the seat of the Land Rover.

You pull out your camera and take a snap. No point in letting these opportunities go by. You want to document your adventure so that when you get back you'll have lots of pictures to show your family.

After walking for half an hour or so, you figure it's safe to climb up the bank and have a peek at the savannah. When you peer over its rim, you see a plain full of animals. Mainly wildebeest and zebra, but you also see a number of elephants, giraffes, impalas and gazelles grazing on the long grass and spindly shrubs. You are pleased to see that there aren't any leopards or lions, although you know big cats are likely to be lurking nearby as they are known to follow the herd's migration.

From up on top of the bank you can see what look like people moving around the base of a tree further along the creek. With all the dust kicked up by the animals, it's hard to see through the shimmering heat haze, but you hope like crazy that whoever it is can help you contact your family.

You pick up the pace, hoping to get to them before they move off. Five minutes later you can see them much more clearly. What looked like people from a distance, turn out not to be humans at all. Instead it is a troupe of baboons foraging for food. You are not sure you want to get too closed to the baboons because, as with any wild animal, they are unpredictable and can be dangerous if they are frightened or feel threatened.

You are about to sneak around the troupe when one of the females, carrying a small youngster on her back, screeches an alarm.

The others in the troupe immediately start climbing into the branches of the nearest tree. You wonder what it is that has startled them. You don't think they are screeching at you because the noisiest baboons are looking and pointing the other way. Maybe there is a predator nearby. Should you head for the trees too?

Then you see the hyena pack again. Are these the same ones you saw earlier or are they another one?

You sprint for the nearest tree and climb up as fast as you can. Unfortunately, it's not a big tree, and a young baboon has had the same idea.

The hyenas are right behind the young baboon as it runs for the tree. A mother baboon screeches from nearby. Without thinking you lean down and hold out your hand. The young baboon sees your offer of help and grabs on to your wrist.

Just as a hungry hyena leaps up towards the young baboon's legs, you pull with all your strength and hoist the baboon out of harm's way.

You and the baboon sit side by side and look down at the drooling pack. The young baboon is shaking with fear. You don't think it is used to being separated from its mother. Then to your amazement, the young animal slides closer and wraps one arm around your waist. As it snuggles into your side you can feel its heart beating wildly against you.

The baboons in the other trees are making a racket, screeching and hooting at the pack. They raise their fists and bare sharp teeth at the intruders. One baboon watches you intently. Is this the young baboon's mother?

In one of the trees a baboon is breaking off branches and throwing them down at the pack circling below. You are surprised at his accuracy.

It doesn't take long before the members of the hyena pack decide they are not likely to find anything to eat here and move off towards the migrating herds. As soon as they are gone, the baboons climb down from the trees and start looking for insects and grubs again.

The young baboon sitting next to you relaxes and starts picking through your hair looking for nits. You've seen other monkeys do this in documentaries and know that grooming is how the animals bond with each other. It feels funny to have a wild animal picking through your hair but it's not unpleasant.

After grooming you for a few minutes, the young animal climbs down and joins the others in their search for food. The baboon troupe seems relaxed. They obviously don't see you as an enemy.

Now that the threat of the hyenas has passed it is time for you to make another decision. Do you:

Keep following the creek in the hope of finding the village? **P183**
Or
Stick with the baboon troupe for protection? **P186**

You have decided to throw the hyenas your sandwiches.

You've been in the tree for over an hour now and the Land Rover hasn't come back. Why aren't your family looking for you? Where have they gone? Are they just going to leave you here on the savannah amongst all the wild animals? They must have driven quite a distance before they noticed you were missing, otherwise they would have found you by now.

The hyenas are lying in the shade of the tree, tongues hanging out of their mouths. Occasionally one will make a funny 'eu eu eu' noise like it is trying to imitate a chimpanzee. Could these be the laughing hyenas you've heard about? The noise they make does sound a bit like someone chuckling under their breath.

Occasionally one hyena will snarl at another. Are they grumpy because they are hungry? Most of the animals are a bit scrawny with ribs showing through their patchy fur.

You reach into your daypack and pull out the two sandwiches you packed earlier. One is ham and cheese and the other peanut butter.

You take the peanut butter sandwich and peel the two slices of bread apart. Then you take the top piece of bread and fling it like a Frisbee as far from the tree as you can. One of the smaller hyenas wanders over to investigate and then gobbles it up. The other hyenas stand up and look up at you. The next piece of bread is the one with all the peanut butter on it. You fling it in the middle of the pack.

A large female snarls and makes a move towards the bread but is beaten to the morsel by a quickly moving male. The female, in a sudden frenzy at missing out on the food, nips at his rear leg. The male yelps and drops the bread and she snaps it up.

You figure the female must be the pack's leader. She is certainly the biggest animal and you remember reading that the females are often the leaders when it comes to hyenas.

You are not sure if feeding the pack will make them want to move on or not, but you figure you've got nothing to lose but your lunch. You break the last sandwich into pieces and line them up along your thigh. You throw one of the pieces to the left and another to the right. Hyenas scatter chasing the scraps. Then you do it again with two more pieces, one left and another right. Again the pack argues over the morsels.

By now the hyena that have missed out on their share of the sandwich are snapping at those that didn't. When you throw the last piece out towards the big female she swallows it whole before the others can get to it.

Seeing how hungry the hyenas are makes you wonder what they would have done to you if you hadn't been able to climb up the tree. It isn't a pleasant thought.

You always knew that life on the African savannah was tough, and that it was a survival of the fittest sort of place. You just never thought you would have a ring side seat for the show.

You lean back against a limb and wait to see what the pack will do now. Not far in the distance, a large herd of wildebeest are getting closer. The wildebeest make a grunting noise that sounds a bit like a cow crossed with a pig. Many of the animals have young with them.

The young wildebeest have long legs for their bodies. Some of them are prancing around, playing, like young animals do. But little do the young wildebeest realize the danger they are in. You have spotted movement in the long grass on the edge of the herd. The lions are nearly the same color as the light brown grass, and they are moving very slowly towards the grazing animals.

When one of the lions breaks cover and rushes at a young wildebeest, the rest of the herd runs off in a wild panic. The animals raise a huge cloud of dust as they run from the lions. You can hear the thump of beating hooves even though they are quite some distance away.

The lions have missed out this time. But no doubt they will try again soon. They stalk after the wildebeest herd.

Hyenas, like dogs, have sharp hearing. It doesn't take the pack long to realize that there may be a meal to be had scavenging around after the lions. The lead female raises her head as if she's smelled lunch, and gets to her feet. Then with a yip to the others, she trots off in the direction of the herd.

Even as you lose sight of the wildebeest that the lions are following, hundreds more appear in the distance. Zebra and gazelles are also on the move towards the greener pastures in the north.

Before long the hyenas are nothing but tiny brown specks as they run off after the lions. The two vultures have flown off too. They've gone to join the twenty or so other birds circling up high in the thermals created by the hot air rising off the savannah, waiting for the lions to make their kill so they can eat.

After watching the lions and hyenas move further and further away for half an hour or so, you can no longer see any predators on the savannah. All that remain are a family of giraffe munching on the leaves of a nearby tree and a small herd of zebra trotting to catch up with the others.

It is hot, and your water is getting low, if only you could find a village.

It is time for you to make a decision. Do you:

Climb down from the tree and head back towards the road? **P177**

Or

Climb down into the creek bed? **P168**

You have decided to keep your sandwiches for later.

You have decided to hang on to your food. Surely the hyenas won't stay under the tree forever. You lean back against a limb and try to relax.

Off in the distance you see more wildebeest moving in your direction. Maybe the hyena will go off and try to catch one of them and leave you alone. You certainly hope so. At least you've got some shade, a little food and what is left of your bottle of water.

Some of the hyenas are skinny. You can see ribs poking out through their fur. It must be a tough life for the animals out on the savannah scrounging for scraps or trying to bring down much larger animals. A serious injury would mean certain death in this unforgiving environment.

After waiting an hour or so, with no sign of the hyenas moving on, you start to get hungry. You take your sandwiches out of your backpack and decide to eat just one. The other you will keep for later.

The hyena's noses twitch as they watch you bite into the cheese sandwich. They lick their lips and make that funny laughing sound again.

The biggest female in the pack stares at you like you are nothing more than a tasty chunk of meat. Her stare makes you a little nervous even though you are well out of her reach.

After you finish the sandwich you take a small sip of water. The bottle is getting low. Only about a third of it remains. You remind yourself not to get greedy. It might be a long time before you have a chance for a refill.

It's not long before you are starting to nod off. Maybe it's the heat, maybe it's because you have just had something to eat. In either case, you know that falling asleep could be fatal. If you fall out of the tree the hyenas will pounce.

You change position and try to wedge yourself into a place where you can't fall, but it's no use. You are going to have to stay awake for as long as it takes the hyenas to go.

As you sit in the tree, you wonder what your family are up to. Are they still looking for you? Why hasn't the Land Rover come back?

Finally the hyena pack gives up on you. The lead female stands and yips to the others and then trots off towards a group of pointy-horned eland grazing in the distance.

Once the hyenas are far enough away, it will be safe to climb down and start looking for a way to get back to the lodge and your family.

You have just started to climb down when you hear the steady whump, whump, whump of a helicopter. It must be someone looking for you!

You make your way down the tree as quickly as you can, but the helicopter is moving fast. By the time your feet hit the ground they have passed overhead and are heading towards the horizon. You run out into the open and wave your arms, but it is too late. The search party is gone.

Will they come back for another sweep? Was it really a search party? Maybe it was just another group of tourists looking at the animals.

Discouraged, you look around and wonder what to do.

It is time for you make a decision. Do you:

Head back to the road and try to walk back to the last village the tour passed through? **P177**

Or

Climb down into the dry creek bed where you will be less visible to predators? **P168**

You have decided to climb down and head towards the road.

After sitting in the tree for so long your legs are a bit stiff. You have decided that getting back to the road is a good idea in case the Land Rover or another vehicle comes past, but the idea of walking across open grassland makes you a little nervous. What happens if another predator comes along while you are out in the open?

There are a pile of broken branches by the base of the tree, so you grab one to use as a weapon and start walking. After a few minutes, you turn and look back at the line of acacia trees that run along the dry creek bed and wonder if you are making a mistake.

The dirt road is really little more than two narrow ruts running through the grassland like railway tracks of dried earth.

You rest the branch on your shoulder and start walking back towards the last village your tour passed through. As you walk you try to calculate how far it is. The Land Rover was only travelling slowly, and with all the frequent stops for photographs you figure it is between five and six miles. That's about two hours walking. That's not so bad you think.

But then, when you think of it another way, it is two hours of being exposed in the open, and when you put it like that, it doesn't sound very good at all.

As you make your way along the dirt road, you continually look around. You are also keenly aware of where the nearest tree is. At times you are quite some distance from a climbable tree. It's then that you keep the sharpest look out for suspicious movements in the grass. You want to see potential danger before it sees you. The grass is only knee high, but you are pretty sure if you drop to the ground and lie still you will be hidden from view. Unfortunately, that works for predators too. Especially the lions, as they and the drier patches of grass are similar in color.

Grazing animals are on the move on the grassland all around you. Most are heading in the same direction as you, towards Tanzania's northern border with Kenya. A large group of eland, a type of antelope, is off to your left. Their sharp horns look like they'd be good protection. You figure if the grazing animals are relaxed there probably aren't large predators nearby. If there were, the animals would be nervous.

After walking for nearly an hour you hear a strange sound behind you. You immediately drop flat onto your belly. You can feel your heart beating like crazy. You tilt your head and try to figure out what the noise is. Then you hear it again. It sounds like human voices.

Could it be a search party out looking for you? You slowly rise up on your hands and knees and poke your head above grass level.

A group of young Maasai are trotting along the track in your direction. The young men wear red robes and each carries a long spear and patterned shield. A couple of the men have brown head pieces covered with brightly colored beads. They move with grace and efficiency and cover the distance between you remarkably fast.

You've never been so pleased to see people in your life. You stand full height and walk slowly towards them, grinning from ear to ear.

The young Maasai are surprised to see you out here on your own. One asks you a question, but you can't understand what he is saying and shrug your shoulders. Then you try to ask them if they are going to the village, but unfortunately they don't speak English any better than you speak their native tongue, Maa. You decide to try sign language.

After waving your arms and making gestures you are pretty sure they understand that you'd like to come with them. One member of the group nods to you and they move off again. You trot along behind them, but keeping up isn't that easy. These young men have longer legs than you do and they are used to the heat and to travelling long distances across the savannah at a pace that is more run than walk.

Just as you think they are about to leave you behind, they stop.

Once you've caught up they point towards a low range of hills to the west and then at their spears.

Are they going hunting that way? Are they asking if you want to come with them? Isn't it better for you to stick to the track if you are going to get to the village?

You point at your chest and then point down the track and make a walking movement with your fingers trying to make them understand that you want to go in that direction. They point off to the hills again and smile. You repeat your gestures, but you're not getting through to them.

One of the men has a talk with the others. He points at the tree branch you are carrying and has a chuckle. Then he takes a spare spear he has looped over his shoulder and holds it out to you with two hands like some kind of offering, bowing his head as he does so.

You hesitate, not knowing quite what to do. Giving you his spare spear is such a generous gesture. You point to your chest and then the spear, trying to ask him in sign language if he is really giving the spear to you. He understands. Again he bows and holds out the spear.

The spear is a much better weapon than a piece of tree branch. Its tip looks sharp and deadly. If these men are about to take off and leave you behind, you'd be silly not to take it.

You reach into your bag and pull out the pocket knife you were given on your last birthday. You hold it up and open the blade. When fully open the blade locks into place. Then you show the man how you push a button on the side of the handle so you can fold the blade away. You hold the knife out on the palm of one hand, as you take hold of the shaft of his spear with the other.

The man smiles and picks up the pocket knife. He opens the blade again. The others crowd around as he runs his finger lightly along the edge of the blade testing its sharpness. He makes excited comments you can't understand to his friends, but from all the smiles you are pretty sure he thinks he's got the best of the trade.

After completing his examination, the Maasai smiles at you once more, folds the blade away and tucks it into his robe. He points down the road, makes walking motions with his fingers and nods to you, as if to confirm that it is the right way for you to walk. Then after a quick word with the rest of the group, the men take off at a trot across the savannah.

You adjust the straps of your daypack and continue on your way, feeling a little better now that you have a proper weapon. The spear has a heavy wooden shaft with a blade on one end. The blade starts out narrow, then widens out to about the same width as your hand, and then narrows into a point again, much like a large gum leaf. You can just imagine the damage it would do to an animal if thrown with any force.

You remember reading that young Maasai have a rite of passage into adulthood that includes hunting for lion. You wonder if you've just witnessed a lion hunting party.

You look at your spear and try to imagine taking a big cat on with it. "No thank you," you mumble under your breath. "Give me a tree to climb any day."

The sun is getting lower in the sky and you still have quite a distance to cover. You try to imitate the gait of the Maasai men, but you don't have the stamina. In the end you settle for a quick walk.

It is nearly an hour before you see a stockade in the distance. Stout poles, sharpened on one end, are joined together to form a boundary fence. Behind the fence you see the cone-shaped roofs of Maasai huts.

A group of smiling children come running out a gate in the fence and gather around you. Their eyes are wide with curiosity. Are they wondering why you are out in the Serengeti all alone?

They look a happy lot dressed in their bright patterned robes of orange and red. If you'd been in Scotland you could have made a half decent kilt with some of the patterned fabric on show.

With a big grin on his face, one of the boys takes your hand and pulls you toward the gate. The other children crowd around and you all move as a group into the village compound.

The Maasai huts are thatched with bundles of grass. Women sit about outside doing various tasks while the younger children play games with pebbles and sticks.

An older man sees you come into the village and walks over. 'Welcome to our village,' he says.

"Great! You speak English. Do you have a phone?" you ask, before realizing what a stupid question it is. You are out in the middle of nowhere. This village doesn't even have electricity.

"Yes. Welcome to our village," the man says once more.

"Do you know any other English?" you ask.

He grins and nods. "Yes English! Welcome to our village!"

A village girl wearing a traditional red dress and bright beads hands you a wooden bowl filled with milk. She looks about 13 years old.

"Those are all the words my grandfather knows. He learned them so he could greet the tourists that come here sometimes. I learned a little English from the missionaries. My name is Abebi. Drink, you must be thirsty."

You introduce yourself and then thank Abebi for the milk before taking the bowl and downing it in one go. You wipe the milk moustache off your upper lip and nod in appreciation before handing the bowl back. "Do you know how far it is to Habari Lodge?"

"About three hours walk," Abebi replies. "But you need to know which tracks to take. There are many that crisscross this area."

"Do many tours come through here? Mine left me behind by mistake. I need to get back to the lodge where my family is staying."

"Not many tourists come to this village these days. They usually go further north along the river to follow the herds and the big cats. They might come once a week, sometimes less."

Now what are you going to do? The villagers are very friendly and the village is probably a safe place to stay, but you don't want to wait a week before another tour comes through.

You are sure your family is looking for you, but you've come quite a distance from where you were left behind. Will they even think to look here?

If it takes three hours to walk to the lodge, you might just make it before dark but you can't be sure.

It is time to make a decision. Do you:

Ask to stay in the Maasai village until morning? **P196**

Or

Keep going along the track and try to get back to the lodge where your family is staying? **P200**

You have decided to follow the dry creek in the hope of finding a village.

The young baboon you shared the branch with is digging into a rotten log looking for grubs. Like the others, she is so intent on finding food that she doesn't notice as you walk off.

You stay near the creek bed where there are more trees. Having something to climb in case of emergency seems a good survival plan. If you take off across the plain, it would be too easy for one of the predators that live here to chase you down.

Hopefully the lions and leopards are more interested in following the herds and catching big juicy wildebeest than they are in eating you. You'll just have to keep your eyes peeled and make sure you stay away from the edges of the herd where the cats lurk waiting to strike.

As you walk, you think about what you should do if you come across a lion. Maybe a weapon of some sort would be a good idea. You look around for a branch you can use as a spear, something with a sharp point would be best.

You also keep an eye out for snakes. Being cold blooded, snakes will often lie on patches of bare ground where they can soak up the warmth of the sun. You've read that there are cobras and puff adders in this area, both of which are extremely venomous. Also large pythons that kill by wrapping their bodies around their prey are common in this part of the Serengeti National Park.

A bit further along you come across a tree that looks like it has been ripped apart by elephants in their efforts to reach the leaves near the top. A couple of branches are lying on the ground at its base. One in particular looks about the right length to make a spear with.

You remember the pocket knife in your pack. Maybe you could lash the knife to the end of the branch. Then you'd have a proper spear.

You find a shady spot, sit on the ground and open up your bag.

The pocket knife is one you got for your last birthday and has a long thin blade that locks open. But what can you attach it to the branch with? It will need to be strong if it's going to work as a spear.

There may be something you could use in your daypack, so you tip the contents out on the ground and see what you've got. The only thing you see that might work is the leather strap for your camera. But the strap is too wide to use for binding.

You set about cutting the strap into two thinner pieces with your knife. Then you carve a small notch in the end of the branch to fit the knife's handle. You remember that leather stretches when wet and shrinks when dry, so you pop both strips into your water bottle for a five minute soak.

Once the leather has soaked you can stretch it out and bind it quite tightly around the handle of the knife and the branch. After the second strip of leather has been wrapped around the branch, the blade feels pretty secure.

In the African heat the wet leather doesn't take long to dry. As it does so, it shrinks and tightens around the knife's handle.

You test your spear a couple of times by jabbing it at the mangled tree trunk. It works perfectly. The point of the knife sticks quite a way into the wood without coming loose from the shaft of your homemade spear. You feel a little safer now that you've got a proper weapon, but even with the spear you still plan on climbing up the nearest tree if you see a predator.

But wait. Can't big cats climb trees too? And even if you wanted to, how are you going to climb with a spear in one hand?

You scratch your head and think.

After a bit of thought, you rip off the bottom couple of inches of your t-shirt and use the fabric to make a shoulder strap for your spear. This way you will have a way to carry the spear and keep your hands free for climbing.

Once the strap is tied onto the shaft of the spear, you test your theory by looping the strap over your shoulder and hoisting yourself up into the lower branches of the nearest tree. With the spear resting along your back, the climb is easy. Once you're wedged into the branches you take the spear and point the sharp end downwards. Now if anything tries to climb up after you, you can give it a sharp poke. But will that be enough to fend off a lion or a leopard? Hopefully you won't have to find out.

After climbing back down to the ground, you start walking again. You know you've got a lot of ground to cover if you are going to get to the village before the sun sets. Dusk on the savannah is the start of hunting time for some predators. You certainly don't want to spend the night out here all alone.

As you walk along the creek you keep a lookout for potential threats. When you come around a slight bend, you see a shallow pond. The water in the pond looks a bit stagnant. The pond's edges are covered in green slime and its surface is alive with insects.

You think about filling your bottle, but then you're not really sure how safe the water is to drink. There are animal droppings and hoof prints everywhere.

You look at your water bottle and see that it is only one third full. You know that will only last you a short while. You are thirsty.

It is time for you to make a decision. Do you:

Fill your water bottle from the pool and have a big drink before moving off? **P192**

Or

Don't fill your water bottle. Keep walking towards the village? **P194**

You have decided to stick with the baboon troupe.

Sticking with the baboon troupe is a good idea. The troupe posts lookouts while other members forage for food. They are much better at spotting danger than you are. After all, you never saw the hyenas coming. If it weren't for the baboon troupe raising the alarm you would probably be hyena food by now.

The young baboon you shared the tree with is sticking close to his mother as she strips the bark off a rotten log looking for grubs. Other baboons are picking the seed pods off the various grasses that cover much of the Serengeti.

As the troupe searches for food, its members make their way along the bank of the creek. They may not move fast, but at least they are going in the right direction.

You are startled when the mother baboon moves quickly towards you. You've seen how sharp baboon teeth are, so you hope she's going to be friendly. When she is only a couple of steps away, she holds out her hand. A big fat grub is wriggling between her fingers.

She is offering it to you. You've heard of people eating grubs, but you've never tried one. Would she be offended if you didn't take her offering? What would the grub taste like?

If you are going to be accepted by the troupe, you'd better get used to eating the food they eat. Baboons are reasonably close relatives to humans and you're pretty sure that you could eat most of the things they do without getting sick.

You reach out and pluck the grub from the mother's hand. 'Thank you,' you say, hoping that she will understand the friendly tone of your voice. Then, holding the grub by the head you pop it between your lips and bite down, leaving only the head between your fingers.

"Yum peanut butter," you say as the taste explodes in your mouth.

The mother tilts her head at your words, sees you lick your lips, and seems satisfied that her debt to you for saving her baby has been paid.

After making a couple of soft sounds, she moves off to continue her search for food.

There is another log nearby. Using a sharp stick you peel off some bark exposing another big juicy grub.

After a couple of hours, a mature male baboon makes a low whoop and the troop suddenly stops what they are doing and moves off in single file. You wonder what they're doing, but you're happy to tag along. At least you're making progress towards the lodge. You attach yourself near the end of the line. Two young males bring up the rear.

For half an hour or so, the baboons march along the bank of the creek. The youngest of the babies ride on the backs of their mothers. Some of the juveniles play games along the way, jumping on each other's backs and wrestling in the dirt. Occasionally a mother screeches at one of her youngsters when they stray too far from the main group.

The bank on the opposite side of the creek is getting steeper. Layers of rock within the bank form distinct lines. Many layers are reddish brown in color, but every now and then there is a layer of darker or lighter rock. Is this darker layer compressed plant material? Maybe the light layer is ash from some ancient volcanic eruption.

Finally the troupe stops opposite a crack in the cliff on the far side of the creek. The rocks below the crack glisten with moisture. The troupe descends into the creek bed and then enters the narrow ravine on the other side. Not far up the ravine, you see fresh water trickling into the sand at your feet.

The ravine is cool from being in the shade. A light breeze flows down between the rocks from above. Compared to the heat out on the savannah, this crack in the cliff feels as cool as an air-conditioned room.

When you reach the head of the ravine you see a deep pool formed by the rocks. A steady flow of water seeps out of the cliff face. The baboons gather around the pool and use their hands to scoop the fresh water into their mouths. You do the same. After you've had your fill, you open your daypack and refill your water bottle. Then you take a few pictures of the spring and the baboons with your camera.

Without having pictures as proof, would anyone believe that you were once a member of a troupe of baboons? You somehow doubt it. Half your friends at school didn't even believe you were going to Africa on vacation.

When the baboons have drunk their fill, the troupe leader heads back down the ravine. Like the others, you follow the leader in single file. Once you get back to the creek bed the troupe once again continues its journey northward.

Before the troupe goes very much further along the creek, you see a flash of light reflecting off something up ahead. You are sure the baboons have seen it too, but they aren't afraid of whatever it is.

Then you see it again. Is the sunlight reflecting off a piece of glass or metal? What would those things be doing way out here on the Serengeti anyway?

The troupe keeps walking. As you near the spot where the reflection was, you see movement. Then you spot a tent set up on an area of flat land not far from the creek. What is a tent doing way out here? Then you remember ... a tent means people!

When a man holding a movie camera stands up from behind a bush, you catch your breath. Then a woman stands up next to him with a fuzzy looking thing on the end of a pole. It must be a microphone.

"What are you doing here with our baboons?" the man with the camera says.

"Your baboons?" you ask. "How are they your baboons?"

The baboons ignore your conversation with the two people and continue moving towards a large acacia tree. The tree has big branches that stretch out like arms. The sun is low, and you wonder if this is where the troupe plans to spend the night.

"We're making a TV documentary. These baboons come to drink

at the spring every evening and then sleep in that acacia tree over there. We have been filming animals in this area for two months. Why are you here?"

After explaining about the hyenas and how you came to be travelling with the troupe, the couple invites you into their camp. You're not sure if they believe your story. You must admit it does sound a little unlikely.

When you walk into their camp, a Maasai man is stirring a pot over a fire.

"This is Koinet. He is our guide and cook."

"Would you like something to eat?" the cook asks. "You must be starving if you've been walking all day."

"I'm not too hungry. I've been eating grubs with the troupe. Did you know they taste like peanut butter?"

Koinet nods and smiles.

The white man looks at you like you are nuts. "Koinet, give our young guest a bowl of your stew." Then he turns to you. "I'm sure you will find it far tastier than grubs."

You're not sure it will be. Peanut butter is one of your favorite flavors, but you eat the stew anyway. It's not bad for something so meaty. When you finish eating, you have a sip of water from your bottle and then turn to the film makers. "Can you help me get back to Habari Lodge? My family will be worried if I don't turn up soon."

"Habari Lodge? I'm not sure where that is," the man says. "But did you know habari means hello in Swahili?"

"That's all very interesting, but how am I meant to get back to my family?"

"I know Habari Lodge," Koinet says. "The only track from here goes around those hills and across the river. It's about two hour's drive."

"Could Koinet take me to the lodge?" you ask. "I would be very grateful.'

The man scratches his head. "I suppose he could, but not until late tomorrow afternoon. We need him for the balloon pick-up in the morning."

"Balloon?"

"Yes Marie and I have a hot air balloon." He nods toward a big cane basket and a bundle of canvas sitting on the far side of the camp next some other equipment. "Tomorrow we'll take it up and fly silently over the herds to the west. The filming should be spectacular. Koinet will track us in the Land Rover and pick us up when we land."

The woman smiles at you. "It is too late to go tonight anyway. You can sleep in the back of the Land Rover. Then tomorrow you can fly in the balloon with Pierre and I or, if you prefer, you can ride in the Land Rover with Koinet. Then, after the flight, Koinet can give you a ride to the lodge."

"Sleep on it," Pierre says. "You can let us know what you decide in the morning."

You nod. "Okay I will. Thanks."

The four of you sit around the fire and watch the sun go down. Sunsets here in the tropics are very short. One moment the sun is up, and then, bang, it's gone. This is so different from where you live.

As you huddle around the fire, the couple tells you about their lives as documentary film makers. It sounds like an exciting life. Maybe you could do something like that when you get older. You've always loved taking photos.

Before long it is dark and the stars have come out like a garden of lights. You've never seen so many stars.

When you start yawning, Marie finds you a pillow and a blanket and shows you to the Land Rover. The back seat is just long enough for you to stretch out on.

Before long you are dreaming of life with the baboons.

In the morning, you wake up to the sound of movement. You peer out the Land Rover and see Pierre fiddling with some equipment on a patch of flat land just beyond the edge of the camp.

Koinet sees you and waves.

You open the door and walk over to the fire where Marie sits drinking coffee. Koinet is cooking breakfast. Sausages and eggs sizzle in a big frying pan. They smell wonderful.

"So," Marie says from her seat by the fire. "Are you riding or flying today?"

It is time for you to make a decision. Do you:

Go flying in the balloon with Marie and Pierre? **P222**

Or

Ride in the Land Rover with Koinet? **P227**

You have decided to fill your water bottle from the pool.

The water looks a bit dirty but you're thirsty and it is the only water you have found since you were left behind. You use your hand and sweep the insects off the surface and then lower your bottle into the water. The water that fills your bottle has bits of plant material and other things floating around in it but at least it is wet.

You have a couple sips to try it out. It doesn't taste quite as bad as it looks. After drinking your fill you top up the bottle again and put it in your daypack before slinging your spear back over your shoulder and moving off.

You climb the creek bank and have a look around to get your bearings. You decide to leave the creek bed and head north, hoping to reach the village before it gets dark. The winding creek is making your journey much longer than it would be if you were walking in a direct line.

You walk across the savannah quickly, scanning the terrain as you go. Off in the distance you see a large group of antelope grazing. Thankfully no predators are in sight.

Walking is easier now that you've left the uneven ground of the creek bed, but it is hot, and you are thirsty.

Sweat drips down your forehead and back. The more you drink, the thirstier you get. Your mouth stays dry no matter how much water you have. Before you know it your bottle is almost empty.

You don't feel very well. Your stomach hurts and your vision is getting blurry. The next thing you know, your hands are on your knees and you are throwing up into the dust.

The water must have been contaminated. Now you are wishing you'd never had any to drink.

As you throw up again you drop to one knee. You have never felt so sick in your life. By the time you finish throwing up your forehead is burning with fever. You curl up in a ball on the ground to try to make the pain in your stomach go away.

You are getting dizzy and feel like you are about to faint. Then blackness closes in.

Unfortunately this part of your story is over. You made a bad decision by drinking contaminated water. Hopefully someone will find you before a predator does.

It is time for you to make a decision. Would you like to:

Go back to the beginning of the story and take another path? **P163**

Or

Go back to your last decision and make a different selection? **P194**

You have decided not to fill your water bottle.

You are thirsty and the water in the pond is tempting, but you know that drinking contaminated water can make a person very sick. All of the animal footprints and droppings so close to the pond might mean that drinking the water here is a bit risky.

You'll just have to make do with what little water you have left until you can come across a cleaner source. Hopefully you'll find some soon. You know that moving water is the best. In a moving stream or river the water is purified by running over rocks and gravel and is a lot safer to drink than water from a still pond like this.

After walking for another hour, you crest a small rise and see the circular stockade of a Maasai village in the shallow valley below. Stout poles, sharpened on one end, have been joined together to form a protective fence. Behind the fence you see the round sloping roofs of the villager's huts. These huts are also arranged in a circle. Inside this circle of huts, another circular fence has been built. This is where the Maasai keep their small animals. A number of goats have already been put away for the night and are eating piles of grass provided by their owners. Off to the left of the main village is another larger pen for their many cattle.

As you approach the village, a group of children dressed in colorful robes come running out and surround you. Their eyes are wide with curiosity. You suspect they want to know why you are out in the Serengeti all alone. With a big smile on his face, one of the boys takes your hand. The other children gather around as you are escorted into the village compound.

The Maasai huts are thatched with bundles of grass. Women sit about outside doing various tasks while the younger children play games nearby.

An old man sees you enter the gate and walks over to greet you. "Welcome to our village." he says.

A village girl wearing a traditional red dress and strings of bright beads is holding a bowl filled with milk. She looks about 13 years old.

"Those are the only words my grandfather knows. He learned them so he could greet the tourists that come here sometimes. I learned a little English from the missionaries. My name is Abebi. Here drink this, you must be thirsty."

You introduce yourself and then thank Abebi for the milk before downing it in one go. You wipe the milk moustache off your upper lip and nod in appreciation before handing the empty bowl back. "Do you know how far it is to Habari Lodge?"

"About two hours walk," Abebi replies. "But you need to know which tracks to take. There are many to choose from in this area."

"Do many tours come by here? Mine left me behind by mistake. I need to get back to the lodge where my family is staying."

"Not many tourists come to our village these days. They usually go further north to follow the herds and the big cats. We might see a tour once a week, but sometimes many days pass without us seeing anyone at all."

Now what are you going to do? The villagers are very friendly and the village is probably a safe place to stay, but you don't want to wait a week before another tour comes through.

You are sure your parents will be frantically looking for you, but you've come quite a distance from where you were left behind. Will they even think to look here?

If it takes two hours to walk to the lodge, you might just make it before dark.

It is time to make a decision. Do you:

Ask if you can stay in the Maasai village until morning? **P196**

Or

Keep going along the track and try to get back to the lodge where your family is staying? **P200**

You have decided to ask to stay in the Maasai village until morning.

"Do you think I could stay here in your village overnight?" you ask Abebi. "I don't think it's safe for me to be out here alone."

The girl nods. "It is not our custom to turn guests away. I am sure mother will let you stay with us until something can be arranged to get you safely back to the lodge."

"Thank you so much," you say. "I was getting a bit worried out there."

The girl grabs your hand and tugs you gently over to a woman sitting on a mat outside the door of one of the huts.

The circular hut is constructed of tree branches tied together into a framework. Between the large branches, thinner sticks are woven around in layers to form walls. Over these walls is plastered a mixture of mud and straw. In the dry African heat the mud hardens like concrete. To keep out the rain and the hot sun, bundles of grass thatch form a thick protective roof.

Abebi says a few words and the woman looks up at you, smiles and nods in welcome. With a sweep of her hand she directs you inside.

"Come," Abebi says as she leads you into the hut.

It takes a minute for your eyes to adjust to the dim light.

The hut is divided into two sections. The first part is a cooking and living area. Through a small doorway, you see sleeping platforms. It is a simple and efficient use of space.

In the living area is a small fire pit dug into the ground. Over the ashes of a previous fire sits a metal grate to hold pots above the flames. A wooden shelf on the wall holds cooking utensils and containers of maize and other foodstuffs.

"You can sleep here," Abebi says, pointing to a clear space along one wall.

You put down your daypack, open the flap and take out your

camera and a chocolate bar. You hand Abebi the chocolate. "Here, I want you to have this."

Abebi's eyes light up. "I have had this once before," she says. "It is wonderful."

Abebi opens the chocolate bar, takes one small square and pops it into her mouth. She closes her eyes and rises up onto her toes as the taste sensation runs through her.

"Ummmm..." When the square is gone, she carefully wraps up the rest of the chocolate and puts it on a small shelf. "I will save the rest to share with my family. Thank you for this wonderful gift."

You are amazed at how something so simple can give such pleasure.

Abebi reaches out and takes your hand once more. "Come. Let me show you around the village."

Abebi leads you back outside and over to the circular fence in the center of the village. Here, tucked away from predators, are the village's goats.

"The goats are allowed to graze during the day, but we put them away at night, otherwise the leopards get them."

You take a few photos of the goats and then one of Abebi with her hut in the background.

"Come, let's watch the sunset," Abebi says, as she walks towards the outer wall that surrounds the village.

Along the inside of the wall a mound of earth has been built. Abebi climbs up the mound so she can see over the wall onto the savannah beyond. You scramble up and join her.

The grassland stretches off into the distance. Acacia trees are silhouetted against the sky. Some of them look like umbrellas with their tall trunks and outstretched branches.

"Look over there," Abebi says, lifting her arm and pointing. "See the cheetahs?"

It takes you a moment to spot them on a slight rise a couple hundred paces from the village. There are three of them lying on the ground. Their dark spots stand out against the lighter fur of their bodies. The cats are long and sleek, with tails that swish back and forth.

These cats are built for speed and unlike the much heavier lions and leopards, can run fast enough in short bursts to catch even the quickest gazelle.

"Do they often come near the village?" you ask Abebi.

"They sometimes steal our goats when other game is scarce. But these cheetahs are well fed. Now that the migration has started, there is plenty of game around."

You take your camera and zoom in on the animals. Their coloring reminds you of a tabby cat. Then you notice two cubs tucked up close to one of the females. About the size of a normal house-cat, these two baby cheetah are so cute you want to go out and cuddle them.

"They've got cubs," you tell Abebi. "Here look on the screen you can see them."

Abebi comes closer as you zoom in on the cubs.

The sun is almost at the horizon when you see an old Land Rover coming towards the village.

"Who is that?" you ask Abebi.

"Oh, that's Dr Nelson. He is working in the gorge two day's walk from here."

"Dr Nelson? Does he run a clinic there?"

"No he's not that sort of doctor. He studies old bones and fossils. He is a ... um ..."

"Oh, you mean he's a paleontologist."

Abebi smiles at you. "Yes that's the word."

The children of the village are already running out towards Dr Nelson's Land Rover. The Doctor pulls up outside the gate and jumps down from the driver's seat. In his hand is a bag of sweets that he starts passing out to the children.

Once the bag is empty, he walks in and addresses Abebi's

grandfather in the local dialect. After a brief discussion Dr Nelson turns to you.

"So you're the one everybody's been looking for. I heard a report on the radio a couple of hours ago when I was in town picking up supplies. Your folks are very worried."

"So was I for a while," you say. "Is there any chance you could give me a ride to Habari Lodge?"

"I can, but first I have to drop off this stuff at my camp. These supplies include antibiotics for one of my assistants whose foot is badly infected."

"Can you radio my family and let them know I'm okay?"

"We are out of range here, but I have a satellite phone at my camp. I'm going to stay here tonight. There have been reports of poachers operating in this area. Travelling at night is too dangerous. We can call the lodge tomorrow once we get to my camp."

You like the sound of the doctor's offer but you are only a couple of hours walk to the Habari Lodge. If you go with the doctor you may not get back to the lodge tomorrow at all.

It is time for you to make a decision. Do you:

Go with Dr Nelson to his camp? **P212**

Or

Walk along the road to the lodge in the morning? **P218**

You have decided to keep going along the track to the lodge.

You tell the village girl, that you are going to try to make it to the lodge before dark so you can see your family.

"It is dangerous for someone to travel alone," Abebi says. "I will talk to my mother. Maybe my older brother and I can guide you to the lodge. Predators are less likely to attack a group, and my brother is a warrior. He is sixteen and has already hunted lion."

The idea of an escort to the lodge is the best news you've had all day.

"That would be great," you say.

Abebi runs over and speaks to a woman with short cropped hair wearing a flowing blue dress, and red and white cape. Strings of white beads hang around her long graceful neck. After a brief discussion with her mother, Abebi enters a nearby hut.

A few minutes later she comes out of with a tall, lean young man. He wears a short length of patterned fabric around his waist and carries a shield and spear. Strings of multicolored beads adorn his muscular chest. Abebi carries a length of fabric and a plastic water container.

"This is my brother Biko. Mother says it is okay for us to guide you to the lodge."

"Hi Biko," you say, giving him a smile. "Thank you so much for agreeing to do this."

Abebi translates what you've said and Biko smiles.

Abebi holds up her water container. "Come let's fill our water bottles before we leave."

Abebi leads you over to a well in the corner of the compound and pumps the handle. She unscrews the lid of her water container and fills it to the brim. As you fill your bottle, Abebi wraps her container in the length of fabric and then ties the two ends of the cloth together. She swings the bundle onto her back and loops the fabric around her forehead like a bandanna.

You can't help thinking that Abebi must have a very strong neck to carry water this way. To test your theory, you interlace your fingers together and place your hands on top of your head. Then you pull down with all your strength. It doesn't matter how hard you pull, you hardly feel any weight on your neck at all. All the pressure is straight down.

Abebi laughs when she sees you.

"Before the well was drilled," she says, "the village women use to have to carry water a long way each day. It was very hard work. Most of the village women use a sling like this. Others balance their water containers on top of their heads. It is hard on your arms otherwise."

As Biko leads the two of you out of the gate and onto the track towards Habari Lodge he scans the surrounding area for danger. It almost looks like he is watching a game of tennis the way his head swings back and forth.

Not far down the track, Biko has a few words with Abebi.

"Biko says that if we are attacked by a predator, stand back to back with him and hold your spear level with the ground with one end braced against your thigh. It is important that we all stick together in a group. Predators always try to separate one out from the others. He says if we stick together we will be fine."

You are pleased to hear Biko's confidence, but you hope you won't need to put his defense tactics to the test.

Now that you are with others and feeling more relaxed, you have a little more time to enjoy the beauty of your surroundings. On both side of the track, wildebeest, zebra and eland are on the move. The fine dust raised by so many hoofs reflects the light and gives the air a golden quality.

Biko says something and points with his spear off to the left.

You look to where he is pointing and see a tribe of meerkats. They are sitting on their haunches on top of a mound of dirt a hundred paces off the road. The older meerkats are watching for predators as the young ones run and leap about in the dust. They aren't worried about your group passing by.

You stop and rummage in your backpack for your camera, but after a few photos Biko is moving about restlessly and you know he is keen to get moving again.

You are about an hour into your journey when Biko stops. He speaks urgently to Abebi.

"A vehicle is coming," she tells you.

"Great. We can flag them down and get a ride back to the lodge," you say.

"Biko says they might be poachers. These are very bad men. It is best to hide until we see who is coming."

You follow Biko and Abebi off the road and into a clump of scrub not far away. Biko gestures you to lay flat on the ground. You and Abebi lay side by side in the long grass while Biko stares through the branches.

Biko speaks softly to his sister.

"It is poachers," Abebi whispers to you.

Biko drops to the ground as the vehicle nears.

You lift your head ever so slightly and peek through the stalks of long grass. A flatbed truck carrying a group of men with rifles rumbles along the track leaving a cloud of dust in its wake.

Once the truck has passed you start to rise, but Biko's hand on your shoulder presses you back down. It doesn't take you long to realize why. The truck is slowing down.

You wonder if the men on the truck saw you. Are they coming back?

The truck pulls off the track a couple of hundred paces past your position and you hear one of the men shouting. Even though you can't understand what he is saying, you can tell the man is issuing orders to the others.

Gradually you hear the noisy men move away from you. You lift your head once more and see the poachers fanning out across the savannah. Their backs are to you but you can see they are all wearing camouflage gear and carry weapons over their shoulders.

Biko gets to one knee and watches the men intently. He says something to Abebi. It sounds like Biko is angry.

"Biko says the men are hunting Rhino. He hates them for harming such wonderful animals. There are so few left."

As the poachers move further away from the track, Biko stands in a crouch and says three words to Abebi.

"Biko says we are to wait here."

Then keeping low, he streaks across the ground towards the truck.

"What is he doing?" you ask Abebi a little concerned.

"I don't know, but I hope he doesn't do anything stupid. He is so hot headed sometimes."

It doesn't take Biko long to reach the truck. He takes his spear and sticks its point into the two tires on the near side and the next moment he is sprinting back to your position. He is almost back to you when you see a puff of dust kicks up at Biko's feet and you hear the sound of a shot.

Biko shouts as he pumps his legs even harder.

"Run," Abebi say as she grabs your hand and pulls you to your feet.

By the time you are both up and moving, Biko has streaked past you. He looks like he is heading towards a dense patch of scrub a hundred or so paces away. He waves his arms for the two of you to hurry. There is no need for him to tell you twice. You run after him as fast as you can.

You can hear angry men yelling behind you, but you don't slow down to take a look. You hear a couple more shots. One shot pings off the ground beside Biko. Biko starts zigzagging from side to side as he runs. You and Abebi do the same.

By the time you reach the patch of scrub, you are panting. Biko slows to a quick walk but keeps leading you further into the bushes. As you walk you reach into your pack and take out your water bottle. You take a deep drink and pass the bottle to Abebi. She has been forced to leave her water container behind in the rush to flee the poachers. She sips and passes the bottle to her brother who shakes his head as he pulls some foliage aside for the two of you to pass deeper into the undergrowth.

The ground is climbing as you work your way through this rough bit of country. Biko motions you both to stay as low as possible as you traverse a patch of open ground toward a pair of large boulders bigger than houses. Biko leads the way as he squeezes into the gap between the two boulders and up a steep dirt slope that comes out on top of the big rocks. He lies down on his belly and creeps forward to peer over the edge towards the men following below. You and Abebi follow suit.

You can see the truck on the savannah. A couple of men stand at the edge of the bush wondering if they should pursue you into it. But then their leader calls them back and you see the men start to take the tires off so they can begin their repairs.

Abebi is talking to her brother. She isn't very happy with the danger he has put you all in.

After a heated discussion Abebi turns to you. "It looks like we have two choices. We can move across country for a little while and then rejoin the road a bit further on. But if the poachers fix their tires they might come back down the road and catch us. Or we can get to Habari Lodge by circling around that range of hills over there. But that means we will need to spend the night somewhere, and won't get to the lodge until tomorrow.

It is time for you to make a decision. Do you:

Try to rejoin the road a bit further on so you get to the lodge today? **P205**

Or

Circle around the hill and get to the lodge tomorrow? **P208**

You have decided to try to rejoin the road a bit further on.

"I really want to try to get back to the lodge today if possible," you tell Abebi. "If the poachers come back, we can just hide in the bushes again."

Abebi has a word with her brother. In the beginning he shakes his head no, but after a little convincing, he shrugs his shoulders and agrees.

"Okay we will try," Abebi says. "But my brother says that we will have to walk without talking so he can listen."

You nod in agreement.

The three of you stand up and start back down the gap between the two boulders. Once you get into the undergrowth, rather than heading back the way you came, Biko turns to the right and works his way along the side of the hill. You notice that Biko makes sure there is a barrier of trees and scrub between you and the road at all times. Once again he speaks to Abebi.

"Biko wants us to walk quietly in single file so we don't disturb too many animals and give away our position," Abebi tells you.

After walking for fifteen minutes or so, Biko turn down the slope and starts making his way back towards the dirt road. When you finally exit the undergrowth and look back towards where the flatbed truck had stopped, you can only see haze and wildebeest. The poachers must be a couple of miles away. Most likely they have resumed their hunt. Why would they bother looking for you when they have rhino to hunt?

You secretly hope the rhinos charge at them and wreck their truck. Or that the rangers catch them and put them in jail.

By the time you've rejoined the road the sun is low in the sky. The horizon has turned red and orange with intense patches of gold and yellow. The trees are now silhouetted against the sky and look like structures you'd see in a science fiction film set on an alien planet.

The sun sets quickly near the equator. As the three of you walk you can see the sky changing, getting darker minute by minute. Biko's pace has increased and you know why. Getting caught out in the open, at night on the savannah, is just asking for trouble.

Just as the sun drops behind the horizon, you see the lodge in the distance. Like the Maasai village the lodge also has a strong fence built around it perimeter to protect the guests from the many predators that hunt at night.

"There it is!" you say breathing a big sigh of relief.

Biko says something to Abebi as he starts walking even faster.

"Hurry," Abebi says. "Biko has seen movement in the grass. He thinks it might be lions. Get ready in case we need to protect ourselves."

You can't believe that you might get eaten within sight of the lodge.

A roar to your left is so loud you nearly poop your pants. Biko breaks into a run for the lodge. You and Abebi do the same.

You hear movement behind you. Expecting to be dragged down by a pair of gigantic claws at any second, you run even harder. Then a man runs out of the gate. He has a rifle in his hands and points it into the air. Bang! Bang! Bang! The noise is deafening.

"Quickly, into the compound!" he yells, waving his arm.

You don't need to be told twice. The three of you run pass the man. He fires two more shots and turns and rushes through the gate after you, slamming it shut behind him.

"You three youngsters were nearly cat meat," the man says. "What are you doing out here at dusk?"

You explain to the man how you came to be in the company of the two Maasai and how they helped you get back to the lodge after being abandoned on the savannah.

"Oh so you're the one who ran off from the tour."

"I didn't run off!" you say. "The stupid driver left me behind!"

"That's not what he says. He says you deliberately snuck off. Your family is very disappointed in you."

You can't believe what you are hearing. "But why would I..."

"Never mind, you're safe now. I'd better get onto the radio and let the searchers know you've been found. Your family will be pleased to see you when they get back."

"Get back? Where have they gone?"

"They're out looking for you of course. They've been out all day. Come. Bring your friends. You three must be hungry after your long walk."

This was the first thing the man had said that made any sense. Why would any sane person get off a tour and walk out onto the savannah alone? Was he crazy?

You are just finishing dessert when your family comes into the dining room and rush over to greet you. After a few hugs, and an explanation of how you came to be left behind, you introduce you family to Abebi and Biko.

Your family thanks the two young Maasai for getting you back safe and promise to organize a ride for them back to their village the next morning.

"Thank you," Abebi says. "I've never had a ride in a Land Rover before."

"Oh and we must take lots and lots of chocolate," you say. "The village children love chocolate."

Congratulations you made it back safely to your family. This is the end of this part of your adventure.

Have you tried all the possible paths this story takes?

You have a decision to make. Would you like to:

Go back to the beginning of the story and take another path? **P163**
Or

Go to the list of choices and start reading from somewhere else in the story? **P320**

You have decided to circle around the hills to get to the lodge.

As the three of you watch from above, some of the poachers start work repairing the truck. A man on the back lifts up a cover to reveal two spare tires and a toolbox. He lifts the tires up and rolls them, one at a time along the deck and over the edge to the ground.

You can see Biko's scowl as he watches the men jack up the truck and undo the nuts that hold the wheels on. He grumbles something to Abebi.

Abebi translates and tells you that if Biko had known the men had more than one spare he would have damaged all of their tires.

You pull your camera out of your daypack and put on the telephoto lens so you can zoom right in on the poachers. Abebi and Biko are keen to move on, but you want to take photos of the poachers. You zoom in on face after face, clicking photo after photo. You also take photos of the men's truck with its distinctive green stripe down the side. Perhaps the photos can help to stop them.

Before long the poachers have replaced the two tires and have driven further onto the savannah. Once again they get off the truck and spread out towards a pair of rhino.

You feel like yelling a warning to the rhino, but you know there would be no chance of them hearing you. And even if they could, the men would hear you as well.

Once you are satisfied with the photos you've taken, you tell Abebi you are ready to go.

Just as the three of you walk back into the bush and turn towards the north, you hear shots in the distance. Each shot makes you wince. You know what the shots mean and it makes you sad that people would kill such magnificent animals just for their horns. You decide some humans are worse than animals. You look towards Abebi. A tear trickles down her face, leaving a line in the fine dust. Biko's jaw is clenched in anger. You grit your teeth. You are glad you took photos so the police have proof of these men's actions. Hopefully they will help bring them to justice.

After walking for another hour, Biko stops next to a large rock. It looks like he has found you a place to stay the night.

Biko and Abebi start collecting firewood. You drop your pack and do the same. Before long you've got a good stack. Biko drags over a couple of bigger logs to throw onto the fire once it is burning well.

Biko builds the fire about three paces out from the face of the rock.

"We will sleep between the fire and the rock," Abebi tells you. "We don't want the fire going out during the night. As long as the fire is burning, the predators will keep away."

You nod and sit on the ground with your back to the rock. The rock face overhangs a little so you don't have to worry about animals sneaking up on you from behind.

The sunsets are brief near the equator. Within half an hour the sky is full of stars. Being so far from the city lights means you can see the stars of the Milky Way much clearer. You try to imagine how many stars there must be out there. There are more than you could possibly count in a thousand years.

Abebi sits down beside you. "We will take turns sleeping and feeding the fire," she says. "Try to sleep now if you can, Biko will wake you when it is time for you to be on lookout."

You scoop out a shallow hole in the ground for your hip and lie on your side with your back to the rock. You can feel the rock's warmth as it sheds the heat it has absorbed from the sun during the day.

The physical exertion of walking and running has tired you out. It is not long before you start dreaming that you are riding amongst the herds of wildebeest on horseback. It reminds you of the cattle-drives there used to be in the Wild West. Then before you know it, Biko is shaking your shoulder.

The night passes without any problem. At dawn, Biko leads you and Abebi across the grassland in a big arc around the hill.

Within an hour you see a track heading northwards.

"Is that the track to the lodge?" you ask.

Abebi has a word to her brother. Biko nods and says a few words.

"Yes, we are about an hour from the lodge."

Soon you will be reunited with your family. You cannot wait to see the look of relief on their faces when you walk into the compound.

The three of you walk into the compound just as the Land Rovers are loading up for the day's search. Your family is talking to the driver who left you behind. When they see you with Abebi and Biko they shout out in surprise and rush over to hug you.

The driver also seems relieved.

When your family finishes hugging you, you walk over to the driver.

"You owe me an apology," you say. "Why don't you count that everyone is on board before you take off?"

The driver kicks the dirt with his foot. "I'm so sorry. I didn't realize you were out of the vehicle. Is there any way I can make it up to you?"

The driver seems genuinely sorry.

"I owe these two something," you say, turning to Abebi and Biko. "Without them I might not have made it back. They put themselves at risk to help me."

"I will make sure they are well rewarded," the driver says.

While you've been talking to the driver, the lodge manager has wandered over. You explain about the poachers and how you've taken photographs of them.

"We're in luck," the manger says. "Normally poachers leave the area before we have a chance to call the authorities, but because of you getting lost, there are police all over the area. I'll radio them now and let them know you've shown up so they can concentrate on catching the poachers."

Abebi looks ecstatic when she hears this. She explains what the manager has said to Biko. His grin is even bigger.

Abebi takes your hand and smiles. "Sometimes good can come from things going wrong. If you hadn't gotten lost today the police might never have had the chance to catch the poachers."

You smile back. "And I wouldn't have made some new friends."

Congratulations, you made it safely back to your family. This part of your adventure is over, but have you found all the possible paths?

It is time to make another decision. Would you like to:

Go back to the beginning of the story and try another path? **P163**

Or

Go to the list of choices and start reading from another place? **P320**

You have decided to go with Dr Nelson to his camp.

Deciding to go with Dr Nelson is the safe option. You could have tried walking to the lodge, but being out on the savannah alone is not a good idea, especially for someone who isn't familiar with all the possible dangers.

After saying a final goodbye to Abebi and her family you climb into Dr Nelson's Land Rover. The back of the vehicle is filled with boxes. Everything is coated in a fine layer of dust. You wipe your finger along the dashboard amazed at how thick it is.

"You wouldn't believe I gave this vehicle a good clean before I left town. The fine dust seeps in, even with the windows closed. These old Land Rovers are reliable, but they certainly aren't dust proof."

You wave to the children as the two of you drive out of the village. A few of the older boys run along after you. It is nearly a mile before the last of the boys give up and return to village.

At a junction about half an hour out of the village, Dr Nelson turns to the west and heads towards a low range of hills in the distance.

"I've been working in the gorge for nearly ten years," Dr Nelson tells you. "We've uncovered some of the oldest remains of early man ever found."

"Really?" you say, turning towards Dr Nelson. "How old are you talking here?"

Dr Nelson raises his bushy eyebrows a couple of times and smiles. "Two million years or so..."

You must admit you weren't expecting it to be quite that old. You try to imagine how far back that is and how many generations of people that would be.

"And you've been digging for ten years?"

"And writing about my findings. It's incredibly exciting to discover a stone tool used by a person who lived long ago. When I see these tools I know they weren't all that different from us."

"But isn't it lonely working so far from civilization?" you ask. "Don't you miss TV?"

"Living here is like watching a reality show. There are always interesting things happening all around you if only you take the time to look. We see so many animals, and have the excitement of our discoveries. Plus I have the research team to keep me company. We have a great time."

You must admit, being here in Tanzania, does make you feel like you are in an episode of Survivor or one of those documentaries on The Discovery Channel.

For a while the two of you are silent, both absorbed in your own thoughts. The track has turned further north and runs along the river. Water levels are low because of the lack of rain, but the river is still deep enough in some spots to make a good bathing place for elephants and hippos. Dr Nelson obligingly slows as you take lots of photographs.

As you near the hills the road starts to climb. When you turn and look back, you get a fantastic view of the savannah below. It is only from this higher altitude that you get an idea of how many animals are on the move. Herds stretch as far as you can see. This has got to be one of the most incredible sights you have ever seen.

"Still think you need TV out here?" Dr Nelson asks.

"I see what you mean. This is amazing." You lift your camera and take a couple more shots. "I'm going to get one of these pictures blown up and put it on my bedroom wall."

After crossing the river you enter a wide valley. With the gain in altitude, the landscape is changing. Towering cliffs, layered with different colored rock, appear in the distance. The lower layers are pale like sand, but then higher up, the rock face turns almost red.

"Looking at the strata in these cliffs is like looking back in time," Dr Nelson tells you. "Each layer spans a time longer than you can imagine. It is the erosion of these layers that has exposed the fossils and artifacts my team and I are looking for."

The further you go, the narrower the valley becomes. Finally you drive around a corner and spot Dr Nelson's camp set on a level piece of ground above a shallow creek bed. There are two tents. A large awning is tied between some trees to provide extra shade.

"Come and meet the others," Dr Nelson says.

You are not sure why, but you expected the other members of Dr Nelson's team to be old like him. These people are not that much older than yourself.

"Meet Jeremy and Alice. They are university students from California here for the season."

Alice smiles at you and holds out her hand. Jeremy doesn't look too well. He is leaning on a makeshift crutch and his foot is wrapped in bandages.

Dr Nelson sees how pale Jeremy is and goes to the back of the Land Rover to get the medicine. Then he gets Jeremy to sit down and starts to unwrap his dressing.

Jeremy's foot is red and oozing pus. You can smell the infection from where you are standing a few steps away.

"Here take these capsules," Dr Nelson says. "I'm going to wash this and put some antiseptic cream on the wound. You'll need to rest up for a few days and let the antibiotics do their job."

Once Dr Nelson finishes dressing Jeremy's wound, he comes over to where you are sitting. "Well I suppose we'd better phone the lodge and let your parents know you are all right."

"That would be great," you say, smiling at the thought of talking to your family.

It takes a few minutes for the doctor to phone town and get the lodge's number, but then he hands you the phone and you hear a familiar voice.

"We've been so worried!"

"Well I'm safe now. Sorry I scared you all."

After a chat with your family, you pass the phone back to the doctor for a minute.

He talks to the lodge manager and then hangs up and looks at you. "They're sending a Land Rover out to pick you up. It will be here in about three hours .In the meantime would you like to have a look around the site?"

"Sure," you say, excited to see with your own eyes what doctor Nelson has been telling you about during the drive. "Can I have a go at digging?"

"If you like," he says. "With Jeremy out of action, we could use some extra muscle."

After sandwiches for lunch, Alice and the doctor lead you along a narrow path to a spot where there are piles of earth and a series of trenches. Wooden frames on short legs with screen mesh bottoms sit on the ground. Alice explains what you are looking at.

"We sift the dirt through these frames to make sure we don't miss anything. Even the smallest piece of bone can be important. We've been finding quite a few tools in this area."

Then the doctor points to a bank of earth and rock.

"Most of the interesting stuff is coming out of that bank there. You still interested in doing some digging?"

"Sure, what should I do?"

Dr Nelson hands you a shovel. "Just fill the wheelbarrow with dirt from that bank and wheel it over to where Alice is sifting."

You nod, put the shovel into the wheelbarrow and grab its handles.

"Slow is good," Dr Nelson tells you. "If you notice any bones, stop digging right away and call one of us. We want to avoid any damage if possible."

It takes you about ten minutes of hard work to fill the wheelbarrow. As you and Alice sift the clumps of dirt through the sieve you spot a teardrop shaped bit of grey rock about five inches long. The rock's edge has small chips on its surface.

"This looks interesting," you say, holding it up for Alice's inspection.

Alice's mouth drops open. "Wow!" she says. "You just found a stone age tool in your very first load. How lucky is that!"

Dr Nelson hears Alice's words and comes over to investigate. He holds the adze in his fist and demonstrates how this rock would have been used for chopping. "See how the edges of the stone have been chipped away to sharpen it? We might have to keep you around as our lucky charm. Alice here didn't find a single thing her first week."

On a trestle-table, set up under a sun shade, all the artifacts and pieces of bone the team has found are laid out in neat rows. Each item has a card tucked beneath it noting when, where and who had found each piece.

Alice takes the tool you found and writes a description of it on an index card with the date and time. She places the adze on the table beside the others and then asks for your details and adds those to the card too before slipping it under your find.

"Well you're part of the team now," she says. "This piece will end up in a museum somewhere and your name will stay with it. How cool is that?"

You find yourself grinning. You have to admit you like the idea of having your name attached to a scientific expedition. It's like being a part of history.

You are keen to get digging again. Time goes by fast when you're hunting for artifacts. Each new shovel full of dirt could contain the next big discovery. After half a dozen more wheelbarrow loads, you all go back to check on Jeremy and have a drink.

This is turning into one of your best holidays ever, despite being left behind by the safari.

When you hear the sound of a vehicle coming up the track, everyone rises to their feet. It's the Land Rover from the lodge.

As soon as the vehicle stops, its doors fly open. Your family rushes over to greet you.

"I didn't realize you were all coming to pick me up!" you say, pleased to see them.

"Of course we all came. We wanted to make sure you weren't left behind again!"

Congratulations, you've made it to the end of this part of the story, but have you followed all the possible paths?

It is time to make another decision. Would you like to:

Go back to the beginning of the story and try a different path? **P163**

Or

Go to the list of choices and start reading from another part of the story? **P320**

You have decided to walk to the lodge in the morning.

After spending the night in the hut with Abebi and her family, you step outside and notice Dr. Nelson getting ready to leave. Abebi has told you there are many tracks in this area and you want to make sure you take the right one. You are hoping that Dr Nelson can draw you a map.

"Are you sure you don't want to come to my camp?" he asks. "It's not safe walking on the savannah alone you know."

"I've made it this far okay," you tell the doctor. "If what you've told me is correct the lodge is only a couple of hours walk from here."

"I'll tell you what," Dr Nelson says. "I'll give you a ride to the next junction. Then at least you'll be on the right track to the lodge."

You accept the doctor's kind offer and after saying goodbye to Abebi and her family, you jump into the passenger seat.

He explains how he'd like to take you all the way, but the supplies he's carrying include antibiotics for one of his crew who has a bad infection. "He might lose his foot if I don't get these antibiotics back to him soon."

You nod and explain to the doctor that you understand and that it's okay. You have your spear for protection. And now that you only have to walk half as far you are sure you will make it without any trouble.

"Lucky for you, most of the big cats are further north following the herds at the moments. Otherwise it would be suicidal to go on foot alone."

After bumping along the narrow track for half an hour or so, you come to a junction.

Dr Nelson points towards two ruts heading towards the northwest. "That's the one you want. When I get to my camp, I'll phone Habari Lodge and tell them you are on your way. They'll probably send out a Land Rover to pick you up if you haven't made it there already." Then he grabs an oily red rag from the back seat. "Here take this. Throw it in the middle of the road if you have to leave it for any reason. Then the Land Rover will know where to start looking."

You tuck the red rag into you back pocket and hop out of the vehicle. 'Thanks for the lift,' you say before slamming the door.

"Good luck!" the paleontologist yells as he drives off.

You watch as the Land Rover disappears behind a row of tree and all you can see is a dusty cloud heading towards a low range of hills.

Apart from some squawking birds in a nearby tree, it is silent. Once again you are alone on the Serengeti.

After adjusting your backpack you rest your spear over one shoulder and start walking. You can see the herds off in the distance. From where you stand they look like a swarm of ants stretching from one end of the grassland to the other.

You slept well and are feeling refreshed. The morning sun is still low in the sky, but you can already feel the temperature rising. Before long it will be scorching. It is time to pick up the pace before it gets too hot.

As you come over a slight rise, you see a wisp of smoke in the distance. Could this be the lodge? You doubt it somehow. There is no way you have come far enough to be at the lodge already.

Still, smoke usually means people. Maybe it is one of the safaris having a coffee break. Then you see the vultures. Twenty, maybe more, are circling above. Others are on the ground feeding.

You duck down and move off the track. As you creep forward you use the long grass and scrubby bushes as camouflage. If this fire is man-made, where is their vehicle? Would the vultures be on the ground if there were people about? You don't think so.

After scanning the surrounding grassland and seeing no people, you slowly stand up for a better look. The camp is deserted. Vehicles and footsteps have flattened the grass in places, but whoever was here has gone.

The carcass of some dead animal lies on the ground twenty or so paces from a smoldering fire pit. As you approach, some of the feeding vultures fly off, only to have their places taken by others. The ugly looking birds stare at you unafraid. Some have pieces of meat hanging from their curved beaks.

You turn your head away. Vultures ripping flesh off the carcass is not a pretty sight.

You are almost back to the road when you hear the sound of flapping wings. The vultures are flying off. They have been frightened by something.

You can see the whole carcass now. It is a rhino, minus its horn. You feel like screaming at this horrible waste of an animal's life. It must be those awful poachers. How can they do this? You shake your head and feel tears forming.

Then you spot what has scared off the vultures. A mother lion and her two cubs have come to investigate.

You move as fast as you can back to the track. Thankfully there is no need for the lioness to chase you when she has an entire rhino to eat. She immediately starts pulling pieces of flesh off the rhino for her young cubs to eat. When you are a safe distance away, you take out your camera and zoom in on the action. After getting a few shots, you move off again. If one lion has been attracted by the vultures, there may be others. You don't see any point in pushing your luck.

Forty five minutes later you are pleased to see the stockade fence of Habari Lodge in the distance. The ground where you stand is slightly higher in elevation than the site where the lodge is. This enables you to see over the barricade into the compound where a number of vehicles are parked up.

This seems a bit odd to you. Why aren't the Land Rovers out looking for you, or at least out on safari? Why are they parked in the compound at this time of day?

Then you hear shots.

You crouch down behind a small shrub and stare down into the compound. What is going on? Why is someone shooting? Something is definitely wrong.

You reach into your bag and pull out your camera. Using its 10x zoom function you study the compound and try to figure out what is happening. Then you see a group of men dressed in a variety of old army clothes and camouflage gear, pushing the lodge guests into a line along the veranda. The men are carrying rifles. They must be the poacher gang.

One of the men is waving his arms and yelling. Another shoots his gun into the air. You see your family lined up with the other guests.

What are you going to do now? These are violent men with guns.

It is time to make a decision. Do you:

Sneak down to the lodge and try to help your family? **P235**

Or

Go back the Maasai village for help? **P241**

You have decided to go flying in the balloon.

You've always been a little afraid of heights, but how often do you get a chance to fly in a hot air balloon? It is an opportunity too good to pass up. Just imagine the photographs you will be able to take.

Koinet puts two fat sausages and a couple of eggs on a plate and passes it in your direction. You are starving after all your walking yesterday and dig right in.

"Juice?" Koinet asks.

The orange juice tastes freshly squeezed. It isn't that cold, but the flavor is wonderful.

You catch the woman's eye and nod over towards the man. "What's he doing?"

"Pierre is setting up the fan to fill the balloon."

"Fan?" you ask.

"Yes we have a small generator that runs an electric fan. We lay the balloon out on the ground and hook up the basket. Then, with the mouth of the balloon held open, the fan blows air into it. Once the balloon has partially inflated, the burner is fired up to heat the air inside so the balloon stands up."

"That makes sense," you say.

"Then the burner is fired in short bursts and more and more hot air rises up into the balloon until there is enough lift for us to take off."

"We tie the basket down until everyone is aboard," Koinet says with a grin. "Then I chase you in the Land Rover."

"How do you steer?" you ask.

The woman laughs. "You don't really. Sometimes the wind blows from a slightly different direction at different heights, but mainly we just wait until the wind is blowing in the right direction and go with it. Today it is coming from the southeast. This means we will fly towards the northwest, which is the same direction the herds are migrating. Today should be perfect for filming."

You hurry to finish breakfast and then ask if you can help.

"Sure," Pierre says. "Help me unpack the balloon and get it laid out on the ground."

The two of you pull the balloon out of its protective bag and drag it out through the short grass. Cords are then attached from the balloon to points along the top rim of the basket.

"See those hooks along the side of the basket? We will attach bags of sand to those so we can drop them quickly if we need to reduce weight and climb quickly."

It does not take long before everything is hooked up, and the fan is blowing air into the gaping mouth of the balloon. Soon, the brightly colored sections of fabric that make up the balloon's panels are billowing in the breeze.

"Hey Marie," Pierre yells to the woman. "Fire up the burner!"

With a roar like a jet engine, a tongue of flame shoots out from the burner and fires hot air into the balloon. Thirty seconds later, another burst rips through the air.

The balloon is rising. After a few more bursts it is standing up and only a rope tied to a stake in the ground is keeping the balloon from taking off.

"Okay you two, get your stuff and climb aboard," Pierre says.

You grab your camera, check that your water bottle is full and walk towards the basket. Marie has a pack of equipment and Pierre is checking that his movie camera is working.

The three of you climb into the basket, which settles back onto the ground with the extra weight. Pierre pulls the lever and shoots another couple of burst of flame into the balloon.

You feel the basket shift, and then lift slightly. Koinet unties the rope from the stake and wraps it around his wrist. His extra weight keeps the balloon down.

"Ready for take-off," Pierre says to Koinet as he fires another long burst.

Koinet releases the rope and up you go. Another short burst and you are above the acacia trees and climbing.

"Wow," you say as you watch the ground fall away. "This is amazing!"

Marie puts her hand on your shoulder. "See how we are drifting towards those wildebeest in the distance? The idea is to film from just above as we glide silently over them. With a little luck, they won't even know we are there."

You rest your arms on the edge of the basket and look out at the savannah below as you drift with the breeze. You look back towards the camp and are surprised how far you have come already. What is most unexpected is the quiet.

Every now and then Pierre breaks the silence by giving the burner a quick blast to maintain your height, but otherwise it is unbelievably peaceful.

Spread out in front of you are a series of ponds reflecting the early morning light. A narrow band of water connects them together so they look like a necklace. A line of acacia trees follow the course of the river.

As you pass over the first pond you see the grey backs of twenty or so hippo swimming and splashing in the water. A baby hippo sticks close to its mother. A bit further along you see why. Crocodiles are sunning themselves on the river bank.

The silver reflection of the water contrasts with the golden grasses of the savannah as it stretches towards the purple hazed hills at the horizon. Dirt tracks crisscross the landscape. They must be animal highways.

A leafless tree by one of the ponds is covered in black and white flowers, but as you get closer to the tree, the flowers suddenly take off and you realize they are not flowers at all but a flock of storks.

Beyond the river a small gang of buffalo trot northwards. You see a parade of elephants too. One of the elephants has a young one trailing behind.

Ten minutes later, you are silently hovering over thousands of wildebeest, zebra and antelope making their way northward. Pierre starts filming and Marie dangles her microphone on a cord down from the balloon so that it hangs not far above the animals.

Marie looks at you and holds her finger to her lips. "Shhhh…"

The sound of so many animals around you is astounding. Soaring just above the herd makes you feel part of one of the most spectacular migrations on earth. You remember reading that more than one million wildebeest, 200,000 zebra and 400,000 gazelle migrate each season. An uncountable number of them stretch out before you.

You are taking shots as fast as you can push the button on your camera. Off near the edge of the herd you see a pride of lions stalking from the long grass. It looks like the lions are waiting for a chance to isolate one of the wildebeest from the herd.

You have glided over the herd for as long as possible without firing the burner so the balloon is getting quite low.

Pierre puts down his camera and reaches for the lever to ignite the burner, but when he pulls the handle nothing happens. "Marie, please release a sandbag, there is something wrong with the burner."

Marie reaches over the edge of the basket and unhooks one of the sandbags. She lets it drop to the ground below, just missing a zebra. You feel the balloon rise a little, but before long as the air in the balloon continues to cool, you start sinking towards the ground one more.

Pierre is frantically making adjustments to the equipment. "Another sandbag," he says, looking in Marie's direction.

You detect a hint of concern in his voice, but Marie calmly follows his instructions and releases another bag of sand.

"This ignition isn't working," Pierre says. "We need to look for a landing spot."

When you look ahead, along the balloon's flight path, all you can see are animals and a number of large acacia trees.

"I see a landing spot past this row of trees," Pierre says. "But we need to lose some more weight if we are going to make it over them."

Marie releases the last two sandbags and you rise once more. The balloon makes it past the first few trees but as the balloon slowly descends again you realize you are not going to get past the last of them.

"Stay down below the rim of the basket," Marie says. "And hold on, we're going to clip the top of that tree."

You can see she is right. The balloon is sinking fast and you are heading right towards the upper branches of the big acacia.

"Hang on ... here we go!" Pierre yells.

The sound of snapping branches you expected. What you didn't expect was for the basket to tip on its side when it hooked up in the tree. You are no longer sitting in the bottom of the basket but kneeling on its inner wall.

A good sized branch is right in front of you. Maybe if you jumped out of the basket onto the branch, the balloon will lighten and have enough lift to clear the tree. You could save the day.

It is time to make a quick decision. Do you:

Jump out of the balloon onto the branch? **P231**

Or

Stay in the basket? **P232**

You have decided to ride in the Land Rover.

"I think I'd rather stay in the Land Rover with Koinet," you tell Marie.

You've decided not to fly in the hot air balloon with a pilot you don't know, despite it sounding like fun. You've never been very good with heights anyway and going up in the balloon sounds scary.

Koinet serves you a breakfast of eggs and sausages. While you eat, Marie drinks her coffee.

"No problem," Marie says. "Koinet will be pleased to have some company for a change."

After eating your breakfast you wander over and help Pierre ready the balloon. He's rigged up a big fan to blow air into the mouth of the balloon. Once it's nearly full Marie fires the burner to heat the air inside.

Slowly the balloon stands up, tethered only by a rope tied to a stake in the ground.

Pierre and Marie load up their gear as you and Koinet hold the balloon steady. When Pierre gives the signal, you both release the balloon and watch it sail up into the sky.

"Quick now," Koinet says. "Into the Land Rover, we don't want them to get away on us."

The next thing you know, you are thundering along a dirt track giving chase.

The balloon looks spectacular. Its multicolored panels really stand out against the powder blue sky.

Koinet drives like a crazy man to keep up. Unlike the balloon that flies in a straight line, he needs to find a way around different obstacles. When the balloon reaches the river, things get really tricky.

While Koinet looks for a shallow place to cross, the balloon flies on. The first possible crossing spot is surrounded by hippos.

"We can't cross here. Too dangerous," Koinet says. "Did you know that hippos kill more people each year than lions?"

"I remember reading that," you say. "Did you know that more people are killed by cows than sharks each year?"

"Really?" Koinet says. "Just goes to show that any animal can be dangerous if you don't watch out."

The next place Koinet finds to cross the river is wide but shallow. A couple of crocodiles lie on the riverbank in the sun but Koinet manages to drive around them and ease the Land Rover into the water. A small wave surges in front of the vehicle as it pushes its way through the murky river.

On the opposite bank, Koinet points to a flock of black and white storks sitting in a tree. Their call sounds like clacking wood. You get a good shot of them just as they fly off.

Once the two of you are across the river, you speed off across the savannah after the balloon again. There are wildebeest, zebra and gazelle everywhere. Never before have you seen so many animals in one place.

Off in the distance the balloon has come down to cruise just over the herd. You see Marie's microphone dangling from the basket of the balloon.

"We'll stay back a little so the vehicle doesn't disturb the animals," Koinet says.

Just as you are about to ask Koinet a question, he stomps on the brakes.

"Look," he says pointing off to the right. "There in the long grass. Do you see them?"

You squint and try to see through the heat haze and dust. It takes a few moments, but you finally see a lion. Koinet creeps forward in the Land Rover. Then you see two more lions just beyond the first. They are eating a gazelle.

Koinet points up at the sky where the vultures are circling. "They always know where the food is."

You take out your camera and zoom in on the lions. Their mouths are red with blood. You take a few shots and then Koinet moves off after the balloon again.

After following the balloon for another hour or so, the radio crackles and Pierre informs Koinet that they are about to land. Koinet speeds up so he is close by to help secure the balloon and so he can chase away any predators that might be in the area.

Koinet turns to you. "When the balloon is down, you can help us roll it up. Then once everything is back at camp I'll drive you to the lodge. How does that sound?"

"Perfect," you say.

Pierre and Marie make a soft landing. With the four of you working to pack up the balloon, rope, burners, and basket it only takes thirty minutes.

After dropping the trailer off at camp, Koinet and you drive off towards the lodge.

You wonder what your family is doing. Are they out somewhere looking for you? Have they got helicopters out scouring the Serengeti?

An hour later you get your answer. As you come out from behind a line of trees you meet your family coming in the opposite direction in the distinctive black and white zebra patterned Land Rovers the lodge uses. Your family are standing up in the back hanging on to the roll bars scanning the savannah for any sign of you.

Koinet stops his Land Rover in the track and you fling the door open.

You can't believe your eyes. Your whole family is there. When they see you they yell for the Land Rover to stop and then rush towards you with outstretched arms calling your name.

Tears of joy are flowing.

"So are we going to do another safari tomorrow?" you ask. "I know a couple of good spots we could check out."

Everyone laughs and gives you a big hug. Then they thank Koinet for driving you back.

Koinet smiles and then reaches into his pocket. He hands you a string of red beads. "Here, for you, a souvenir of your adventure."

"Thanks Koinet," you say, putting the beads around your neck. "I've got Pierre and Marie's address here in Tanzania. I'll send you some photos once I've got them printed. I've got a couple good ones of you."

Koinet smiles, waves one last time and drives off into the Serengeti.

You climb into the back of the black and white Land Rover.

As the Land Rover starts to move off, you yell "STOP!"

The Land Rover skids to a halt.

"What's the matter?" your family asks.

"I just wanted to make sure everyone is here. We wouldn't want to make the same mistake twice now would we?" You do a quick headcount. "Right, all present and accounted for. Let's get back to the lodge. I need a shower and a big bowl of ice cream."

Congratulations, you have completed this part of the journey and made it safely back to your family. But have you followed all the possible paths?

Now it is time to make another decision. Would you like to:

Go back to the beginning of the story and try another route? **P163**

Or

Go to the list of choices and start reading from another part of the story? **P320**

You have decided to jump out of the balloon's basket onto the tree.

You are on your hands and knees on the inside wall of the basket. The tree branch is right there in front of you. The branch is reasonably wide and there is another smaller branch you'll be able to hang on to for stability.

You rise slowly into a crouch and then jump.

"No!" you hear Marie yell from behind you.

But it is too late to heed her warning. You are already out on the limb. You wrap your legs tight around the branch and grip the smaller branch for balance.

With the sudden reduction of weight, the basket shoots up and smacks you in the side.

Before you can regain your balance you are falling. You try to grab hold of another branch as you fall, but miss. Your head smacks into something hard. You head is spinning and your ribs ache.

The ground is coming up fast.

Then everything goes dark.

You have made an unwise decision by climbing out of the balloon without first checking with the balloon's pilot. Remember when he said for you to stay below the rim of the basket? That was for a reason. The cane basket is designed to protect those inside it like a crash helmet protects your head if you fall when you are riding your bike.

Unfortunately this part of your story is over.

It is time to make another decision. Would you like to:

Go back to the beginning of the story and try another path? **P163**

Or

Go back to your previous choice and choose differently? **P232**

You have decided to stay in the basket.

You've made a wise decision by staying in the basket and waiting for instructions from the balloon's pilot. If you had leapt from the basket the sudden reduction in weight would have caused the balloon to shoot upward and would have put everyone at risk.

A gust of wind pulls at the balloon, tipping it further onto its side. Pierre leans out of the basket and kicks at a branch in an attempt to get the balloon clear of the snag.

With a sharp crack the branch gives way. The balloon swings forward, tipping the three of you into a heap in the bottom of the basket.

"We're clear," Pierre says, struggling to regain his feet.

Marie and you untwist yourselves and stand up too. Pierre pulls a cord to release air from one of the side vents in the balloon. The more air he releases the further you drop.

"As soon as we hit the ground I will pull both flaps and release as much air as I can," Pierre says. "We may drag for a while so duck down and make sure you keep your head and arms below the rim. There are handholds inside the basket. Just hold on tight and wait until we stop."

You remember reading once that it isn't flying a balloon that is dangerous. It's the landings that are the tricky part. Now you understand why. But at least here in the Serengeti there aren't any power lines to get tangled in ... just trees and stampeding animals!

Bending your knees slightly, you get ready to duck down and brace yourself. The ground is getting closer.

"Almost there," Pierre says. "On my count, five ... four ... three ... two ... okay down everyone."

A jolt shudders through the basket as it hits the parched savannah. The basket tips on a slight angle and you can hear it scraping as the balloon drags it through the grass. Pierre has pulled both flaps fully open and air is rapidly spilling from the balloon.

After twenty seconds or so, the movement slows and then you finally stop altogether. The basket is resting on its side. When you look out, you see the balloon flapping in the light breeze as it lies on the ground shrinking rapidly as the air continues to escape.

Once enough air has escaped, Pierre tells you it is safe to climb out of the basket. You all run over to the top of the balloon and start rolling it up, forcing the remaining air out the mouth at the bottom.

It is less than a minute before Koinet drives up in the Land Rover. "How did you find your first flight?" he asks you as he joins in the rolling.

"The flight was wonderful," you say. "I'm not so sure about the landing."

Koinet smiles, "I thought I might have to rescue you all for a moment."

"Ignition wouldn't fire for some reason," Pierre says. "We might have to go into town for parts before we launch again."

The four of you set to work packing everything up and loading it into the covered trailer attached to the back of the Land Rover. Once everything has been put away, you jump into the back seat with Marie.

On the drive back you look through the shots you got on your camera.

Marie leans over and has a look too. "Some of those are great," she says. "You could be a wildlife photographer when you get older if you keep taking pictures like these."

You are pleased that a professional thinks your pictures are good. Maybe you will study to be a photographer one day. What a great job that would be, travelling to exotic countries and taking photos of the many beautiful and unusual animals there are in the world.

After getting back to camp, Pierre takes the faulty burner apart and finds the part that needs replacing. It's just a simple valve. He gives the damaged piece to Koinet who will pick up a replacement in town after he drops you back at the lodge.

You are pleased to be heading back to the lodge at last. You miss your family and are sure they will be worrying themselves sick.

Koinet unhooks the trailer and climbs in behind the wheel. You sit with you camera at the ready in the passenger seat. Hopefully there will be some photo opportunities on the way to the lodge.

Two hours and thirty eight photographs later, the Land Rover pulls into the lodge compound. You see your family members talking to a man in uniform. When they see you, they all rush over and surround you. They are asking you so many questions at once you can't hear yourself think.

"Slow down," you say. "I'll answer all your questions in a few minutes. Let's find a computer so I can transfer my photographs. Then I'll give you a slide show and tell you all about my adventure in lion country."

Congratulations, this part of your story has come to an end with you safe return to the lodge despite the many dangers you faced. Have you followed all the possible paths yet?

It is time to make a decision. Would you like to:

Go back to the beginning of the story and try another path? **P163**

Or

Go to the list of books and try another story? **P5**

You have decided to sneak down to the lodge and try to help.

You can't bring yourself to run off and leave your family. There must be something you can do. You zoom in again with your camera to see what is going on and take a few shots for police to use as evidence.

The poacher gang is forcing the lodge guests to turn out their pockets and take off any jewelry they are wearing. You look on as your family and the other guests put their valuables into a bag.

All the gang members have their backs to you, so you sprint down the hill and stop outside the fence just by the gate. There are only narrow spaces between the poles, but they are big enough for you to look through into the compound. You lie on your belly and listen.

The gang leader is yelling at the lodge guests.

"You better give us everything!" he shouts. "If we find out you are lying, we will beat you!"

One of the male guests reaches down into his sock and pulls out a wallet. He tosses it over to the poacher.

"Is there any more?" the poacher asks as he points his gun at each guest in turn.

The guests are shaking their heads. Some are crying.

"We've given you everything," an older woman says. "Please don't hurt us."

What will the poachers do? Will they harm the guests? What can you do to help?

Then you remember that there is a satellite phone in the lodge's office. But how will you get there?

You study the compound from outside the fence. The office is the last room on the right hand side of the main building. The poachers and the guests are on the veranda near the dining room on the left.

Then you have an idea. Staying low, you run through the gate and hide behind the first of the lodge's Land Rovers. You check to see if the poachers still have their backs turned and then sprint over to the poacher's truck. It is higher off the ground than the Land Rovers so you hide behind the truck's tires, otherwise if a poacher turns around, he will be able to see your legs under the vehicle.

Your luck is holding.

You take a peek under the truck. The men are now searching the guests to make sure they haven't kept anything back. You sprint to the next Land Rover.

"What about this?" a poacher screams at a woman. "Why didn't you give us this ring?"

"I can't get it off," the woman cries.

Another poacher comes over to investigate. He grabs the woman's hand and starts to pull.

"Ouch that hurts!" the woman yells.

While the men try to get the woman's ring off her finger, their attention is distracted. You run over and hide behind the last Land Rover in the row.

The office door is just up the steps on your right. Luckily the door is ajar.

As you peek around the back of the vehicle, one of the male guests spots you. He turns his head to disguise the fact that he has seen you, but then turns back and gives you the slightest of nods as if to say he knows what you are trying to do.

You just need the poachers to keep looking the other way long enough for you to cross the last part of the compound, climb the four steps onto the veranda, and duck through the office door.

The male guest sees your problem. The distance you have to cover might be too far to run without the poachers seeing you. Some sort of distraction is required. He winks at you and nods again.

The next thing you know the man is on the ground rolling around in agony clutching his chest. All the poachers stop what they are doing and look at the man. A woman drops to her knees and tries to help.

She looks horrified.

Not wasting any time, you sprint across the compound, run up the steps and rush through the office door. A quick peek out the window and you see the man sitting up on the ground, his wife is mopping his sweaty brow with a tissue.

Now where is that phone?

Then you see it sitting on top of the filing cabinet behind the main counter. Next to the filing cabinet on a cork notice board is a list of emergency numbers. Police is second on the list. You punch in the numbers. Thankfully, the woman who answers speaks a little English. She understands the words emergency, poachers, guns, Habari Lodge, and help.

"Will send police," she says.

You breathe a sigh of relief. Help is on the way. As long as the poachers don't hurt your family before the police arrive, everything should be okay.

But how long will it take for the police to get here? The lodge must be at least an hour from town, if not more. Will the poachers still be here in an hour?

You peek out the window again. It looks like the gang is getting ready to leave. Apart from the bag of goodies they have collected from the various guests, a couple of the gang members have just come out of the kitchen carrying boxes of groceries.

The leader is yelling at them to hurry. While two of the gang guards the guests, the others go back inside the lodge to get more stuff.

You want the poachers to leave, but you also want the police to be able to catch them. What can you do to make that happen? After thinking for a moment, you decide to take a chance.

You check what is happening outside. When all the poachers are looking the other way, you sprint back over to their truck. The truck's fuel tank is on the side facing away from the poachers. You unscrew its cap and grab a couple of handfuls of dirt and pour them into the tank.

Then you screw the cap on again.

Hopefully the poachers will get their truck out of the compound, but the dirt will block their fuel line before they get too far away so the police can find them.

You run back towards the office.

"Stop!" a poacher yells.

You've been seen. You run into the office, slam the door, and push the lock button in the middle of the door knob. You slide your camera along the floor and under the sofa to keep the poachers from stealing it.

The poacher who saw you doesn't even bother to try the door handle. Instead, he kicks the door with such force that it flies back and hits the wall so hard that the window in the door breaks, showering the floor with shards of glass.

You look around, but there is nowhere to hide. "Come here!" the poacher yells as he grabs your arm and drags you out onto the veranda.

There is no point in resisting. If you do, you will only get hurt.

You try to regain your feet as the man pulls you towards the other guests. Then he flings you down on the ground at your family's feet.

"Stay!" the poacher says. "Stay here or I will shoot you!"

You look at your family and shrug. Their eyes are huge. No doubt they are wondering where you came from.

"I'm back," you say. "I was ..."

"Shut up! No talking!" the poacher yells.

You can see the anger on the poacher's face so you do as he says and keep your mouth shut. There is no point in getting shot when you are less than an hour from being rescued by the police. You move over and sit with your back to the wall.

The gang is loading everything they can onto the back of the truck, food, alcohol, TV's, even a table and chairs from the dining room. You can hear the sound of things breaking as the gang ransacks the place.

Once the men have loaded all they can on the truck, the leader yells for his men to climb aboard. Then he turns to the guests. "If you follow, you will die!"

By the crazy look on his face, you don't doubt he is telling the truth. Your body is shaking with fear. All you want is for these horrible men to leave. You look at your feet and keep quiet.

Once all the men are on the truck, you cross your fingers that their truck will start. With all the dirt you put into the fuel tank, you can't imagine them getting very far.

When the truck starts first try, you relax a little. Then with a puff of black smoke and a couple of shots into the air, the poachers drive out of the compound and head off across the savannah.

"Where did you come from?" your family members ask.

You are about to tell them how you came to be in the compound when you hear the poacher's truck splutter and then backfire.

"Oh no ... not yet ... please truck, don't stop now," you say. "This is too close to the lodge. They may come back."

As your family asks you what you mean, you see a couple of the men get down off the back deck and walk around to the front of the truck. They start looking into the engine compartment.

"I put dirt in the truck's fuel tank," you explain.

"Quick, lets close the gate," the lodge manager says. "Unfortunately they've taken all our weapons."

As a couple of the men move across the compound, you hear a steady whump, whump, whumping sound.

"What is that?" a woman guest asks.

The sound is getting closer.

"Sounds like a helicopter," the lodge manager says. He turns and looks at you. "Did you call the police?"

You nod. "I used the phone in the office."

The police helicopter hovers over the compound and then slowly descends into its center. The guests run back onto the veranda as the dust swirls around.

The lodge manager runs over and has a quick word with one of the policemen, then runs back to join the others. The helicopter lifts off again and heads toward the poacher's truck.

"Well those poachers will be out of action for a while thanks to your bravery," the lodge manger says as he rests his hand on your shoulder. "Even those idiots won't be stupid enough to argue with the big machine gun the police have on board that chopper."

Your family gathers around. They all give you a big hug.

"Can I use your computer?" you ask the lodge manager. "I've got some evidence the police can use on my camera."

"Sure," he says.

You run up the steps and into the office. Once you've retrieved your camera from under the couch, you take out the memory card and slot it into the lodge's laptop. You take a copy of the pictures and paste them onto the desktop.

"There you go. Now the police will have all the evidence they need to convict those awful men."

"Well you've certainly done very well for someone lost in lion country," the manager says.

Your family are smiling. They all agree. "We'll have to leave you behind more often!"

Congratulations you have saved the day. You have not only successfully made it back to the lodge and your family, but you've helped capture a nasty gang of poachers. Well done!

This part of your adventure is over. Have you followed all the possible paths yet? Have you travelled with the baboons? Flown in a balloon? Met the film-makers? Seen all the animals?

It is now time to make another decision. Would you like to:

Go back to the beginning of the story and try another path? **P163**

Or

Go and read a different story? **P5**

You have decided to go back to the Maasai village for help.

You are shocked at what is happening in the lodge, but you realize that on your own you are unlikely to be of much help. The poachers are armed with semi-automatic weapons and knives. What is the point of you getting caught? What help would you be then?

You start jogging back the way you came. If you can keep up the pace, you might get back to the village in an hour and a half, assuming you don't run into trouble along the way.

You take a good drink of water and then jog for ten minutes, then you walk until you've cooled down. You drink again and then jog again.

After repeating this jog, walk, drink routine three or four times you stop to rest and look around the savannah for potential danger. The second time you stop for a rest, you see something a little worrying. It is only for a moment, but you are sure you saw a tail swish above the swaying grass a few hundred paces to your right.

Was that a lion's tail you just saw? Is it stalking you?

Where is the nearest tree? You see one you think you can climb fifty paces off the track to your left. Should you run or walk? If you run will a lion sprint out after you? You have no doubt you'd lose if it came to a straight footrace.

You start moving towards the tree at a walk, trying not to show the panic that is thumping in your chest. When you are about half way to the tree, you turn and look back. There is no sign of a tail, but the long grass just over a hundred paces away is moving.

You want to run but your knees feel weak. You look at the tree and plan exactly where you are going to place your hands and feet when you make your break. You carefully loop the strap of your spear over your shoulder to free up your hands for climbing.

When you are twenty paces from the tree you take off, pumping your legs and arms for all they are worth. You don't look back. That would only slow you down.

You hit the tree trunk with your right foot and use it to spring up and grab a lower limb. With the upward momentum of your leap, you pull with your arms and hook your knee over the limb and swing up so you are sitting. Grabbing onto the main trunk you pull yourself up into a standing position and reach for the next branch.

You hear something running thought the dry grass. It is getting nearer.

You don't look anywhere but up to the next branch, up to your next step. Your grip slips and a big splinter jabs into your palm. Blood trickles down your arm, but you don't have time to worry about that now. You scramble higher and higher into the tree.

Now it's time to fight for your life. You turn and wedge yourself in the crook of two branches and pull the spear off your shoulder. You spin the point downward as the lion starts up the trunk. It is a large male with a magnificent mane of golden hair. Around its mouth and chin the hairs are almost white. The lion digs his claws into the trunk. Powerful muscles in the cat's front legs pull the body up past the first branch. The cat's eyes are yellow with narrow black pupils.

It stares at you and snarls. You can smell the cat's bad breath and see its huge front teeth.

"No!" you yell at the top of your voice. "Go away!"

The only thing stopping the lion from lunging at you are a couple of stout branches blocking the way. You yell again and jab your spear downwards.

Then you hear gunshots. The cat hears them too. Both of you look for the source of the noise. Another shot pings off the ground near the base of the tree. A dark green Land Rover is tooting it horn as it nears.

The cat looks up at you, roars one last time, and then slides back down the tree and sprints off into the long grass.

Your hands shake. Sweat drips off your forehead. You sit between two branches for a moment, afraid that if you don't you might fall.

"You okay up there?" a deep male voice yells.

A man dressed in uniform is at the base of the tree looking up at you. He wears a green cap with a yellow badge sewn onto its front. Over his shoulder is a rifle. His dark skin shines like ebony and his smile is the brightest and friendliest you've ever seen.

You smile back at him. "I am now that you are here!" You loop your spear's strap over your shoulder and start down. When you reach the ground your knees nearly buckle.

"Here let me help you," the man says taking hold of your elbow. "Come and sit, you're probably in shock."

You allow the man to lead you over to his vehicle. When he sees the blood on your hand he pulls out a first aid kit, removes the splinter and patches you up.

Four other men are standing around the Land Rover. All are dressed in the same uniform and carrying automatic weapons. On the side of the Land Rover is the same yellow and green logo as on the man's cap.

"Are you wildlife rangers?" you ask.

"Yes," the man replies. "We are looking for poachers. What are you doing out here alone?"

Then you remember your family. You'd been so busy trying to stay alive that for a moment there you'd forgotten all about them.

"The poachers are at Habari Lodge robbing the guests," you say.

"Habari Lodge?"

You explain what you saw and how you were on your way to the Maasai village for help when you saw the lion and made a dash for the tree.

After listening to your story, the ranger has a word to his men and they all pile into the Land Rover. You are directed to sit in the back seat between two men. The last man jumps onto the back where a machine gun is mounted on a tripod. Its barrel points over the roof.

"You've got a lot of fire power here," you say to one of the rangers.

"Believe me, when it comes to dealing with these heavily armed criminals we need it."

The driver turns the Land Rover around and starts down the track towards Habari Lodge. On the drive you fill the head ranger in on everything you saw, the number of guests and staff at the lodge, and everything else you can remember about the poachers and the lodge's layout.

The ranger's Land Rover stops behind a row of bushes on a rise overlooking the lodge. It is close to the spot where you first noticed the poachers. Their flatbed truck is still in the compound.

The head ranger studies the situation with his binoculars. The poachers have tied up the guests on the veranda and are loading stuff onto their truck.

"I think they are getting ready to leave," he tells you.

The chief ranger wanders over to chat with his men. Then he comes back to you. "We are going to wait until they come out of the compound before we strike. This should reduce the chance of injury to the guests and staff."

You nod. It sounds like the right thing to do. The last thing you want is for your family to get hurt.

"We will leave you up here during the attack. After it is safe we will come back and pick you up."

One of the men rushes over to the head ranger and has a few words.

"It is time," the head ranger tells you. "Stay here. Hopefully we won't be long."

You are about to be left in the Serengeti once again. Only this time you will have a ring side seat to something few people will see on holiday, a poacher group being brought to justice.

The faint sound of a motor starting brings all the rangers to the alert. All but two of the rangers jump into the vehicle. The other two get on the back deck to operate the big machine gun.

Inside the vehicle, the men roll down their window and point their guns outside ready for action.

"Let's go!" one of the men on top of the ranger's Land Rover yells.

The ranger's vehicle revs up and races down the hill. You pull your camera out of you bag and move to a spot where you can watch the action below.

The poachers have come out of the lodge and have turned onto a track that heads west towards the hills. The rangers are gaining on them. You snap pictures of the action.

When the ranger's big gun opens up, the ground around the flatbed truck erupts with puffs of dirt. Some of the bullets hit their front tires. Their truck swerves sharply, and then starts to roll. The men on the back leap for their lives just as the truck lands on its side and slides through the dirt.

Rangers pile out of their Land Rover and surround the poachers. Two are pulled from the wrecked cab. With a machine gun pointing at them, the poachers see sense and give up. They raise their hands above their heads and sink to their knees.

It is not long before the rangers have the poachers in handcuffs.

You figure it is safe to go down to the lodge, so you put your camera into your daypack and pick up your spear. You can't wait to see your family.

When you enter the compound all the guests and staff are lined up along the veranda, their hands tied in front of them. Your family are shocked to see you. They have heard all the shooting but don't know what is going on.

You start untying people. As people are freed, they help others. Your family gives you big hugs as you release them, and ask how it is that you are here.

"I'll explain later," you say. "Once I've loaded my pictures onto my laptop, I'll give you a slide show and tell you the whole story."

You wave your family towards the dining room. "Let's all go and have something nice and cold to drink. It sounds like everyone's got a tale to tell. This has turned out to be quite some holiday!"

Congratulations, you have made it safely back to your family. This part of your story is over, but have you followed all the possible paths and had all the possible adventures?

It is time to make another decision. Would you like to:

Go back to the beginning of the story and try another path? **P163**

Or

Go to the list of books and pick another story to read? **P5**

Once Upon An Island

A little into the future.

The arms of the giant squid slither and tighten around you. You struggle to pull yourself free, but the giant sea creature is strong. You gasp for air before it tugs you down into the depths of the sea. You hold your breath, but how long will you last?

How did you end up like this? If only you'd made different choices. If only you could start again.

Wait a minute – you can!

You are about to enter a story that depends on YOU. You say which way.

Here is how it starts, but you will decide how it's going to finish:

You have been invited to New Zealand to spend the school holidays with your cousins, Stella and Max. They are going to stay on an island called Arapawa. If you don't want to go, you can stay with your mother's friend.

It is time to make your first decision. Do you:

Go to Arapawa Island? **P249**

Or

Stay with you mother's friend? **P248**

You have decided to stay with your mother's friend.

Your mother's friend teaches mathematics. As soon as you arrive at her house she gives you a long test.

Then she organizes a three week course in algebra, trigonometry, and calculus. She says you will have a great time, but you wonder if things might have been a little bit more fun if you had chosen to go to Arapawa Island in New Zealand.

It is time to make another decision. Do you:

Change your mind and go to Arapawa Island? **P249**

Or

Stay and do math problems? **P301**

You have decided to go to Arapawa Island.

Out of the airplane window the sun is rising over a large green land surrounded by an aquamarine ocean. There are rolling hills, forests, and lakes. The plane touches down and in no time you are meeting your cousins, Max and Stella.

Dressed in t-shirts and shorts they definitely look like brother and sister.

Together you head to a ferry to sail to the top of the South Island. From there you will take a smaller boat to Arapawa Island.

The ferry is huge with cars on the bottom level, a playground and shops in the middle, and a movie theatre and restaurants on the top. There is a shudder as the ferry leaves the dock and glides into the harbor. The harbor is large and dotted with other boats ranging from massive container ships to small sail boats. Tall city buildings cluster on the flat ground between sea and green hills beyond them colorful houses are stacked along steep, curving streets.

When the ferry leaves the shelter of the harbor and enters Cook Strait, the strong engines beneath your feet crank up the pace and the vessel starts to move up and down in the ocean waves.

You and your cousins get lockers for your luggage and then take a stroll around the boat, getting to know each other again – it has been a while since you were together.

Max and Stella are twins about the same age as you. They ask you questions about your home and school and family.

Then it's your turn. "What are you guys into?" you ask.

The two of them look at each other wondering what to say.

Stella begins. "I've been working after school at a bird sanctuary for two years. I show people around and take care of some of the animals and birds. I'll be keen to see what's roosting on Arapawa."

"And you think you might do some diving too," cuts in Max. "She's a fantastic swimmer and won the regionals this year. We think there might be places around the island to do some snorkeling and maybe free dive to find shipwrecks."

Max explains that he likes drawing and riding his dirt bike, and he plays guitar and trumpet. He wishes he could have brought the bike to the island.

They tell you what they know about the island you are travelling to. The water is very deep on one side of Arapawa Island – great for fishing off the rocks, but probably quite dangerous for swimming.

"I'm not afraid of deep water!" you say.

"It's not so much the deep," Stella says ominously. "It's what is *in* the deep."

The ferry is well out to sea now and the rise and fall from the waves makes walking around strange. Sometimes the floor meets your feet too soon and sometimes it falls further than you expected. The cafeteria is full of people doing the same unbalanced walk as you. You slide trays along a bench, picking your food from cabinets above. There are sandwiches, hot savory pies, sausage rolls, and fries. Stella has the money for food and she chats with the man who serves you as she pays.

"Is it going to be a rough crossing?" she asks.

"No, love, I think it's only about a three foot swell. It's just rough going out the heads."

As the crewman says this, you envy the easy way he holds himself as the ship moves.

You lurch between tables, looking for somewhere to sit. It's hard to balance a tray of food on a boat and you all stagger about trying not to spill your lunches.

At the back is a big table with just one person sitting at it. He is reading a newspaper. Max asks the man if it would be okay to share the table. He grunts and shuffles his chair across to make room. He lifts up the paper and hides behind it. The headline reads *Tuatara Missing from Sanctuary*. What, you wonder, is a tuatara?

Then you remember something else you were wondering about.

"Who is the woman we are staying with, Max?" Things have happened so fast that you haven't had a chance to find out much about your host.

"Madeline. But we call her Aunt Maddy," Max says. "She's an old friend of our parents, not really our aunt. She lives on the island when she isn't teaching science at a university. We went to the island with our parents when we were young. I don't remember too much, though. Aunt Maddy is very nice but a bit eccentric. I think she'll be happy to let us do our own thing."

You are about to ask about the missing tuatara, but then you see that a woman at the next table is sneaking food into a large handbag on the chair beside her. A snout and a pink tongue emerge to take the food. The woman tries to close her bag but she is too late. The head of a fox terrier pops up to inspect the table. It wears a red leather collar with an odd pendant dangling from it.

You aren't the only person who noticed the dog. A steward quickly comes over and glares at the woman.

"You can't have a dog loose on board," he says. "It will have to be caged or stowed in a car below deck."

The little dog yaps at the steward.

"Shhh, Trixie!" her owner says. "I'm sorry. I'll go and put her in my car right away."

Later, up on the deck, the boat slows as it enters a wide channel with land on both sides. The water here is much calmer.

"That's Arapawa Island," Max says.

The three of you hang over the rail to look at the place you'll be going. You pass some little harbors and inlets with boats in the water. There are a few houses near the coastline. The hills are mostly pasture near the sea, but further up there are places covered in trees.

"Some people farm there," says a nearby passenger to his friend. "Others have weekend houses they get to by boat."

"The fishing must be out of this world," his friend says, admiring the clear water.

You don't see any roads on the island, just a few tracks.

"Looks like a fun place to explore on a dirt bike," Max says wistfully.

"It's a pity you don't have your bike then," Stella says. "I guess your legs might be an alternative way to do it."

The two of them start arguing good-naturedly. Then Stella gives a shout and points out a small harbor.

"Look! That's Maddy's house just there," she says.

"Do you remember it from when you were young?" you ask.

She laughs. "No. I looked it up on Google Earth."

The old fashioned yellow house is a short way up the hill. Some farm buildings are above that. There is a sailboat tied up to the jetty.

"Looks like Maddy hasn't set off to meet us yet," says Max.

You hear barking and shouting.. The little dog Trixie is springing along the deck with both a steward and her owner trying to catch her. The steward corners the dog as she reaches the end of the walkway, but with a leap Trixie jumps onto the hand rail and runs along it. The steward makes another grab, and the dog loses its footing and tumbles over the side.

Her owner shrieks. You and everyone else rush to see if they can see the dog in the water. You look over the rail but can't see the dog anywhere.

A short yap draws your attention to a thick rope hanging from the rail. Trixie is balanced precariously on the rope! You might just reach her in time if you lean over and hook your leg around the rail.

It is time to make a decision. Do you:

Try to rescue the dog? **P304**

Or

Let the crew deal with the dog? **P253**

You have decided to let the crew deal with the dog.

The steward hooks his leg over the rail and leans over. He scoops up the dog – which is now very willing to be in his grasp. People cheer and the steward bows then heads toward the cargo area with Trixie under his arm, and her owner following hurriedly behind.

The ferry finally docks. Huge ropes are used to secure the vessel to the wharf. Tourists and other passengers get ready to go ashore. Most people go down below to their cars. You, Max, and Stella are part of a small crowd to walk off the ship through a gangway that connects with the ferry terminal and land.

A man and a woman have a sign that says 'MAX AND STELLA'.

"Is this Maddy?" you ask Max.

"No," he says, shaking his head. "I don't know who they are."

"Hello!" the man says as the three of you approach. "I'm sorry your aunt Maddy couldn't be here, but we'll look after you. We Islanders take turns getting supplies from the mainland, so we'll take you to the island. Here's a note from your aunt to say it's okay to come with us."

Stella studies the note.

"I'm Damon and this is Sandy," the man says.

You all introduce yourselves and then walk to their sailboat where you help them finish loading cargo – boxes of food, bags of mail, and big red cans of petrol.

Soon, you are all on board and Damon steers the boat out into open waters. The waves seem a lot bigger on a smaller vessel. The warm wind smells of the sea. When you are clear of the other boats Damon puts the sails up and cuts the engine. Under sail, the boat cuts smoothly through the water. Without the engine noise you hear the water, gulls, and each other much better.

Dolphins swim ahead of the boat. You grab your camera from your backpack and take some pictures of them leaping out of the water. Damon offers to take a photo of all three of you in the prow of the boat. The beautiful creatures have fun for a while surfing on the boat's bow wave, but then disappear to chase a school of fish.

"It's not unusual for dolphins to come up to swimmers and play with them," Sandy says. "You might get a chance to swim with some while you're staying on the island."

There are not too many large boats on this side of the Strait but you see a number of sailboats and fishing boats in the distance. The ferry you travelled on is beginning its home journey. As it passes it sends a huge wake towards your boat. Luckily, Damon is an experienced seaman and handles the wave by turning the boat into it.

"Look there's Arapawa," Max says, pointing ahead.

In front of Arapawa are some smaller islands – they are like a pod of dolphins swimming in a group while Arapawa looks like a great whale.

To your surprise the boat begins to turn away from Arapawa and toward one of the smaller islands. "Where are we going?" you ask as the boat slips between two rocky outcrops, and Damon heaves the anchor over the side.

"We're dropping off some supplies at the weather station," explains Damon. "Tell you what, you kids can go up to the station and tell them the supplies are here. Don't take cell phones up there though – the radar will scramble all your data."

After putting your cellphones safely away, they lower a row boat filled with supplies and help you climb in. Damon climbs down last and rows you all over with a few strong pulls on the oars.

"Just walk straight up the track," he says, pointing up the hill. "I'll unload this gear."

The narrow path slopes upward and changes from sand to rock, and then dirt and a tangle of tree roots. Just as you are picking your way between the first trees Max turns around and cries out.

You spin around and see that the sail boat is leaving the little inlet. You all race back down the hill, but by the time you reach the shore, the boat is well out to sea. You yell and throw stones but soon it's clear that they are not coming back.

You make your way to the pile of things they have left behind. There are a couple of crates of food and other supplies.

"Is this for us?" Stella says.

Max shrugs.

"But why have they left us here?" you ask.

Max crouches to look at the boxes of supplies and finds a note addressed to himself and Stella:

"Don't worry," Max reads from the note.. "You will only be here a few days. Take the food up to the hut and stay there."

"It's a kidnapping," says Stella.

"But Mum and Dad aren't rich," Max says. "Why would anyone want to kidnap us?" He turns to you. "And I doubt they were kidnapping you – they didn't have your name on their sign. I don't think they even knew you were coming!"

You are confused too, but try to keep calm and think. "The note says to go up to the hut, let's do that. Maybe there is someone there who can help."

The three of you pick up the supplies and head up the path.

Now that you've made a decision to take some action, you feel better. It is a beautiful place. Birds soar overhead, while others flit about in the trees. The sea is blue and the sun feels warm on your face. The path leads you away from the coast, up the hill and into a forest of green trees. It then opens out to a pretty clearing with a cabin in the middle.

The cabin has wooden walls and a metal roof. There is a small porch with one wide step leading up to it from the grass. You put down the supplies on the porch and see that there is the clasp holding the door shut, but it isn't locked. You push the door open.

Inside there is one large room with four bunks built against a wall. On the other side are a sink, bench, a stove, and cupboards. In the center of the room is a wooden table.

There is no sign of anyone.

You go back outside and walk around the hut. A large plastic tank with a pipe running to it from the roof catches rainwater.

There is a small shed a short distance away, in amongst the trees, which Max investigates. "Poo!," he announces. "I've found the outhouse!" Then he grins. "We could burn the hut and draw people's attention to rescue us."

"Maybe we should burn the woodpile instead?" you say.

"Maybe we should spend the night here and see if they come and get us in the morning?" says Stella.

It is time to make a decision. Do you:

Burn the woodpile? **P257**

Or

Don't burn the woodpile, get ready to stay the night instead? **P266**

You have decided to burn the wood pile.

Burning the wood pile might make smoke that will attract people's attention and get you rescued, so you pile some wood in the clearing well away from the hut, and set it alight with paper and twigs.

At first there isn't much smoke, so you try adding some green branches to the top. But even that doesn't work that well. Then you see a bicycle inner tube on the porch. You grab it and drop it on the fire. Thick, smelly smoke billows upwards, and there is a terrible smell of burning rubber.

"I'm going down to the sea again to signal to any boats that come by," you say.

Max and Stella stay behind to mind the fire as you hurry back down the path. Once on the beach, you see that the fire isn't very noticeable. There are no boats in sight.

The plan isn't working, so you head back to the clearing.

Max and Stella are still tending the blaze, but they have done too good a job. Your fire lights the dry grass and spreads quickly to a pile of sticks right beside the water tank. The plastic tank starts to buckle and melt in the heat, and as you watch, water seeps out of a hole in the tank. Then, with a rush, water pours out over the ground and extinguishes the fire with a hiss.

Your nose and lungs are filled with the sharp stink of melted plastic. Within a couple of minutes the tank has almost run dry, leaving a pile of wet firewood and a partly melted container.

You feel terrible about destroying the tank. You also realize that there may not be another source of water on the island.

There are only a few more hours of daylight.

It is time to make another decision. Do you:

Explore the island? **P258**

Or

Get ready to stay the night? **P266**

You have decided to explore the island.

There is another track heading out of the clearing. The three of you leave your gear at the hut and follow this path. Before long the path becomes very overgrown. Nobody has been along here in a long time but you can still make out where it leads. You crash through weeds — another hundred yards around the hill, you start to hear bees buzzing, and when you round a corner you find an orchard of gnarled old fruit trees sitting in a field of grass. Soon you are all munching on juicy apples.

One tree is much taller than the rest and stands on its own. It's a walnut tree. You climb up into the wide branches hoping to get a better view of the island. Max climbs up behind you. You can see Arapawa. It's infuriatingly close but the rocks, heavy sea, and deep water means there is no way any of you could swim there.

You feel something smooth in the fork of the branch you are holding and pick it up. It looks like it's made out of stone. It's almost white and very smooth. It's a small carving in the shape of a whale. At closer inspection you realize it's made of bone. A wave passes over you and for a moment you feel like you are losing your balance, but then everything seems fine again.

You are just about to share your find with the others when a boy comes into the little orchard. He is carrying a cloth sack and begins to pick. He doesn't see any of you. As you watch him, you put the carving in your pocket.

You are about to call out to him when he sees Stella. Then he looks up and sees you and Max.

"Hi!" says Max. "Did you see our smoke signals?" Your cousin quickly explains that you have been left here and you are trying to get to Arapawa.

"My name's Jack," the boy says. "Sorry, I didn't see the smoke signal at all. I just sailed over from Arapawa Island to get some apples.

Do you want me to take you there?"

"That would be great," Stella says. "Can you take us to our aunt Maddy's house?"

"That's odd, I don't know her, but I suppose there are a few people on the island I don't know. If she's there I'm sure we can find her."

You are all excited to be rescued and you help him put apples into his sack. You make picking the apples into a bit of a game. One person picks an apple and calls out "Hey!" Then they throw the apple to one of the others. You try to trick each other by looking at one person and throwing to another. Jack is great at it and soon you are all laughing like old friends.

"Come on," Jack says when his sack is full. "We'd better get going. It's so good you'll be staying on the island. We can come back one day and I can show you the tunnels I found."

You follow him down a path leading to a small cove. Jack's sail boat is very old fashioned and small. There are no life jackets.

He tells you all where he wants you to sit to balance your weight in the water, and then has you help to push the boat out into the water. Jack barks out instructions and expertly maneuvers the boat past rocks – a bigger boat would not have made it into the small harbor.

"I can only go in and out at high tide," Jack says. "There's a cave to explore in the cove as well. That's how I found the tunnels."

When you are between the two islands the wind picks up and some of the waves are as tall as the boat. You have to yell to be heard over the wind and the splash of the waves, and Jack is too busy to talk much.

Sitting in the boat you look at him closely for the first time. He is dressed strangely, in trousers made of a rough grey material and a cotton shirt with wooden buttons that look handmade. Maybe he is from some alternative, back-to-nature community? You notice he is wearing a carved necklace exactly the same as the one you found at the orchard.

You are about to show him your carving when Jack swings the sail about and you begin to go away from Arapawa Island – and looking toward the island you can see why. Larger boats are busy in the water ahead and it would have been dangerous to sail among them.

A huge, dark shape suddenly bursts out of the sea between your boat and the big boats. The men in their boats leap into action, running around on deck, frantic with their ropes. A harpoon is launched from the prow of one boat. It arcs up in the air and falls short of the target.

"It's a whale hunt!" Max says.

"We have to do something!" screams Stella. "Those men are hurting the whale – they might kill it!"

Jack looks at her as if she is crazy. "We can't stop them," he says.

"Yes we can!" yells Max. "Put your boat between the whale and the men – they won't shoot us!"

"That's my father's men. If I did that, he'd skin me alive."

Jack shakes his head and looks to you for support.

Something about this isn't right. Surely whaling stopped in these waters years and years ago? Fortunately, the whale has avoided the hunters. It leaps high into the air and then dives. You hope it's heading far away.

You are closer to the shore now. On the beach there are other boats and beyond them, some big sheds. Jack is making ready to land, pointing the boat towards the beach as he lowers the sail and ties off ropes. You see his whale carving again and remember the one you found.

You take it from your pocket and show it silently to Jack. When he sees the whale carving he looks confused and reaches for his own at his throat.

"But that's just like the one I carved," he says.

As he touches his carving, you get the same dizzy feeling you felt in the tree earlier. The boat and Jack begin to fade. A moment later you, Max and Stella are all in the waist-deep water, catching hold of each other and struggling to stand against the waves. The three of you pull yourselves onto the beach. When you look back, there is no sign of Jack or his boat.

Standing dripping on the beach, you see that it is now bare of boats and buildings. The sheds you saw earlier are gone.

"I think he was a ghost," says Max.

"Then what about the whalers?" Stella asks. "Do you think they were ghosts too? I think we went back in time!"

That makes sense – or at least, as much as any of this makes sense. You look around to try and figure out where you are and how far Maddy's little harbor might be.

A little way up the beach you see the ruins of a small building. They were regular buildings from the boat with Jack.

After a bit of discussion about what to do next you all set off down the beach together, with the warm afternoon sun drying your clothes. After ten minutes you can see an old house a short way up the hill. There is smoke coming out the chimney.

You follow a path through the trees towards it. As you near the house a large dog rises from the porch and begins to bay. A man comes out of the door, but your excitement at being able to tell someone about your bizarre day turns to terror as you realize he is holding a shotgun!

"This is private property – keep moving!" he yells.

"We need to call the police! We need to use your telephone!" Stella shouts back. The dog leaves the porch and starts to head towards you. A low growl comes from its throat. None of you are keen to go closer.

"I don't have a phone – keep moving! Don't let me catch you on my land again!"

You don't need to be told again and decide to keep walking in the direction Stella thinks Aunt Maddy lives.

The path that you followed to the house continues on up the hill, so you keep walking up it. Before long it brings you to the top of the low hill and you walk along, keeping to the top of the hills so you can look down each valley. It's starting to get late in the day and you're feeling tired, but as the sun starts to set you can see her yellow house in the last of the daylight.

You head down, following a rough sheep or goat track and trying not to trip up in the dark. Lights come on in the house as it gradually gets darker. The path ends behind an old shed beside Aunt Maddy's house, and you are about to follow Max and Stella around the corner when they stop in their tracks.

You peer around the side of the shed and see two figures on the porch. It's your kidnappers! You, Stella, and Max duck back behind the shed and listen.

"Did you hear something?" says a woman.

"That sounds like Sandy," you whisper to Max and Stella.

"Sheep, she has them running loose all over the place," says Damon.

There is a slurping sound as one of them sips from a cup, and then Damon speaks again. "Do you think she'll crack?"

"Yeah, she's very close to giving up. Now it's dark she'll be really worried about those kids."

"Let's hope so."

So your kidnapping has something to do with Maddy. But what? You have to get word to her that the three of you are okay so she won't do whatever it is they want her to do.

Signaling for Stella and Max to stay where they are, you creep around the back of the house. The back door is unlocked, so you slip inside and stealthily tread down the corridor.

The tiniest sound seems so loud. You can hear your own heart beating like a drum. In the lounge you find a woman tied to a chair. She is not looking your way so you tap lightly on the door frame. You put a finger to your lips as she looks towards you.

"We are free," you whisper. Then you shrink back into the shadows as Sandy comes into the room.

"Maddy," Sandy says, "the kids will be safe tonight, but by tomorrow they are going to get hungry and scared. We have all the time in the world – but they don't. We just want you to sign a paper – it's as simple as that."

"I've told you, Sandy, this process needs to stay with the university. We can't tie it up with one company."

"We are your research partners. This device is as much a part of our work as yours! Why don't you trust us?"

"Trust you?" said Maddy. "You are kidnappers!"

What can you do? In your pockets there is nothing except the bone carving. You rub its smooth surface as you think. Then there comes a loud crash from the porch, and growling and barking. Sandy rushes to the door and you leap forward to untie Maddy.

"Hands up where I can see them!" instructs a man's voice.

Through the open door you can see Sandy comply.

"Maddy, are you in there?" the man shouts.

"Yes! I'm just being untied," she yells back. "Those people are kidnappers and thieves."

In a few moments, Maddy joins the angry old man you met earlier and together they use the ropes to tie Damon and Sandy back-to-back. Before you know it, the three of you kids are munching thick slabs of melted cheese on toast. You were famished! The police have been called and say they will be over in the morning.

As you sip a hot chocolate, Maddy introduces you to her gruff neighbor, Jack. Jack was born on the island. His father and grandfather grew up here too. His family was one of the last to hunt whales in New Zealand.

"I'm glad to say that whaling died with my father," he says. "I'm sorry I was so rude earlier today, kids. I didn't recognize you. But after you left, I realized I had met you before."

"No, Jack, I don't think you could have met them before," says

Maddy.

"Oh, we didn't meet on this island," you say. "We met on the island we were marooned on. But ... it's complicated."

"Now Maddy," says Jack, "tell me why these people wanted to tie you up?"

Maddy sighs. "For years I've been researching ways to generate power from the tide. It's a natural source of energy with almost no environmental problems. Finally I have some very promising results. My colleagues have been talking to some private companies and they have been offered a lot of money to sell our technology. That's not what I intended. I want this technology to be used by everyone – not patented by a few companies who just want to make lots of money from it instead of giving people cheap electricity."

You and Jack look at each other and smile.. Silently, you hand him his carved whale.

"I made this when I was 11 years old," he says.

"The day I took you across in my boat I was so excited I was going to have friends my own age on my island. You showed me your carving just as we were about to land. As I looked at it, you all faded away. I could sort of see you in the water, but when my boat landed, all I had was a sack of apples.

"I put the carving in the walnut tree that same summer. I went back often to see if you had reappeared, and when I got older I built the hut there in case you or some other group were marooned there and I wasn't around."

He laughed to himself. "Well guys, welcome to Arapawa. And now we've had the welcome party, what do you want to do with yourselves?"

"I'm thinking of serious sleeping and eating," says Max.

Everyone laughs.

"Sounds good to me," says Maddy.

"When you've done with that you'd be welcome to come over to my cove and try some surf casting," says old Jack. "I would take you back to the little island, but I've leased it to a film crew who are doing a project in the caves. They, and one other tenant over there, like their privacy. It's odd you didn't meet them though."

The rest of your time on the island is a blur of land and sea adventures. You are almost eaten by a giant squid, you rescue a sailor, and you explore abandoned homesteads and find a ship wreck. You catch your own fish and, finally, swim with the dolphins!

The End (sort of!)

It is time for another decision. Do you:

Go back to the beginning and try another path? **P247**

Or

Go to the list of choices and start reading from another place in this story? **P320**

Or

Try another story? **P5**

You have decided to get ready to stay the night.

You rummage through the things you have been left. There are only two sleeping bags, but there are some extra blankets. You give the sleeping bags to Max and Stella and offer to use the blankets, as long as you get a top bunk.

Now – food.

There is a little gas stove in the kitchen area and it has a tank of gas, so you unload the supplies and look through everything, trying to decide what you can make for dinner. You combine three ready-made camping meals to make one big pot of macaroni cheese. Luckily there is bottled water with the supplies, or you would be in trouble.

After eating dinner the three of you sit out on the porch as the rest of the day slips away and the sun sets. Around you, birds are settling noisily in the trees, but as it gets dark it becomes quieter again. You can hear the sea lapping against the beach down below.

Max heats up some water to make hot chocolate, and Stella sets up a battery lantern on the table. She hunts around in the supplies and brings out two packets of biscuits.

"Well, we aren't going to starve here," says Max.

"As long as you aren't in charge of the food, that is!" laughs Stella.

You all nibble biscuits and drink your hot chocolate in silence. Max and Stella both yawn and you realize how tired you are. Soon everyone is wrapped up ready to sleep.

"Should we tell some stories?" Stella asks.

"No offence, you guys, but I'm not in the mood for ghost stories," says Max.

You agree. It's been a strange day. After a game of I Spy, you hear Stella climbing out of her sleeping bag.

"I need to go to the toilet," she says. "Max, can you come with me to the outhouse?"

He groans, but gets out of his sleeping bag and follows her outside.

They take the lamp with them, and Stella carries a roll of toilet paper. Lying in the dark you wish you had a brother or a sister with you for stuff like that. Max and Stella tease each other, but they also look after each other.

A few minutes later, Max and Stella come in laughing. As Max puts down the lamp, Stella accidentally drops the toilet paper and it unravels as it rolls across the floor. It veers off on the uneven floorboards. She follows the paper and bends to pick it up.

"Hey," Stella says. "I think there's a trap door or something here."

"Don't be crazy," says Max.

Together they look at the floor, and sure enough there are lines forming a large square.

"It looks like maybe something fits in here," says Max, pointing at a small metal hole in the wood.

"What do you think would be down there?"

"It's probably just more firewood or something. We should just leave it till morning."

"I want to know what's down there," Stella says. "I won't be able to get a wink of sleep."

All three of you look around the hut for something to use as a lever, and you spy a big metal spoon on the bench. It doesn't fit too well, but you can make the trapdoor lift a little. Stella grabs a spatula, and the next time you try to lift the floorboards she slides it in the gap you've made. Max grabs the edge with his fingers and heaves, and soon the three of you have the trap door open.

Under the trap door there are stairs carved into rock leading down to blackness. The stairs are manmade but the hole looks very old. Someone has cleverly built the hut to disguise this old tunnel entrance. You look at each other, grab the lamp, and head underground. At the bottom of the stairs there is a door with a big, old fashioned lock. You are surprised to find it's not locked. The door looks a lot older than the hut.

Holding your breath, you silently push at the door. It might be old, but the hinges are well oiled and it opens noiselessly. You see a corridor sloping downwards made of concrete and rock. Here and there are braces in the ceiling made of wood. It looks like a cross between a mineshaft and a small railway tunnel.

"This place is cool!" whispers Max.

"What if someone's down here?" Stella asks.

You creep forward, and are just about to speak when you see a light around the corner up ahead. Stella snaps off the lamp.

Around a bend the tunnel joins a larger corridor to form a T. The light you saw is coming from a fluorescent tube on the ceiling. The pool of light fades out to black in both directions.

It is time to make a decision. Do you:

Turn left? **P269**

Or

Turn right? **P278**

You have decided to turn left.

Turning left, you walk down the widening tunnel. You can make out chisel marks in the rock where people have widened the space, but the rest of the tunnel looks natural. More lights stud the ceiling and there is a strange noise overhead. It seems incredible that you are walking around inside the island. The noise you can hear is the sea – the tunnel has taken you under the ocean!

You walk on, looking out for any signs of people, and enter a wider antechamber. The first room you come to contains lots of food and other supplies, a lot with strange pictures on the packets and foreign words written on the cans. On a shelf to one side are chocolate bars and biscuits, and on the floor below the shelf are large sacks of rice and potatoes.

As you leave the room to continue exploring, you hear another noise – a sort of slow stamping sound. In a room off to one side you see a machine. A man stands beside it with his back to you. With all the noise from the machine he has not heard you. You wonder: Is he friend or foe?

You signal to Max and Stella to stay hidden, then bravely walk up to the man and tap him on the shoulder. He jumps and spins around with an astonished look on his face.

"Who you are?" he gasps. "Is anyone else here with you?"

"No…" you say, sensing he might not be friendly. "I'm on my own. I found my way down from the hut. Can I get a lift over to the other island, or use a phone? My aunt will be looking for me."

The man shakes his head. "No phones here. Where's your boat?" You can't really tell what the man's accent is, but you don't think he is a local.

"My boat sank," you say. "I did something really stupid."

The man laughs, but it isn't friendly. "We'll get you sorted – come with me."

He leads you out of the work room and further down the corridor. You hope that Max and Stella keep hidden – you don't dare to look behind you, you might give them away.

The man leads you past a few doors. Some of them are open, and you can see small cell-like bedrooms cut into the rock

Then the tunnel is heading upwards again. Soon you reach another large room where there is music quietly playing. On one side of the room is a pool table, an exercycle and bench for lifting weights. On the other side is a kitchen and dining area. Two men are eating at the dining table. They watch as you are led past them to a closed door.

The man opens it and leads you though into a sort of office. It has three regular walls, but the last wall is mostly rock with a window set into it. You think that it must look out to the sea. There is a desk on one side of the room, as well as two couches.

"Welcome to my island!" a woman says as she enters the room. She has tousled red hair and is dressed in jeans, sneakers, and a polo-necked sweater.

"Congratulations on making your way into the inner sanctum. I'm Mrs Rogers, but most people around here call me The Director."

"What is this place all about?" you ask.

"The cave system was carved out by the sea. There was once a large blowhole that spouted up through the main cavern – but earthquakes have raised the island and left the chambers dry. This place was first used by the native Maori people as a place to shelter when they were bringing precious greenstone from the South Island to the North."

You have heard of the Maori. They were the first people of New Zealand. Their descendants still live here today. What Maori call greenstone is called jade in other parts of the world. It's worth a lot of money.

"Next," Mrs Rogers explains, "early whalers used these caves to shelter in when the seas got rough. It was nearly forgotten until World War II when this place got a major overhaul. It was used by the army to look out for Japanese ships and planes. After the war it was sold into private hands. Today, it is leased to my company."

"And what does your company do?" you ask.

"Before I answer you, how about we invite your friends to join us?"

Stella and Max walk into the room, escorted by a young man with a clipboard. You all sit down on the couches and a plate of toasted bread dripping with honey appears from somewhere, along with another plate with crisp slices of pear and kiwifruit. Mrs Rogers clicks some buttons at her desk and a video begins to run on a screen set in one of the walls. You see pictures of the three of you coming down into the caves!

"We were alerted to your presence on the island when you entered the trap door and tripped our sensors. After that our cameras followed you. It was a smart move to split up and see what would happen when you approached Hank. You have every reason to be suspicious about people in a strange underground hideaway. We hadn't had time to tell him that we had unexpected guests, so you certainly surprised him!

"This is the setting for a reality TV series. There will be people up above and people down below, and they won't know about each other's existence in the beginning. The people aren't here yet, though."

"I wonder how long they will take to find each other?" says Max.

"Excuse me Mrs Rogers," Stella interrupts. "Do you have a boat that can take us to Arapawa Island? We think our aunt is worried about us."

"Sure! I'll get you over there as soon as we have a camera crew together," Mrs Rogers purrs.

"A camera crew?" you ask.

"Of course! I want you to be part of my reality show. "How long will it take to get the film crew together?" you ask.

"No more than two days."

You start thinking that Mrs Rogers isn't being very helpful. Maybe she is more interested in ratings than anything else. Before you can think of what to say, she points out that it's not safe to navigate the rocks at night, anyway.

"It's getting late. Let's get you kids to bed!" She points to one of her staff and tells you to follow him.

Mrs Rogers sends you all off to the bedrooms you saw earlier. They are small rooms, perhaps originally used for soldiers.. After the assistant leaves, you meet in Max's room.

"There is something weird about all this," says Stella. "I don't think I believe Mrs Rogers."

"I don't either," you say.

"Me neither," says Max, "but it's too dark to take a boat over to the island now, so there's no point trying to escape yet. In the morning we should scout around for one and try to escape."

You agree, but wonder if a bit of scouting later tonight might be useful too.

You climb up into your bunk and fall asleep almost instantly. In the middle of the night you wake and wonder where you are, and then the whole drama comes flooding back. While it makes sense to wait till morning to leave the island, it doesn't make sense to wait a few days. Your parents and Aunt Maddy will be worried. Maybe there is something else that Mrs Rogers is trying to hide.

You decide to have another look at the room where you met the first of her assistants. You slip out of your bunk and pull on your clothes.

Remembering the cameras in the corridor, you don't switch on any lights and instead decide to feel your way. You leave a sneaker outside your door so you will know which room is yours when you return. Then, you start creeping up the tunnel. You run your hand along the wall to feel the doors – one, two, three, this next one might be it...

As you start to open the door, you hear snoring. You must have counted wrong. You quietly shut the door and keep going up the corridor. You stop at the next door – okay, *this* must be it.

You listen carefully and then step inside and close the door softly behind you. It takes a moment to find the light switch. The light is so bright after the pitch black you have to squint. Your heart thumps. You cross the room and look at the machinery, trying to work out what it does. Then it hits you – it's a printing press, and stacked to one side is money, lots of it, all in $100 bills!

There is Australian currency, New Zealand currency, and others you don't recognize. These people aren't making a TV show – they're forgers!

There are some empty plastic bags on the bench. You slip a variety of the fake money into one of them and cross back to the door. Just in time, you remember to switch off the light before opening the door. You feel for the knob and then slip back out in the corridor.

Feeling your way back towards your room, you are relieved when your toe finds the sneaker you left outside. You clamber back into bed, and sleep.

You are awoken hours later by Stella and Max. In moments you are up and ready, with the money stashed in your pocket. You sneak through the big open-plan room with the kitchen, and luckily there is nobody around. Max starts filling his pockets with food.

"There's no time for that!" you hiss at him.

If someone comes now you'll be trapped in this place and you're more certain than ever you are all in danger.

You go through a door in the direction you think might lead to the sea, and maybe a boat. Sure enough, you find yourself outside on a ledge which slopes down to the sea. In the early dawn light you can see that there are three motor boats moored there.

Max and Stella have been in boats before and have an idea how they work, so Max sits in the driver's seat while Stella casts off. She jumps in when Max starts the boat.

"It's like a dirt bike on water," he declares.

"Just get it moving Max!" Stella tells him, glancing left and right, "we're really close to getting away."

As the boat moves forward, you hear a shout from behind you. It's one of the assistants, waving his arms for you to stop.

"Come back! You'll kill yourselves on the rocks!"

It is time to make a decision. Do you:

Listen to the assistant and stop? **P302**

Or

Escape in the boat? **P275**

You have decided to escape in the boat.

Max gives the boat a burst of power and it surges out through a small rocky channel. On the console, Max flips a switch and a screen comes to life showing the terrain underneath the boat. Not far below its hull are rocks!

"Stella, watch the screen for rocks," says Max as he steers. "Help me navigate out to sea."

As the boat leaves the channel the sea floor drops off sharply and you no longer have to worry about running aground. In fact, you can make out the shapes of fish beneath you. Some of them are very big. Max points the boat towards Arapawa. Stella is no longer glued to the depth finder, and as she looks back she shouts, "Oh no!"

You turn to see another boat emerging from the hidden cove. There are three figures on board, and one of them has red hair blowing in the wind – Mrs Rogers. Her boat picks up speed as soon as it is past the rocks and starts to close the gap between you.

"We have to speed up!" you yell at Max.

He pulls on the throttle and the boat leaps forward. Out here the waves are bigger, and the increased speed makes the boat feel very unstable. Arapawa Island is getting closer. You are more than half way there. Hopefully you'll get there before Mrs Rogers catches up.

"She's on a bigger boat," you say, "Watch out she might try to ram us."

The beach is in sight now, and Max is heading straight for it, rather than the little jetty.

Without warning Stella grabs the wheel and jerks it to one side – the depth finder is showing rocks beneath you again, and Stella has narrowly avoided some big ones!

Looking back, you see a large wave coming up behind Mrs Rogers' boat. She is close enough that you can see her angry face.

The wave picks them up, and then a moment later it lifts your boat too. The surge is like riding on a surf board.

Max increases speed to take advantage of the extra momentum. In moments you are beached on the golden sand, and scrambling out of the boat on to dry land.

Behind you, Mrs Rogers' boat has wedged on the rocks that Stella avoided.

Mrs Rogers doesn't look as scary teetering precariously on the rocks, but she does look as angry as a hornet.

A soft voice speaks up from behind you. "Don't worry, the boat will come loose at high tide and the police can get them off. Who are those people?"

A friendly looking woman has joined you on the beach. Stella and Max throw themselves into her arms. It's Aunt Maddy.

Maddy explains that your 'kidnappers' had left you on the little island to try and press her into selling her rights to the little harbor.

"They want to set up a business there. But I don't stand for blackmail, and I threatened to call the police straight away. So Damon went over to the island to get you and then came back to say you had disappeared! So then I *did* call the police, and they have been looking for you too. Oh, look, here they are now!"

A powerful police launch has come into view and sweeps into the little harbor. They see Mrs Rogers in trouble and throw a rope over to her boat. The police drag the smaller vessel off the rocks and in no time Mrs Rogers is on shore beside you.

She is busy explaining to the police how she is part of a reality TV show when you remember the plastic bag full of money and. hand it to one of the officers.

"Mrs Rogers might be making a TV show," you say, "but they are also busy making these."

The policeman looks into the bag and his eyes widen in surprise. The scene quickly changes – Mrs Rogers stops explaining about her TV show, and is arrested and taken away on the police launch.

"Well," says Aunt Maddy, "after all that excitement I think you'll want some breakfast and to get started on your proper holiday?"

"Yes!" you all agree and set off up to the house. It's been a great start to your vacation but you wonder what would have happened if you'd made some different choices?

It is time to make a decision. Do you:

Start the story over and make different decisions? **P247**

Or

Go to the list of choices and read from another part of the story. **P320**

You have decided to turn right.

Turning right, you head down a sloping tunnel. The walls are roughly hewn as if people have widened an existing crack in the rock. There are large spider webs across the roof and walls of this section of the tunnel. It's like a giant spider has made this its nest here. Max shudders as he brushes against one of the cobwebs, but Stella, unafraid, puts her hand out to pull it off him.

"Not much for spiders to catch down here," she says, studying the web. "Hmmm … they're fake!"

As you walk further, you begin to hear old fashioned music. You can see light around the next door you come to. It's locked, so you all bang on it to be heard over the music. The song finishes abruptly and the door opens.

The man standing in the doorway is much older than the pictures you've seen of him, but you still recognize him instantly, and when he speaks you recognize his voice.

Max blurts out, "But … you're supposed to be dead!"

"Well, Max – my career is dead, but I'm alive and well."

He lives in a fabulous cave that makes you think of the inside of a genie's bottle. The cave walls are covered in richly colored fabrics, and Oriental rugs cover the floor. Peering in, you see that beyond the main room are a kitchen, and a room through a window that looks like a recording studio.

The old rock star smiles at your curiosity and beckons you in. In the kitchen he makes you all a hot chocolate. He tells you how his fame got too much for him.

"It got so I couldn't enjoy my life at all. I was followed everywhere – so I decided to disappear."

"Hey," says Stella. "How did you know my brother's name?"

"Well spotted, Stella! That's because you've been down here already tonight. We talked and I explained about my private life, and then you kindly let me hypnotize you so you would forget our meeting. It worked, but unfortunately you made the same choice to come back this way. If you don't mind, I'll do it again and try to put in a stronger suggestion that you go another direction. I hope you understand?"

"Okay," says Max, "but only if I can play one tune with the King."

The older man laughs and tells you and Stella to stand by to sing the backup vocals – again!

Five minutes later after the excitement of singing, he lines you, Max, and Stella up by the door and says, "You are feeling sleepy…"

The next time you open your eyes, you are at the fork of a tunnel.

Now you have to make a decision Do you:

Turn left? **P269**

Or

Turn right? **P278**

You've finally decided to go to Arapawa Island.

Arapawa Island is large. Maddy explains there are only a few people spread over its many acres. Maddy has her own harbor in a horseshoe-shaped bay with another little island in its centre. Her boat, the *Seahorse*, is moored in the bay. Maddy explains that her land reaches up to the top of the hills that create the valley, and it is covered in a mixture of green subtropical forest and pasture. You look up at the hills and see some sheep and a few goats.

Maddy lives in an old fashioned farm house with a full front veranda. A fenced garden surrounds the veranda – it's a wild mixture of herbs, flowers, and vegetables.

There are solar panels on the roof and several small wind turbines sit on fence posts around the house.

"I'm pretty much self-sufficient," she says, "which is important because in bad weather the island can be cut off from the mainland for days. Come on, let me show you your digs."

Halfway up the hill behind the house is a large shed with a bunk house attached.

"This land used to be part of a large sheep farm. Each year a shearing gang would come from the mainland and stay here while they sheared the sheep. Nowadays I let writers and scientists use it for a place to do some thinking. Why don't you kids settle in, and then come round to the house before dark."

You wander through the bunk house. The walls are whitewashed and the floors are bare boards worn smooth by all the feet that have travelled over them. There is a small central kitchen and living area. Several old armchairs circle a big stone fireplace. Beside it is a bookshelf, so you have a look at the books. You see books about the history of whaling in New Zealand, a couple of cookery books, a few thrillers and mysteries, books about fishing and sailing, and a semaphore manual. There are cards and old fashioned dice and word games. You wonder what it would be like to live here all the time.

"This is my room!" shouts Stella, rushing through one of the doors.

"This is mine," Max says claiming another.

You hurry to find your own bunk. There are four doors off the main living area. Through one is a short corridor leading to the bathrooms. That leaves one more door – you open it and see a narrow flight of stairs. When you reach the top you see you are above the living area where there is a table and a bed. Stella and Max come up to find you.

"Awesome," says Max, looking at your attic space.

As you grab your bags and drag your gear to your rooms, there is a clanging sound from outside. It's Maddy ringing the dinner bell. The three of you head to the big house. "This bell was here when my family bought the house when I was your age. My mother used to ring it to bring me back home for dinner – now I'm the one ringing the bell."

The smell of fresh bread draws you inside. On the table sits a roast chicken, potatoes, gravy, asparagus and green beans. There is a pile of bread rolls and a huge tossed salad. Soon everyone has full plates.

Maddy suggests you take the leftovers back to the shearing shed.

"There should be plenty for sandwiches tomorrow. You can go exploring or fishing and see if you can catch yourselves tomorrow night's meal. I've left you things for breakfast, so if you don't need me you can just do your own thing till dinner."

Clearly, Aunt Maddy hasn't had children of her own and isn't worried that you'll come to any harm. Great.

That night, you lie in bed and listen to the noises of the island. A sheep or a goat bleats somewhere, there is the constant lapping of the water, and you can hear an owl close by in the trees.

The next day you wake up to the smell of toast. In the kitchen you find Max cheerfully smearing butter and honey onto a stack of thick browned slices of bread. Stella staggers into the room, rubbing her eyes.

Through the window, the sea glistens under a bright blue sky. The three of you take your breakfast outside onto the porch. Sitting on the steps you can see the sea change from green, just below you, to a deep blue out by the horizon. As you sit in the sun and bite into the grainy bread a small goat makes its way up the path and walks right up to you. It bleats a greeting and then snatches the toast from your hand! It looks at you as if it does this every morning and can't work out why you look so surprised. Then it trots back toward the hills. Oh well, there is plenty more toast.

After breakfast, the three of you pack some lunch into your backpacks and grab fishing rods. Stella has a book. What a good idea. You randomly grab a book on semaphore off the shelf and stuff it into your bag's side pocket.

Then you, Max and Stella head down to the shore.

"What shall we do," says Max. "Shall we fish or go exploring?"

It is time to make a decision. Do you:

Go fishing? **P283**

Or

Go exploring? **P288**

You have decided to go fishing.

After walking down to the sandy bay you walk along the beach and then clamber up into the forest. There you find a natural path to follow around the coastline. The waves lap gently down below you, but as the shore turns rocky the water begins to surge and slap.

You pick your way down to where the rocks sit just above the water. Close to the water's edge, rock pools hold multicolored anemones and little fish. The pools are like little cities – busy with life. The fish dart away when your shadow falls over them, making you feel like a giant.

Stella puts her fingers into the water and lightly touches an anemone. It clamps shut like an alien eye. A small fish would be trapped and digested in its grip. You are impressed by these beautiful little monsters. Stella gets out her camera and tries to get a picture of the life inside the rock pool.

"This would make a good app," she says. "It would be cool to manage your own rock pool."

"Come on!" Max shouts from a rocky ledge just above you.

You and Stella follow him up some natural steps. Striped limpets stud the cliff and there are little pockets of water in the rock, showing that the tide can reach this far.

"We'll have to watch out for rogue waves. One big one and we'll be plucked off the rocks," says Max.

A bit further along, you find a wide ledge overlooking the sea and peer over the edge. It's about fifteen feet down to where the waves break against the rock.

There's no cell phone coverage on this part of the island, so you sit down on the edge and pull the semaphore book out of your bag. Leafing through, you think about how people used to communicate.

Stella and Max look over your shoulder.

The book explains how to use one or two flags to represent the alphabet. You don't have flags, but you can use your arms. Before long you are spelling messages to each other and planning how you might be able to signal to each other from greater distances.

"Hey," you say. "Aren't we meant to be fishing?"

The three of you bait hooks and then cast your lines. The reels whirr as sinkers fly and then plop into the sea. Within minutes there is a tug on your line.

"I've got one!" you yell as you reel it in.

Max gives a shout and starts reeling in too. A moment later and Stella is also pulling in a fish. Soon there are three silver fish in your bucket.

"They're blue cod," Stella says. "They're great to eat."

"Let's climb up the cliff face and see if we can find some birds' nests," says Max.

"That's a good way to get yourself killed," says Stella.

"Don't be a spoil sport," say Max.

It is time to make a decision. Do you:

Climb up the cliff? **P285**

Or

Head back with your fish? **P286**

You have decided to climb up the cliff.

With the bucket of fish tied beneath your backpack you feel for hand and foot holds and slowly make your way up the cliff. You catch up with Max and look up. Way above you, at the top of the cliff, is a wire fence. Maybe there is a sheep paddock and a different route back. You hope so, because you don't want to have to climb back down this way.

Shrill squawking interrupts your thoughts. A baby seagull sits inside a nest of grass and seaweed. It seems to think you might have come to feed him. Another noise brings your attention back to your climb.

A large seagull is squawking at Max and swooping so close to him that it looks like it will hit him in the head! Ouch! It feels like stones are hitting the back of your head – another bird is attacking you!

It is almost impossible to shelter your head, but you tuck your face in against the cliff. The gull lands on the bucket swinging beneath you. It's after the fish!

As the bird propels itself skyward with a fish in its bill, it pushes the bucket behind your knees, your legs give way, and you hang for a moment from your hands.

You see the bird flying away triumphantly with a fish as you plummet to the rocks far below.

Arghhhhhhhhhhhhhhhhhhhhhhhhh!

Ooops that didn't end well. But what would have happened if you'd made different choices?

It is time to make a decision. Do you:

Go to the beginning of the story and try another path? **P247**

Or

Go try your luck with another story? **P5**

You have decided to head back with your fish.

You head back toward the shearers' quarters and find Maddy on her front porch, writing at a table.

She waves as you approach and takes you in to her kitchen to show you how to clean the fish. She has a trench outside in her garden for the fish guts. It is an ingenious system. She digs in compost and fishing leftovers and then covers it all with dirt. Later she plants a row of giant sunflowers which benefit from the smelly plant food. Her garden is amazing.

She shows you where you can dig up new potatoes and carrots, and there are tomatoes growing on a vine. You have never been surrounded by so much food outside a supermarket.

Back in the kitchen, Maddie shows you how to breadcrumb the fish ready for tonight's meal. You tell her about practicing from the semaphore book as she puts the finished fish into the fridge.

"That old book! I used to have some flags so that I could signal to a friend on the mainland. We had great fun sending messages to each other. We found if we dropped out all the vowels in our messages we could communicate much faster."

"Um – that's called text messaging, Auntie," says Stella.

The phone rings and Maddy is still laughing when she picks it up. It's Stella and Max's parents.

While you finish tidying up in the kitchen, Stella tells them about your journey here and the shearers' quarters you are staying in. Max tells his parents about fishing.

You wonder what it must have been like to live on the island before telephones and boats with motors. You head back to the shearers' quarters and lie down on your bed with the semaphore book.

After a while Max comes back, and then Stella.

"What should we do now?" Stella asks. "Do you want to go swimming or exploring?"

It is time to make a decision. Do you

Go swimming? **P303**

Or

Go exploring? **P288**

You have decided to go exploring.

Up the valley the smell of salt air and the sound of lapping water is replaced by bleating lambs and the occasional clatter of small rocks disturbed by a goat high on the cliff. The three of you agree to go up the hill different ways and then walk along the ridge to meet at the top. The sun is at your back as the three of you climb up the valley.

Max goes to one side, Stella to the other, and you take the middle track which ought to be the shortest way up. You are thinking about the semaphore book – when you get to the top you might signal to the others. You stop and leaf through the book, thinking about a funny message you could make. After a while you realize you had better get moving or you will be last to the top.

You watch the ground as the path becomes much steeper. Pasture turns to bare rock that sparkles here and there with quartz. One section is shaped like a natural armchair. You sit in it, the stone feels warm from the sun.

Over to the left Stella is climbing below a small group of goats. Whenever she gets close the goats move away, but one young kid seems very curious and is slowly letting Stella get closer. You see that Stella has noticed the kid as well. She reaches into her back pack, takes something out, and throws it toward the kid. The kid comes closer to see what it is. Stella is making a friend.

You reach into your pack, pull out your camera, find Stella through the viewfinder, and zoom in across the valley as she charms the young goat. You take a few shots as it gets closer and closer and then finally scampers away. Perhaps you can find Max on the opposite side of the valley. Without taking your eye from the camera you swoop down toward your feet and fiddle with the zoom so you can have a wider look for Max.

As you pan the camera over the ground, a large rock seems to move – zooming in, you find that you are staring at a dinosaur! You panic, drop the camera and scuttle backwards. Where is it? With relief, you see it sitting on a rock a few yards away. Your dinosaur is a lot smaller when you aren't looking through your camera. No wonder you didn't see it when you sat down — it is almost the same color as the rock, and covered in craggy skin.

Could it bite you? It might be small but you know there are small snakes in the world than can kill with one bite. Meanwhile, your dinosaur hasn't moved — it's just staring up at you. How curious it is — quite different to the little geckos and lizards you've seen before. It's like a miniature dragon without the wings.

Glancing to the left, you see that Stella is nearly at the top of the valley. To the right Max is already walking across the crest of the hill, making his way to your agreed meeting place. Stella is spelling out something in semaphore with her arms:

H
U
R
R
Y
U
P

You grab your pack and get moving, thinking of the story you have to tell about meeting a dinosaur.

When you make the top of the hill Stella is telling her brother about her goat. From this height the three of you are able to see much more of the island. There is a spine to the island, with a goat track stretching as far as you can see along a long narrow ridge. On each side of the island are valleys like the one you just climbed. You can't see too far into them but the nearest one has lots of different trees.

The next valley has a longer, gentler slope to the sea. There is a house and some sheds down at one of the bays, but closer to you, between the trees, you spy an old house and some dilapidated buildings.

It's the trees that catch Stella's attention. "I think those are plum trees! Let's check them out."

Worried that you may be trespassing, you hang back a bit as you climb through brambles and low bushes. It's clear not many people come through this way. As you get closer to the house it's also clear that nobody could live there – there are trees pushing their way up through the old back porch, many of the windows are missing and the rusted roof is sagging.

It is time to make a decision. Do you:

Go in? **P291**

Or

Don't go in. Go check out the plum trees instead? **P293**

You have decided to go inside the run down house.

The old house is too intriguing to ignore. You gingerly make your way up to it. The boards of the porch creak as you approach the door – it's very slightly open and it groans as you push it the rest of the way.

You step into the kitchen first. It is warm and musty. The window is covered by a vine which gives the room a green hue as the light filters inside. The floor is covered in dried bird droppings. There is a large iron oven, its door ajar and filled with grass and branches twisted into a birds nest, a small table, and two chairs – the chairs are pulled out as if the owners had just stood up and walked out without packing or looking back. The door to the next room is closed and for a moment you think it might be locked, but with a bit of wriggling the rusted handle moves and you find yourself in a hallway with a strip of moth-eaten carpet running down its center Light struggles through the grimy windows.

You follow the hallway all the way down, then turn and enter a room, while you hear Max and Stella explore another.

Two large armchairs sit against one wall. Their upholstery is old and tattered. A mouse peeps out of a hole and you crouch to look at it.

Stella and Max enter the room and stand behind you. You suddenly realize you are all keeping very quiet.

You are just about to point out the mouse when you hear a tortured creak from the back door.

You look at each other – Stella and Max look as scared as you feel. Maybe it's the wind?

It isn't. Suddenly there is banging and crashing in the kitchen. All three of you scramble toward the window but as you wriggle the catch the whole frame falls out hitting the ground with a huge bang.

The three of you leap out of the hole in the wall and run into the long grass until you hit a solid wall of overgrown trees and bushes. You stop and catch your breath.

"Let's take a look around the back," Stella says.

As the three of you stealthily make your way round the house, you crouch down as you near the back door. Then you hear it – bleating.

Stella laughs and heads back into the house. You and Max follow, just in time to see the young goat she fed earlier emerge from the kitchen, wearing the bird's nest from the oven on its head.

You shoo the goat away and shut the door, not wanting to cause any more damage to the old place.

What should you do next?

It is time to make a decision. Do you:

Go look at the plum tree? **P293**

Or

Go back for a swim? **P303**

You have decided to look at the plum tree.

The plum trees have formed a tight forest around the side of the old house. It reminds you of the fairy tale Sleeping Beauty.

The air is perfumed by the sweet smell of ripe plums. You pick one and bring it to your mouth. The dark red fruit is a juicy explosion of sweet and sour in your mouth. The three of you wander from tree to tree finding the next perfect treat.

"There's a path here!" Max points to a line of trampled grass leading away from the trees. "I wonder where it leads."

Max takes off. You and Stella follow. As you wander down the narrow path there is a wall of long grass on each side of you. Then when you turn a bend you find a little shed – it's not as dilapidated as the house, but it's certainly old. Suddenly, you are startled by a figure at the door of the shed.

As he moves into the light, you see a boy a little older than you.

He smiles shyly and says "Hello" in a strong accent. "Do you have anything to eat?"

Stella reaches in her backpack and offers her sandwiches to the stranger. He smiles broadly. You all sit down and share your food with him.

"My name is Mikhal," he says. "I swam to shore one night from a fishing boat. My mother and father owed money and when they couldn't pay it, the man took me to work on the boat. I worked on the boat for a miserable year and then knew I had to escape. The debt must have been paid. When I saw land I packed my belongings in a plastic bag and used an old polystyrene box to help me swim to shore."

"Sounds terrible," you say, thinking how fortunate your life has been

He sighs, and looks sad. "I want to find job and get the money to go home to my family."

"We can help," you tell him.

As the four of you leave the glade, you ask him where the other path leads.

"It goes to the sea. I looked, but I see lights and think it might be ghosts or fishermen coming to find me. I walk across hills and find I am on island! I sleep here and try to think of plan."

You take Mikhal back to Maddy's house – on the way you tell the others how you saw a little dinosaur. Stella and Max laugh at you but Mikhal looks serious.

"I know about such things. My captain collects little animals and birds for people. It was my job on the boat to look after the animals – I grew up on a farm and the captain thought I would know what to do. The night I escaped, the fishing boat was close to land because the crew were picking up more animals."

Maddy's house is in sight and Mikhal becomes quiet. He looks nervous about meeting her.

She is in the kitchen when you arrive. You explain in a rush about finding the castaway.

Maddy shakes Mikhal's hand and shows him a spare room where he can put his things. Maddy says she has heard about people exploiting child labor and says that there are laws against it.

"You'll stay here the night, Mikhal. I will call the police," she tells him. "They will be able to send you home to your family."

While she finds him a towel and sends him off for a shower she sets the three of you to work readying dinner. She has you busy frying the fish you caught this morning, while Max is cooking vegetables and Stella is cutting up lemons and setting the table. Lastly, Maddy brings out a large potato salad.

Mikhal arrives from the shower wearing some of Max's clothes. Max and Mikhal are not too different in size, although a year at sea has built Mikhal's muscles. Everyone eats and Mikhal asks the name of everything on the table in English.

When Maddy asks what else you have been up to today you tell her about Stella making friends with a goat. Stella laughs and says at least her friend wasn't imaginary.

"I'm pretty sure I have a picture of it…" you say and then trail off because you've just realized that you left your camera on the hillside where you saw the little dinosaur.

It is time to make a decision. Do you:

Go outside in the dark to find your camera? **P297**

Or

Stay inside? **P296**

You have decided to stay inside.

You sit down to a game of cards. Maddy teaches you the rules. It doesn't take long to learn and before long you are all hooked. After a couple of hours, Maddy shoos you off so Mikhal can get some sleep. He's had little food and rest for the past few days and looks exhausted.

Back in the shearers' quarters, Max and Stella call out to each other for a while before their voices go quiet and you slip off to sleep. Maddy said that in the morning you will all travel to the mainland to take Mikhal to the police and to sort out a plan to get him home.

In the morning you run up the hill to find your camera.

While you stand there fiddling with the camera you see movement. It's the small dinosaur, and wait — there's a second! You pull off your sweatshirt and make a bag and coax the lizard things inside then you carefully take them back to the others. You think you'll release them later but you're in for a surprise.

"Tuatara!" Max and Stella say. Something twigs in your memory, where have you heard that word?

"How did they get to the island?" Maddy says when she sees them.

"I brought them, then I lost them," says Mikhal.

"Tuatara Missing from Sanctuary," you yell, "they were in the newspaper on the ferry." Maddy leaps for the phone and an hour later a news crew arrive with a wildlife specialist to collect your find. They also do a story on Mikhal who gets to stay on the island until his parents are found and he can go home.

Congratulations, you have reached the end of this part of the story. But have you tried all the possible paths?

It is time to make another decision. Do you:

Go back to the beginning of this story and try another path? **P247**

Or

Go and try one of the other stories? **P5**

You have decided to go and look for your camera.

The stars are much brighter than in the city, and there are so much more of them. The moon is full, like a giant white plate in the sky. You have only taken a few steps up the hill when you hear a shout as Mikhal runs up to join you. In contrast to this afternoon you are moving fast, but you can't see any animals on the hillside.

"Look up there. It is Southern Cross." Mikhal is pointing at the stars where they form a shape like a kite. "Old sailors would find their way by the stars."

Soon, you come to the place where you dropped the camera and saw the little dinosaur. When the moon to come out from behind a cloud, you are able to make out a gleam on the ground. The camera! You switch it on and flick through the pictures. The last picture is of the rock and the dinosaur! You are so excited you almost drop the camera again.

You show the picture to Mikhal, and he smiles.

"But this is my little dragon! You saw it here? Good, she is alive. I brought her with me when I came ashore."

You start back to the house wondering what Mikhal is talking about. But before the two of you have made it halfway back down the hill, three figures step out of the dark. You jump back in surprise, and Mikhal grabs you by the arm and tries to run, but the men have the advantage. Someone wraps his arms around you and presses a rag over your face. It has a strong smell and you feel yourself blacking out. You fight to stay awake, but it's useless. The darkness comes rushing towards you as you feel yourself being lifted up...

You come to your senses wondering where you are. There is a rocking motion and the smell of diesel and seawater. You look around and realize that you are on a bunk in a boat, and you can hear voices outside speaking in a language you can't understand. There is the clink of spoons in coffee mugs, and laughter.

Then the cabin door opens and Mikhal enters. He looks scared and pale and there is a bruise on one side of his face.

"Oh my friend. They are angry I ran away, and they are so angry I have lost their little dragon. It is worth much money and now they say we both must work to earn the money back. I am so sorry."

You can't believe this is happening – kidnapped!

A large man enters the cabin and speaks to.

"Mikhal," you say. "Tell him to let us go. The police will be looking for us."

The man laughs, and Mikhal translates his reply.

"Nobody looks for you, the captain says. Now you have a job with us fishing. And if you do not work then you feed the fish! You understand?"

You understand.

You get up and follow Mikhal outside to find that it is bright daylight – you must have slept right through the night. Outside on deck you stagger as the ship moves, and see that you are well out to sea. There is no land on the horizon. You couldn't possibly swim ashore.

It is the start of a long, hard day. With Mikhal showing you how, you clean a huge hold that will contain the next haul of fish. From time to time a siren sounds that alerts you to meal breaks, and together you make your way to a mess hall where you are fed alongside ten men – one of these is Mikhal's friend Stan, who taught him English.

As the days pass you get into a routine, and when there is not much to do Stan sits you both down and teaches you something. You never know what the lesson might be, but it becomes your main source of new information and entertainment.

Another of your duties is to take care of the animals. The captain has a collection of birds and lizards in various cages. You and Mikhal clean the cages and make sure each animal has water and fresh food. In a large glass container you find several more of the little dinosaurs, or dragons, as Mikhal calls them. These are the creatures that caused you so much trouble. Something about them keeps nagging at your memory, but you don't know what it is.

The animals are kept deep in the ship, through a hidden door next to the engines. It's loud in there and you think the birds mustn't like it very much. Some of them are beginning to pull out their feathers, and they look a bit downcast.

The ship is like a factory with processing and freezing facilities. Several times you try to get to the captain's office where instruments and presumably a radio are kept, but each time you are blocked from entering by the crew. Eventually, when nobody is around, you get closer but find that the doors have keypad locks, and you don't know the code. You are a prisoner, but as long as you work you are fed.

The days are getting warmer and you know you have been heading north for a week now. The holds are full of fish. The ship has completed its work and is heading to offload its cargo.

On the twelfth day of your kidnapping, you see land in the distance. The ship gradually gets closer, and just as you are planning to jump overboard a burly sailor grabs you and locks you and Mikhal in the animal room. You stay there for two days – from time to time you are sent food, but no matter how hard you bang on the door nobody comes to let you out until you are out to sea again.

The next morning you and Mikhal are washing down the foredeck when a yacht comes into view. Not wanting to draw attention from the crew, you both move so that you are mopping behind one of the ship's funnels. Calmly, you perform the semaphore signals you learnt on the island, repeating the same message over and over until one of the crew notices what you are doing and locks you below. You hardly dare hope that someone on the yacht saw your message. Even if they did – would they know what it meant?

The next day you are back on deck when you hear a helicopter. You and Mikhal are quickly hustled below deck to the room where the animals are kept. You are there for hours before the door is opened by an Australian naval officer. You can't hear what he is saying over the noise of the engine, but you can see his surprise as he looks at the cages. He signals for both of you to follow him out.

Above deck you find that the crew has been rounded up. A large naval ship is alongside the fishing boat, and there are men and women in navy uniforms everywhere. You and Mikhail are swung across to the bigger ship, and soon you are telling your story to the authorities.

The Australian officers tell you that the yacht you signaled had a retired naval officer aboard – he could read your semaphore message and called the navy. You and Mikhal can be returned to your parents or back to the island – you have saved a number of rare birds, and the little dragons are rare New Zealand tuatara that were stolen from a wildlife sanctuary.

The day after you were kidnapped, Max and Stella found your camera and the picture you had taken of the tuatara. Everyone realized that your disappearance might be linked to the missing lizards, and the New Zealand and Australian navy have been looking for you. If the greedy captain hadn't kidnapped you then the tuatara and other endangered creatures would have been lost to private collectors, and could have become extinct in the wild.

You are returned home and Mikhal goes home to his parents. Months later you hear that you have both come into possession of the fishing boat as reparation for your kidnapping and forced labor.

The two of you set up a trust, and the boat is renamed *Tuatara*. It becomes a conservation vessel, travelling the Pacific Ocean helping marine biologists save endangered species.

Congratulations, you've reached the end of this part of the story.

That means it is time to make another decision. Do you:

Go back to the beginning of this story and try another path? **P247**

Or

Go and try out one of the other stories? **P5**

You have decided to stay and do math problems.

Question One:

A New Zealand giant squid can drag someone your weight and strength down to the bottom of a three mile trench in ten minutes. How many minutes would it take for two giant squid to drag you down to a watery grave?

Question Two:

You find a device which moves you backwards and forwards in time. You move back one hundred years every time you hit the back button and you move forward fifty years every time you hit the forward button. You travel back 300 years and find yourself being chased by a giant eagle. The Haast's eagle was the largest eagle ever known to have lived and has been extinct for two hundred years. How many times do you have to hit the forward button to avoid being a meal for a giant eagle?

Question Three:

While Lost in Lion Country you find yourself left alone with the safari picnic basket. There are 50 ham sandwiches inside the basket. One hyena will be satisfied after 10 ham sandwiches and will head off to sleep in the sun. How many hyena can you hold off until help arrives?

For the answers **P316**

Or to go back to Arapawa Island **P249**

Or to go and stay with your mother's friend **P248**

You have decided to stop.

Seeing you hesitate, the agile assistants swarm onto the boat and pull you back to shore. You are frog-marched to the main room inside, and as one of the men goes to find Mrs Rogers, the bag of money that you took falls out of your pocket.

"Look," shouts one of the men as he snatches it up, "they know everything!"

Mrs Rogers strides into the room.

"Okay, kids, this is going to be a working holiday. I tried to come up with a way you could go home to mummy and daddy, but you had to ruin it by sneaking into things that don't concern you. Well now you'll work. For the next four weeks you can learn how to make money – and when we're done here, we'll drop you off somewhere and you can make your way back to civilization. Behave, or you'll be fish food!"

She bundles you into the printing room. For the next month you work day and night, making fake money and hoping each day won't be your last…

You have reached the end of this part of the story. But have you tried all the possible paths?

It is time to make a decision. Do you:

Go back to the beginning and try another path? **P247**

Or

Go and try one of the other stories? **P5**

You have decided to go for a swim.

It's a hot day and the lapping of salt water on your toes is delicious. The sand has been warmed by the sun and feels like chocolate pudding between your toes as you wade in.

Max and Stella are kitting up with snorkels and masks. You dive under a wave and swim out into the bay. The three of you move out deeper and deeper. Max and Stella dive under and when they come back up they tell you about fish they see. They muck about flicking seaweed at each other. Suddenly the water feels a lot colder.

"That's because it's so much deeper now I've heard it's about two miles deep out here," says Stella.

They dive back down again, and then you feel one of them tickling your leg – it almost feels like a snake pulling at you.

Stella surfaces a few yards away on one side, and then Max surfaces a few yards away on the other side – they are yelling and waving frantically.

Hang on – If they are over there, what is grabbing your leg?

A huge tentacle writhes up out of the water and clamps onto your arm. It is a giant squid! The last thing you think, as you are dragged below, is how incredibly rare a death like this must be. Glub glub glub!

Well that's the end of this part of your story. What a way to go!
It is time for you to make another decision. Do you:
Go back to the beginning of this story and try another path? **P247**
Or
Go and try one of the other adventures? **P5**

You have decided to try to rescue the dog.

You squeeze under the lowest rail and wiggle to the rope the dog is balancing on. Its quivers in terror, looking up at you with fearful brown eyes. You hook your leg around the rail and stretch to reach her… closer and closer, you are nearly there. As your fingers brush against her collar your leg slips and with a splash you and the dog fall into the sea.

The water knocks your breath away and you are barely aware of the cold as you hit the sea and go under. For a moment you think you will keep sinking and never breathe air again, but then you kick towards the surface and start to rise. As you come up, spitting salt water and gasping, you see the ferry moving away with a line of faces looking back at you. Trixie is swimming beside you, her head held high and small paws paddling.

On board a figure hurls something – a life preserver! The doughnut shape flies through the air and lands with a smack not far from you, and bobs up and down in the water.

With a few strokes you reach it and gratefully pull it over your body. Now you can float easily. You turn around to look for the dog. She is not far away, but the choppy waves block her from view every few seconds. The little pendant at her throat shines in the water.

You kick towards her and she scrabbles her front paws onto the red plastic ring. If you stay together you can both be rescued. You lean toward her and she licks your face, probably happy that she can rest. Your hand brushes the pendant on her collar as you get a comfortable grip on the dog, and you hear a strange ringing noise.

You spin around in the water, trying to figure out where the noise is coming from. Seconds ago you could see the big ferry, but now it's disappeared and you can't see it anywhere!

You almost don't hear a shout above the slap and slosh of water.

"Ahoy!"

A small sailing boat appears with a boy in it. The boat comes quickly across the water and pulls up beside you. You pass the dog to the boy, and then he hands you a rope.

"Pull yourself aboard," the boy says with a smile.

It is time to make a decision. Do you:

Climb into the boat? **P307**

Or

Stay out of the boat? **P306**

You have decided not to get into the boat.

You shake your head. "No, I don't want to get into your boat."

The boy looks at you as if you are crazy and then shrugs. The breeze catches his sails and he moves on, leaving you to tread water looking vainly for the ferry or a better rescue vessel. Your legs are getting cold and starting to go numb, but you are sure you can feel something twining about them...

Suddenly, a long tentacle emerges from the water and slides up your arm. It is the extremely rare giant squid – and you are not feeling lucky about finding one.

The arms of the giant squid slither across your skin and tighten around you. You gasp for air as it squashes you, and you struggle to pull yourself free, but the squid is strong and it tugs you down into the water. You hold your breath, but how long will you last as you're pulled deeper and deeper and the water goes dark?

How did you end up like this? If only you'd made different choices! If only you could start again!

Wait! You can!

It is time to make a decision. Do you.

Start this story over and try a different path? **P247**

Or

Go to the list of choice and start reading from another part of the story? **P320**

Or

Go to the list of books and choose another story to read **P5**

You have decided to get in the boat.

Grabbing the rope, you clamber aboard while the boy keeps the boat stable by leaning over on the other side. Soon you are safe in the bottom of the little boat, your sodden clothes dripping as Trixie licks your face.

The hands you a blanket – it is dirty and smelly, but it is also thick and warm. You feel instantly better as you pull it around you.

"I'm Nick," the boy says.

You introduce yourself then nod at the dog. "This is Trixie – it's thanks to her I was in the water."

Trixie huddles in between your legs as you warm each other.

You are in a small, old fashioned wooden sailboat. Inside the boat are more blankets and a couple of sacks. Nick is about your age. He is tanned a dark brown and wears a dirty shirt and torn trousers with a piece of rope holding them up. His legs and arms are covered with bruises. He looks like he might be going to a pirate-themed costume party. From the way he is looking at you, Nick seems to find *you* just as curious.

"Where did you come from?" he asks.

You explain about falling from the ferry, but he looks confused and you're not sure he understands. He examines the life preserver for a few seconds and then shrugs and gets to work with the boat. He puts the sail up and it soon catches the breeze.

As you look at the hills on the nearby island you see that the farmland isn't there anymore – there are dense trees instead. The few buildings you see are rough-looking houses with smoke rising from their chimneys. Further down the channel you see some large wooden-masted sailboats. There is no sign of the ferry, and somehow the world is quieter.

"Where do you want to go?" asks Nick.

"Nick, what year is it?"

He laughs. "Are you mad? It's 1897, of course. Did you bump your head?"

So… you're in a little boat in a huge channel of water over a hundred years earlier than when you woke up this morning.

"I don't know where I need to go because I don't know anyone here, or at least, not in this time."

Nick laughs again, and shakes his head. "I don't have anywhere to go, either," he says. "I've run away from my uncle because he was always beating me."

Great, you think. *Both his parents are dead, and mine haven't been born yet.*

"So, *if* you went back in time, how do you think you did it?" Nick asks.

You explain again about how you fell out of a large boat and when you tried to rescue the dog you touched the dog's collar.

You both stare at the dog. Nick leans forward, one hand on your knee and he pats Trixie's head.

"She seems a pretty ordinary dog. What's this?"

As he touches the pendant on her collar the sail boat lurches violently. When it steadies again, you look about. There is still the sea and the boat but…

"Hey, Fowler's farm is gone!"

You don't know which farm that was, but it looks like some of the houses on the hill might have disappeared too. One thing that's for sure is that the larger boats are gone. Now there is only one.

"Well I never," says Nick. "It's the *Endeavour* – one of the first ships from Europe to come to this land. Captain Cook sailed the *Endeavour* to New Zealand more than a hundred years ago. Cook wasn't the first European to see New Zealand, but he was the first to explore it, and he found this channel between the North and South Islands."

So… now you're in a little boat in a huge channel of water over *two hundred* years earlier than when you woke up this morning.

A longboat is lowered from the side of the *Endeavour*. Four sailors deftly climb ropes from the ship onto the longboat, and then row toward you. They look around as though they expect to see another boat or signs of life – but it is only you and Nick.

As they pull up beside you, one of the sailors pulls out a musket and trains it on you. You hold up your hands to show you aren't armed, and they look you over.

"Are you French?" one asks.

"No," says Nick, "we're lost. Can we come with you? I'm a good sailor."

You notice he isn't saying anything about time travel, and you decide you won't say anything either.

The sailors look inside your boat and is surprised at the sight of Trixie. With help from a grappling hook and a rope they tow you back to the *Endeavour* where you climb aboard to meet the captain.

The captain's cabin has a low ceiling and it is full of plants, so it's like walking into an indoor forest or a greenhouse. You are led to a table, where Captain Cook has been writing. He wears a blue jacket and a white wig. He has a commanding presence and you hope he will treat you kindly. He looks you both up and down and you know he has taken a full measure of you both. This is an intelligent man. He speaks at last.

"My men tell me they have found you on the water alone – who are you, and what are you doing here?"

"We've been adrift for many days after we lost our ship in the islands," Nick says.

The captain looks at you for a long moment. "I do not know where you two came from, but from the look of you... " He turns to Nick and eyes his bruises "– it cannot have been a pleasant place. You are many, many days' sailing from civilization, and yet your dog seems well fed and neither of you are wasting from the scurvy. So let's put you to work."

"We can stay with you?" Nick is incredibly happy as Captain Cook nods.

"You know these islands?" asks the Captain.

Nick chats happily about the channel and the islands. You have little to say – you have no knowledge of these waters and you are very aware of the differences between you and Nick. He is happy to be here, to be useful and to have escaped his uncle, but you feel completely out of time and realize that while Nick will probably thrive you have few skills to help you get by.

As Nick talks, you rise and make your way to the captain's desk – there are charts neatly filed away and a large map is being drawn of the area. There are books about plants, and someone has been drawing the plants that fill the little cabin.

"Do you read?"

You realize this last question is being addressed to you.

"Of course!" you blurt out, before you remember that not everyone would have been able to read and write at this time in history.

"Can you reckon?"

Reckon? What's that? Ahhh, he means math! You nod.

"Well, that explains your soft hands!" Captain Cook exclaims. "I will tell Banks that I have found him an assistant – and I have found myself an extra sailor."

Perhaps you won't be entirely useless in this place after all. Joseph Banks is a botanist on the *Endeavour* and it was he who has filled it with plants. He is busy cataloguing all these new specimens.

A clanging noise announces that lunch is ready, and the captain sends you both to eat. On the way, you hurriedly discuss your situation with Nick. The dog keeps close to you both.

"If we touch that dog's collar again we could end up here a century before now," Nick says.

"Or maybe we'll go back to our own time!"

Nick shakes his head. "I don't want to go back!"

You think it through. When you first went back in time it was about a hundred years. The next time, Nick was touching both the medallion and you, and the boat and you and Nick all went back another hundred years. What would happen if somebody touched it again?

At that moment a sailor plucks up the little dog, and before you can do anything he touches the pendent. The ship lurches violently, creaks, and then steadies in the water. The sailors look around, trying to work out what has happened. They look overboard – perhaps they hit a rock or a whale. You and Nick look to the hills. At first everything seems the same, but then Nick gasps and points upwards. Circling in the sky is the biggest bird you have ever seen.

"Haast's eagle!" says Nick. "They died out a long time ago. Oh no!"

"What is going on?" The captain comes up on deck and looks at everyone for an answer. Most of the crew are pointing to the giant eagle whose wings from tip to tip are wider than a man is tall.

The sailor is still holding Trixie, and to your horror his hand brushes the swinging medallion once more. Again the ship lurches, and the huge eagle disappears. The sailor drops the dog and she runs toward you. Trixie jumps into your arms and buries her nose in your shirt.

There is a bumping against the hull, and two of the sailors move to see what it is. You wonder if the next creature you will meet will be a giant shark. One of the sailors leans a little over the side and shakes his head.

"It was only the little sail boat," he says.

Wait! If the boat you and Nick arrived on is outside the ship, maybe that means you have gone FORWARD in time!

Once more you find yourself in the cabin of Captain Cook. He listens as you explain where you have come from, how you met Nick, and how the *Endeavour* has moved back and forward in time.

"The talisman is dangerous," Cook says, glaring at Trixie. "I don't want it on my ship. You must make a choice – you can throw it overboard now and stay with the *Endeavour*, or you can try to journey back to your own time in Nick's boat."

"I want to stay," Nick says.

It is time to make a decision. Do you:

Stay in this time? **P313**

Or

Try to return to your own time? **P314**

You've decided to stay in this time.

After thinking about it for a while, you decide that it's too risky to try to get back to your own time – who knows where (or when) you might end up.

You take Trixie's collar off and drop it into the deep waters of what will become known as the Cook Strait.

Later that day, you begin working with Joseph Banks. He is an enthusiastic and interesting man, and before long you discover that you too are passionate about botany. Together you travel the world, discovering new species of flora and fauna, and you make more of the world known to people. You live comfortably and Joseph treats you like one of his own children – he is a rich man, and he buys you a home and gives you all you need to be wealthy in your own right. You feel that the work you do leaves something for the future when people will appreciate the environment differently.

You live a long life, make many friends, and always have one of Trixie's descendants by your side.

Congratulations you've reached the end of this part of the story. But have you tried all the possible paths?

It is time to make one more decision. Do you:

Go and read a different story? **P5**

Or

Go back to the beginning of this story and try another path? **P247**

You have decided to try to return to your own time.

You farewell Nick and Captain Cook, and then clamber down into the little boat.

Nick carefully lowers Trixie down to you in a basket.

Then you row a short distance from the *Endeavour* so they won't be affected by the amulet, and pick up Trixie.

If you have this wrong you could be about to go back one hundred years to a time when Maori is the only language spoken in this land, and giant birds ruled the skies…

You touch the pendant and the boat rocks, and you lose your grip on Trixie. You look up, scanning the sky for giant eagles, but seagulls are all you see. With relief you see sail boats in the distance – you went forward in time!

Now to try it again – well, the worst thing that can happen is you'll have to flag down the *Endeavour* again…

The boat tosses and…

Success!

The ferry is once again in sight, and within half an hour the ship has stopped and picked you up. You are congratulated by some passengers for rescuing the dog, but others are very grumpy that your falling overboard means that the ferry will arrive late.

"Thank you so much for rescuing my Trixie," her owner says. "But where has her collar gone?"

"I'm sorry – it must have been lost in the water," you say.

Trixie's owner is upset, and you suspect that she knew Trixie had been carrying a treasure.

Later, you tell Max and Stella about what happened, but of course, they don't believe you. It doesn't matter, though, because in your back pocket you have something that would change their mind. Just for now you are keeping it for yourself – if you ever need to leap back in time, you'll be prepared.

Congratulations you have reached the end of this part of the story. It is time to make another decision. Do you:

Go back to the beginning of this story and try another path? **P247**

Or

Go to the list of books and choose another story to read? **P5**

Answers to questions in Once Upon an Island

Question One:

A New Zealand giant squid can drag someone your weight and strength down to the bottom of a three mile trench in ten minutes. How many minutes would it take for two giant squid to drag you down to a watery grave?

Solutions: The answer is still 10 minutes. Just because there are two squid doesn't mean they can swim any faster. However, while they fight over who gets to eat you, you should swim to safety or tie their tentacles into knots. A third solution might be to point out that a creature that lives so far beneath the ocean wouldn't survive up on the surface – but why ruin a good math problem.

Question Two:

You find a device which moves you backwards and forwards in time. You find out that you move back one hundred years every time you hit the back button and you move forward fifty years every time you hit the forward button. You travel back 300 years and find yourself being chased by a giant eagle. The Haast's eagle was the largest eagle ever known to have lived and has been extinct for two hundred years. How many times do you have to hit the forward button to avoid being a meal for a giant eagle?

Solutions: If the Haast eagle has been extinct for two hundred years and you have gone back in time three hundred years you only need to go forward 100 years to be safe from these giant predators. You move ahead fifty years each time you hit the forward button so you'll need to press it at least twice to be safe. If you want to get back to the present, you need to hit the button another four times.

Question Three:

While Lost in Lion Country you find yourself left alone with the safari picnic basket. There are 50 ham sandwiches inside the basket. One hyena will be satisfied after 10 ham sandwiches and will head off to sleep in the sun. How many hyena can you hold off until help arrives?

Solutions: Strictly speaking the answer is five but what if there are more hyena than that? We think a better solution is to empty out all but a few of the sandwiches into a pile for the pack to fight over. Take a couple yourself and a) if the picnic hamper is very sturdy consider getting inside until help arrives or b) climb up the nearest tree, have lunch, and wait for rescue.

So where do you want to go from here?

Go to Arapawa Island **P249**
Or
Go stay with your mother's friend? **P248**
Or
Go try another story? **P5**

List of Choices

IN THE MAGICIAN'S HOUSE

More 'You Say Which Way' Adventures

Available from Amazon.com

- ❖ *Between The Stars*
- ❖ *Island of Swimming Cats*
- ❖ *Dinosaur Canyon*
- ❖ *Secret of the Singing Cave*
- ❖ *Valley of Flying Dogs*
- ❖ *Dungeon of Doom*
- ❖ *Dragons Realm*
- ❖ *Stranded Starship*
- ❖ *Movie Mystery Madness*
- ❖ *Mystic Portal*
- ❖ *Duel at Dawn*
- ❖ *Secret Project*
- ❖ *Danger on Dolphin Island*
- ❖ *Volcano of Fire*
- ❖ *Secret of Glass Mountain*
- ❖ *Deadline Delivery*
- ❖ *Missing Cat Mystery*
- ❖ *The Sorcerer's Maze Adventure Quiz*

YouSayWhichWay.com